Also by Kelly Durham

The War Widow

Berlin Calling

Wade's War

The Reluctant Copilot

The Movie Star and Me

Kelly Durham

Cover design by Nat Shane

For Mary Kate, Addison and Callie.

"I know this will come as a shock to you, Mr. Goldwyn, but in all history, which has held billions and billions of human beings, not a single one ever had a happy ending."

Dorothy Parker

Prologue

Pepe Ramos cradled the Winchester 4440 rifle in the crook of his right arm and squinted into the late afternoon sun. Lighting was always so critical. You always had to compensate for the position of the sun and where that made the shadows fall. Already the wooden boardwalk in front of the saloon and general store to his left was in the afternoon shadows. Like the expanding shadows, an eerie silence stretched over the storefronts. It had already been a long day and he was tired, his throat dry. Still, he had things to atone for, so he vowed to put forth his best effort.

Dressed in tan buckskins, the five foot, eight inch Pepe was half a foot shorter and forty pounds lighter than the big man standing beside him on the vacant, dusty street of the small western town. Kit Justice, his muscled chest pushing against the light blue fabric of his shirt, rested his hands on the elk horn grips of the holstered single-action Colt .45 pistols slung across his hips. From beneath the brim of a white Stetson, his blue eyes stared in the same direction as Pepe's. There was just enough breeze to ruffle the dark blue kerchief knotted around Kit's throat, to stir up wisps of dust around his black leather boots. Off to the left, out of sight behind a row of store fronts, a dog barked once, twice, then fell silent. No horses were tethered to the hitching posts on either side of the street. No one dared venture out into the open.

"Well, amigo," the big man said, his voice strong and deep, "what do you think those rustlers are up to?"

"I think, Señor Kit," Pepe replied glancing up at the taller man, "they are waiting for sundown."

Kit nodded, his eyes never leaving the street stretching out before them. "Lawless men favor the darkness, their wicked deeds to … hide."

A long pause, then, "Cut! It's not 'hide,' it's '*conceal*!' C'mon Terry," shouted the film's director, Sam Levin, "That's four takes! Can't you get it right?"

The set came alive as technicians scurried to reposition for the next take while they ignored the scathing words directed at star Terry Thorpe, who portrayed western hero Kit Justice in Pacific Pictures' most popular serial. Prop men adjusted the electric fans generating the artificial breeze, lighting technicians tweaked the giant, tripod-mounted Klieg lights and the animal trainer prepared the dog to bark again.

Levin hopped down from his canvas chair and strode out onto the dusty street on the back lot of Pacific Pictures Studios. "That was wonderful, Mickey! Just wonderful!" he enthused to the shorter man. "Just the right emphasis! It's going to be a perfect set-up for the big scene! Mabel!" he called over his shoulder, "we need some makeup here!" Mabel scurried forward with her kit and powdered the scratches on the side of Mickey's face. She stepped back, inspected her touch-up and, satisfied, retreated back behind the camera—and out of Sam Levin's line of fire.

Thorpe pushed the brim of the white Stetson back from his forehead and pulled a pack of Camels from beneath the leather chaps covering his blue denim jeans. "Don't you have something nice to say to your star, Sam?" he smiled. "After all, it's my name above the title."

Levin rolled his eyes, hands on his hips. "Just get the damn line right. It's 'their wicked deeds to *conceal*!' And yes, it does make a difference!" he grumbled. Turning back to the buckskin-clad Mickey Moreno, Sam's natural enthusiasm returned. "Bull's eye, Mickey! That's the line we're going to use to promote the picture: '… waiting for sundown!' It's gonna be dynamite! It's gonna be the best picture of 1941!"

Thorpe lit his cigarette, watching through squinted eyes as his sidekick basked in the director's praise.

Chapter 1

I had not been with the 10th Army when it landed on Okinawa on Sunday, April 1, 1945. The ironic combination of Easter Sunday and April Fool's Day no doubt contributed to the mixed feelings American soldiers and Marines had about the landings. On the one hand, they knew the job had to be done, that Japan had to be finished off step-by-step, island-by-island. On the other hand, I'm sure most of those boys would have been content to let someone else have the privilege. In fact, casualty rates were so high that, in most cases, someone else *did* have the privilege. That's where I came in. I was a replacement officer assigned to a rifle company in the 77th Infantry Division.

From a rear area replacement depot, I was taken by a mud-covered jeep to the forward area, a morass of mud-choked roads clogged with mud-caked vehicles and mud-splattered men.

"This is as far as I can take you, lieutenant," the driver reported as he wheeled the jeep past a shell crater filled with brown, stagnant water. "Any closer and the Japs will start tossing mortars at you, and I wouldn't want that on my conscience," he smiled.

I hopped out near a small shack with its roof half bashed in. I felt a little self-conscious because my field uniform was still green. Everyone and everything else within sight was covered with a brown film of mud. Well, I figured, at least my boots were getting muddy.

I walked as steadily as I could across the slippery ground, hopping when possible onto patches of grass brave enough to poke their blades above the muck. Even so, I managed to half slide, half skid into a soldier exiting the shack.

"Sorry, lieutenant," he said, looking my relatively spotless uniform up and down with weary, red-rimmed eyes.

"It's okay. I'm looking for the CO," I replied.

"You're on the right track sir; he's right inside," he said, tossing his thumb over his shoulder as he slogged on to whatever mission he'd been assigned.

There was no door on the shack, but a filthy, wool Army blanket hung across the doorway, its bottom edge ragged and, like everything else, caked with mud. I pushed it aside and entered, then stopped to let my eyes adjust to the darkness within. I couldn't see anything for a moment. Finally, I realized that I was standing between two blankets, sort of like a trap to make sure no light exited the shack once darkness fell. I pushed aside the second blanket and saw a couple of soldiers hunched over a warped, wooden plank stretched between two makeshift sawhorses.

I cleared my throat. "Looking for the CO," I said.

"You found him," the soldier to the right replied without lifting his gaze from the map spread out on the table. A kerosene lantern provided the only light in the room. "Have a seat. I'll be with you in a minute."

I looked around, but there were no chairs in the small room. The floor was covered in mostly dried mud. I decided to stand. A window to the left of the table was covered with yet another blanket. To the right was what appeared to be another room, but I did not investigate.

"So here's the trail," the CO pointed at the map with a stubby, yellow pencil as the other soldier nodded in comprehension. As both of their uniforms were ragged and filthy, I couldn't tell their ranks. I only knew the CO from his curt greeting. "Battalion wants another probe right here," he stabbed at the map again, "at midnight."

"Again?" the other soldier sighed. His short hair was plastered to the sides of his head as though it hadn't seen soap in a month. "This whole idea's as fouled up as Hogan's goat, sir. The last three times we been up there haven't turned out too good."

"I know. I was with you." The CO eyed the soldier. "Again. Okay?"

"Okay," he said in weary, hopeless agreement.

"Make sure everybody understands passwords and signals. I don't want anybody getting shot by our own boys."

"I don't want anybody getting shot."

"Yeah, well good luck with that. You'll have mortar support up and back. Questions?"

"No sir." The subordinate picked up his helmet and stepped around the table. He nodded at me, as he passed, his eyes sunken in deep, dark sockets. He looked and smelled as though he'd been living for months in a hole in the ground. Which he probably had.

"What can I do for you?" the CO asked without leaving his spot.

I crossed the room in two steps, came to attention and saluted. "Lieutenant Russell reports, sir!" The CO looked at me for a moment with unfocused eyes and then offered a tired salute in return. "I'm a replacement officer, sir." I started digging in my pocket for a copy of my orders.

"I don't need your orders, Lieutenant Russell," he said with an exhausted smile. "Nobody would come here who didn't have to." He thrust his hand across the makeshift table. "Wade Brooks. Nice to meet you. Welcome to Dog Company. You know anything about mortars?"

Lieutenant Brooks was about the same size as me, five ten or so, and like me he had brown hair and blue eyes. But while we may have been similar in appearance, his combat experience trumped mine as surely as an ace beats a jack. Brooks invited me to dine with him that night. We ate our C-rations on the same table that held the map.

"Where you from, Frank?"

"Los Angeles, sir. How about you?"

"We're pretty informal around here. You can call me Wade. South Carolina; Aiken to be precise."

I nodded. I'd heard of South Carolina, of course, but not the town. "How long you been here?"

"Too long," he said, fanning a swarm of aggressive flies away from his open can of chicken. "We landed on a nearby island at first. This was back in April. We cleared that and then came over here as the corps reserve. The 7th Infantry got chewed up pretty bad, so we relieved them and now we're getting chewed up pretty bad." He glanced at his wristwatch and scratched the dried mud off the crystal. "And in a few hours we'll chew and get chewed again."

"How long you been in command here?" I asked.

"Into my third week," he replied as he blew away the flies and forked some more chicken into his mouth. "Another three days and I'll set the company record for time in command."

"That bad?"

"That bad," he nodded without looking up. "What'd you do before the war?"

"I was working at the Lockheed factory in Burbank. I was a production supervisor on the P-38 assembly line."

"The fighter?"

"Right. How about you, where did you work?"

Brooks grunted, a hollow, humorless half-laugh. "The White House."

Before I could inquire further, Brooks shifted the conversation. "I want you to take over the weapons platoon."

He didn't say so, but I understood his thinking; while the weapons platoon was important, it fought from just behind our friendly lines. Brooks wasn't going to trust me with a rifle platoon—and the lives of forty-odd men— until I got adjusted to life at the front—and until he could evaluate my leadership ability.

"Every time we go up against these ridges, we get hammered," Brooks explained, his index finger outlining a terrain feature on the map. "The Japs are dug in so deep we can't get at 'em. Their positions are laid out to give them very effective crossing fires. About the only chance we have is to go up in the dark. That offers us some protection, but of course we can't see what the hell we're doing. Smoke, illumination and suppressing fire from our mortars are about the only advantages we have at night."

"Yes sir," I replied. He shot me a look. "Wade."

Dusk had fallen, but it was not yet pitch dark as Lieutenant Brooks introduced me to the company's other officer, Lieutenant Miller. He was a veteran, having survived the front lines for two weeks already. Miller, Sergeant Thomas and Sergeant Davenport led the three rifle platoons. I was taking over the weapons platoon after dark on the night of a scheduled patrol. I was nervous, not so much about finally facing the fanatical Japanese, but about not letting down my new comrades.

"You can't move around like this in the daytime," Brooks said as a light rain fell, replenishing the slimy, smelly muck. "If the Japs see you out in the open, they'll lob a couple of well-aimed mortar shells at you and mess up your day." He led me away from the positions of the front line platoons. "We keep the mortars fairly close together most of the time." Even in the dark, Brooks had no trouble finding his way. "Pepe!" he called in a soft voice.

"Here, sir," came a quiet response.

Brooks pulled me by the sleeve and half-stepped, half-slid into a shell crater that had been improved to hold the weapons platoon's headquarters. "This is your new platoon leader, Lieutenant Russell," Brooks said to the man I could see only in silhouette. "Lieutenant Russell, meet Staff Sergeant Mickey Moreno."

"Glad to meet you, sergeant," I said, shaking hands in the dark.

"Pepe here will get you squared away and I'll check on you in the morning. Field phone working?" he directed his question at the sergeant.

"Yes sir. Just let us know what you need and where and we'll drop it right in."

"All right. I'll leave you two with it. Stay alert. And don't leave this hole. Anything moving around here once I leave, shoot it."

The shell crater in which Sergeant Moreno and I crouched was filled with about three inches of muddy water, but some smart-thinking soldier had requisitioned a couple of used ammunition pallets and thrown them in the bottom of the hole. While that didn't exactly keep us dry, it kept us from standing in the brown, smelly water. The sides of the crater were slimy mud, but its rim was topped by sand bags laid three high and overlapping like bricks. Another pallet, covered by a tarp, was laid across the sand bags, which were broken here and there by forward facing gaps which would allow us to fire our rifles at any enemy brazen enough to penetrate our company's forward positions. The field telephone was tucked in a nook at the base of the bags, its wire disappearing into the darkness toward the switchboard at the company command post. I looked around for a relatively dry spot to set my gear and my carbine, but there wasn't one. I found the least muddy patch and set my pack there. I was proud of myself for having stashed my poncho in the top of the pack, on top of my dry socks. I pulled it out and slipped it over my head, settled my helmet back in place and slung my carbine back over my shoulder.

The rain was now no more than a steady drizzle and the cloudy sky blocked out any starlight. Occasionally friendly artillery flashed like lightning to our rear, the thunder of the shells racing overhead sounding like a runaway locomotive. Up ahead, obscured in the rainy darkness, was a 350-foot-high coral ridge into which the Japanese had cut miles of interconnecting tunnels. These tunnels included hundreds of holes, some just big enough for a single sniper to aim his rifle at us, others able to conceal artillery pieces that could rain red-hot shrapnel down on top of us.

One thing the darkness couldn't obscure was the sickly-sweet smell of decay. The mud was bad enough, but between our lines and the ridge, some

400 yards away, was a no man's land littered with corpses from both sides. No one liked to see friendly casualties left to bloat in the sun or decompose in the muck, but in truth, the risks to retrieve the bodies were so great that too many were still unrecovered. I guess that was one of the blessings of the darkness—you couldn't see the bodies.

"Why don't you take the first watch, sir?" Sergeant Moreno asked. "I'm used to the late shift."

"Fine," I replied. I had no illusion that I'd be able to sleep in the falling rain and the muddy hole anyway. Within a few moments, Moreno had wrapped himself in a poncho, huddled by the forward rim of the crater just below the sand bags, and begun to snore lightly. I was still standing on the pallets, trying to figure out how to make myself more comfortable. It proved an impossible task. I kept waiting for the tell-tale rattle of the field phone to call our mortars to action, trying to organize my thoughts and actions so I would be ready to take command and deliver the needed fire support to our patrol. I didn't have to come across as Sergeant York, I just wanted to make sure I didn't screw things up.

Fortunately, I never got the chance. While the Japanese occasionally lobbed a round or two in our general direction, our patrol never made contact and Dog Company didn't fire a single round all night. I know, because even after Moreno relieved me around midnight, I was unable to sleep. I was used to a bed, a cot or just a sleeping bag, and the slippery, sloped sides of the hole just didn't meet my standards for comfortable accommodations. I don't think I slept ten minutes all night.

Dawn revealed another cloudy day. Though the rain had mercifully ceased, the war of course had not. Under the supervision of Sergeant Moreno, I spent the morning moving carefully between our platoon's mortar positions and meeting the crews manning each of the three 60mm tubes. The three mortar pits were close to each other for coordination's sake, but not so close that one Japanese round could take us all out. Sergeants Righetti, Danes and Sowell were the squad leaders, each in charge of a five-man team maintaining, firing, and when necessary moving, one of our three mortars.

As we trotted back through the few remaining trees between our mortar positions and the platoon command post where we'd spent the night, we heard a loud *"whap!"* Before I knew what was happening, Moreno had tackled me and we landed all tangled up in the mud. Thirty yards to our front right, a Japanese mortar round detonated, concussing the air and throwing up mud, sticks and stones. "Come on, sir!" Moreno was already up, grabbing me by the collar and jerking me to my feet with surprising strength. He rushed me toward our crater and we both tumbled in just before a second round fell not more than ten yards away.

"Damn!" I exclaimed, wiping the splattered mud from my face, my ears ringing. "That was too close."

Moreno just smiled, reached into his front pocket, pulled out a pack of Luckys, and offered me one. I didn't smoke, but he'd just saved my life and I thought it would be petty to refuse, so I thanked him and accepted a cigarette while trying to control my shaking hands. Moreno had a handsome smile and clear brown eyes. He looked familiar to me, but I was sure we'd never met.

"Where you from, Sergeant Moreno?" I asked, taking a shallow draw on the cigarette. The last thing I wanted was to start coughing and embarrass myself.

"Los Angeles, sir. How about you?"

I laughed. "Small world. Here I come 6,000 miles and I end up in a hole with a guy from my hometown. How about that!"

About mid-morning, Lieutenant Brooks appeared, accompanied by a gangly, taller man wearing relatively clean fatigues and a slouch hat. He had a small ruck sack on his back and a slightly larger, olive-colored canvas bag slung over his right shoulder. I noticed right away that he wasn't carrying a weapon. As he got closer, I could read the green and gold "WAR CORRESPONDENT" patch on his left shoulder.

"You boys been attracting attention this morning?" Lieutenant Brooks asked, stepping into our crater. The tall man stepped in behind him, causing muddy water to slosh up between the slats of our pallets.

"Lieutenant Russell, Sergeant Moreno, meet Oliver Cameron. Mr. Cameron is a newsreel photographer out here to document our tour of the Orient for the good folks back home. Since you two are both from the motion picture capital of the world, I thought this might be a good place for Mr. Cameron to begin." We shook hands all around and it was quickly obvious that Cameron wasn't an American.

"Pleased to meet you both," he said with a crooked-toothed grin. Within a couple of minutes, we learned that Cameron was an Australian working for Pacific Pictures Newsreels. That seemed to pique Moreno's interest, but before I could ask any questions, Brooks pulled me by the sleeve.

"Pepe," he said looking at Moreno, "entertain Mr. Cameron while Lieutenant Russell and I stroll back over to the command post."

"Yes sir," Moreno replied, reaching again for his pack of Luckys.

Immediately, Brooks leaped out of the hole and sprinted toward the nearest trees. I followed as quickly as I could, keeping my ears tuned for the tell-tale *"whap!"* We reached the battered shack where I'd met Brooks the previous day and found Miller, Thomas and Davenport standing around the makeshift table waiting for us. Brooks set his helmet on the end of the table and leaned his carbine in the corner. He massaged his short hair with the fingers of both hands and let out a deep breath.

It smelled bad in the tight confines of the room. I wasn't sure if it was me or the others, and then I realized that it didn't matter. The blanket was still hung over the pane-less window, the kerosene lantern providing a meager yellow light.

"Look here," Brooks began, using his short pencil as a pointer. "Regiment is calling for another attack on the ridge. The idea is to put two companies abreast and one right behind to exploit a breakthrough."

Miller interrupted. "Let me guess. We're leading the attack."

"Right you are, Lieutenant Miller!" Brooks said, looking up from the map. "Here's the deal." We huddled around so we could follow Brooks' pencil as it moved across the map from our current positions to our jumping off points to our routes of advance to our objectives—the top of the coral ridge.

"H-hour is 0400. Brief your men, then distribute water, rations and ammunition. Review passwords and signals. Rest 'em as much as possible. Lieutenant Russell," he said, looking at me, "I'm putting the light machine guns with the lead platoons to help cover their flanks, so don't worry about them. You concentrate on your mortars. I want you to begin firing harassing rounds, say one every fifteen minutes or so, as soon as you get back to your platoon. Once the attack starts, you'll fire some smoke to give us visual cover as we work toward our objective. Just be ready to fire explosive rounds as we come in contact. We'll use the platoon radios once we get moving. Work with Sergeant Moreno to identify the routes to the next two firing positions and move one tube at a time so you can continue to support the advance with the other two. As long as you can hit our targets effectively, we'll keep you in place. But when we say 'move,' you've got to be ready to haul ass."

"Yes sir." I thought "sir" was the right response under the circumstances even though he'd bristled at that the previous day. That seemed like weeks ago now. Spending the night in the mud and getting shot at by the enemy had changed my perspective.

The briefing went on for another twenty minutes or so. Brooks was methodical and thorough. He asked for questions and clarified instructions before releasing us back to our platoons. It was now early afternoon.

Moreno and I were sitting on the left side of our hole, enjoying a rare moment of sunlight and constantly brushing the flies away from our opened ration tins. I quickly found that if you didn't move the food from the can to your mouth with a rapid motion, you got to eat a fly or two along with your ham.

"Where's our cameraman?" I asked Moreno between bites.

"I sent him over to Righetti. They're going to be firing a few rounds." These were the harassing shots Brooks had directed us to launch every fifteen minutes. "I figured that would give him some predictable shots; easier to photograph what you know is coming. In combat, it's going to be aim and shoot."

"Good thinking," I replied, spitting out a fly. Moreno had his face tilted back, exposing it to the weak, but welcome sun. I again had the notion that he looked familiar. "How come Lieutenant Brooks calls you 'Pepe?' Is that some kind of nickname?" I asked.

Moreno straightened up and chuckled. "Yes sir. I did some acting before I joined up. My best role was a character named 'Pepe.'"

I slapped my forehead with the heel of my hand. "Of course!" I laughed. "I knew you looked familiar! You were in the Kit Justice serials!"

Moreno was smiling sheepishly now and nodding his head. "Right. Then just before the war started, Pacific Pictures decided to shift Kit Justice from two-reelers to features. I was on the way to stardom!" he laughed. "We'd just released the first full-length movie when the war broke out." A loud "*toonk*" from our left rear reminded us that Righetti's team was following its orders.

"Yeah. What was the guy's name, the main guy?"

"Terry Thorpe," Moreno smiled and shook his head.

"Yeah, yeah, that's right! What happened to him?"

"He went into the Marines. Got somebody at the studio to pull some strings for him and got a flying assignment even though he was too tall. No special treatment for the Chicano," he said with a wry smile, "and here I am in the infantry."

"Well," I said, scraping the last bite out of the can and blowing on it to keep the flies at bay, "the fliers may get the glory, but the infantry wins the wars." We talked for a little while longer and then heard Oliver Cameron's boots slapping through the mud as he loped back toward our hole. He hopped down beside Moreno, his big feet hitting the pallets and splashing muddy water up on to my pants.

"Sorry, lieutenant!" he chuckled, but it didn't matter. Although my uniform wasn't as worn as my comrades', it was now just as muddy.

"Get any good shots?" Moreno asked.

"Quite a few!" Cameron replied with a lopsided grin that sloped down from his right to his left. "Your Sergeant Righetti was kind enough to explain the firing process step-by-step, gave me the chance to follow along and film the whole cycle several times. I shot a whole roll and started on a second one." Cameron held up a metal can sealed with white tape. With a grease pencil he labeled it with the number "3" and the date. "Much easier and more efficient than filming in combat."

"What else you got in there?" I asked, pointing to his bag where something with a handle had caught my eye.

"Oh, this little gem?" he grinned, pulling a small brown and black pistol from among the film cans. "It's a Nambu, a Japanese officer's pistol. I picked it up on Iwo Jima when I was there with your Marines. As a correspondent, I'm not allowed to carry a weapon, but a souvenir — I think that's allowed." Cameron handed the pistol to me butt first.

"Is it loaded?" I asked.

"Not much good if it isn't. That's the safety on the left."

I looked over the nifty little pistol, then handed it to Mickey who hefted it in his right hand. "Very light." He held it up and aimed along the open sight across the top of the barrel. "Have you fired it?"

"No," Cameron replied. "I'm usually too busy with the camera to shoot anything else," he chuckled. Mickey smoothly spun the gun around his index finger and presented it grip-first to Cameron, who laughed again and stuck the "souvenir" back in his bag. I watched as he refastened the bag's clasps. "Lieutenant Brooks said I could tag along tonight. Mind if I use your hole to catch a few winks?"

"How can you shoot pictures in the dark?" Moreno asked.

Cameron laughed. "Can't. But once daylight comes, you just have to keep your camera loaded, wound up and ready to shoot, don't you? I imagine it's a lot like your rifle. You've got to keep it ready to fire if it's going to do you much good!"

Mickey and I moved to the side of the hole to let him nestle in for some sleep beneath the overhead cover at the front of the position.

Once darkness fell, activity in our area picked up. Our forward platoons began distributing ammunition, rations and drinking water. Socks were changed. Dry socks were our first line of defense against trench foot, which put almost as many infantrymen out of action as the Japanese did. Attack plans were reviewed and challenges and passwords were covered, then covered again.

At last light, Cameron left our hole, his movie camera in hand, film bag over his shoulder. He planned to move forward with Lieutenant Brooks. That would put him just behind the lead platoons. Once daylight dawned, he'd be in a position to film plenty of action.

Sergeant Moreno and I checked again with our mortar team leaders and confirmed ammunition stocks, the presence of firing cards, maps and all the sundry details that would enable us to fire in support of Dog Company's attack.

"Don't worry, sir," he said to me in a quiet, low voice as we made our way through the darkness and back to our hole. "The men know their jobs. They'll do fine. So will you."

"Thanks, Sergeant Moreno."

"Call me Mickey, sir."

"Call me Frank."

By midnight, we were all rested—at least as rested as one can get living in a hole in a combat zone where mortar rounds are being lobbed back and forth all day. Moreno and I had visited all three of our mortar emplacements and reviewed the forward firing positions we would move to and how we would get there if the opportunity arose. My hope was that we would be able to support our company's efforts from our current positions, at least until it was light enough for us to see our way forward. I didn't want to have to move in the darkness. I figured that the weight of our attack on the ridge's Japanese defenders would cause them to focus on the threat immediately in front of them, not on our mortar teams. Boy, did I have a lot to learn!

As the minute hand on the luminous dial of my wrist watch ticked inexorably toward 0400, I could hear men moving all around us. Our harassing fire had stopped about 2200 hours in the hopes that the Japanese up on the ridge would figure we'd gone to sleep. Now, in the dark, I could make out shadowy figures moving up toward the line of departure, that imaginary point on the map from which our attack would commence. Occasionally, a whisper would penetrate the blackness as officers or NCOs issued last minute instructions.

The tactical plan was to fire a rolling artillery barrage before the attack. The infantry would then move ahead staying safely behind our exploding shells as they slowly walked up the ridge, rather like an angry giant stomping his colossal feet down onto the hapless defenders. It sounded like a good plan, except that the defenders weren't exactly hapless. They were well-hidden and protected by heavily fortified positions occupying higher ground—higher ground that we had to wrestle away from them.

Precisely at 0355, the horizon to our rear lit up with what seemed to be a thousand flashes. Seconds later, the ear-splitting "*karump*" of the 105mm and 155mm howitzers rolled over us like a hot summer night's thunder. Mickey and I hunched under our protective cover even though we knew this bombardment was aimed at the enemy. In anticipation of fire missions from Lieutenant Brooks or one of the platoon leaders, Mickey held the handset of our SCR-300 radio close to his ear. Rounds from our friendly artillery continued to streak over our heads and impact near the base of the ridge some 400 yards distant.

Just as we were beginning to enjoy the sound and fury of the bombardment, the home team took the field. On the opposite horizon to the south, new flashes were succeeded by the hollow "*kaboom*" of Japanese artillery. Its objective was not the infantrymen creeping through the muddy, slippery darkness, but rather to answer the American guns now pouring hot steel onto the ridge. Within moments, an epic duel of big guns was underway. Even at our position seemingly center point between the battling howitzers, the noise was tremendous, the dancing flashes temporarily blinding. I was glad Mickey and I were under the arc of the rounds rather than at their terminus. The thunder and crash of the big guns and the rippling explosions of their ordnance drowned out all other sounds.

After fifteen minutes or so, the barrage began to slacken and before long we could hear the rhythmic snap of our light machine guns. We also heard the "*whap*" of the Japanese mortars as they began to fire parachute flares to illuminate the night. As the flares swung beneath their tiny parachutes, the harsh, white light they cast caused shadows to lurch and sway like drunks staggering home after closing time. We began to hear the distant *"pop"* of rifles and carbines and the swift answering rattle of the Japs' machine guns.

Our radio crackled and we could hear Lieutenant Brooks somewhere ahead in the stark, artificial half-light calling for status reports from the platoon leaders. We waited, hunched over the radio set, our shoulders knotted from tension.

"Dog 4-6 this is Dog 6, fire mission." Adrenalin coursed through my body as I heard my call sign.

Moreno keyed the mic and answered, "Go ahead Dog 6."

"Reference Able, add 100, smoke."

"Roger." Moreno shouted instructions to one of our runners who dashed over to Righetti's mortar pit. Within half a minute, Righetti's team sent a white phosphorous round arcing toward the target.

"Dog 4-6, fire for effect."

Now all three of our mortars fired on the target, a hundred yards beyond a predesignated point, in this case labeled "Able," on our map. Three "*toonks*" were followed shortly by three flashes and the muffled "*bump*" of the exploding rounds.

The front line was moving steadily away from us. I began to think about the right time to move our tubes forward and suggested to Moreno that he prepare the first tube, Righetti's, to move up.

"We might want to hold off for a bit yet, lieutenant," Moreno advised. "We can still range the heights of the ridge from here. I'd hate for us to get tangled up with the riflemen moving through here as the other company comes through." There was the voice of experience counseling a newcomer to combat. Fortunately, I was smart enough to listen.

We continued to lob rounds out in front of our advancing platoons, mostly smoke to give them some concealment from the Japanese flares, but occasionally some explosive rounds too. About an hour and a half into the attack, as the sky to our left began to reveal the first gray streaks of dawn, heavy machine gun fire from the ridge opened up on our attacking soldiers. The rattle and thump of the Japanese machine guns was answered by the snap and pop of our rifles and light machine guns. We began to receive urgent calls for explosive rounds to the front of our advancing line.

"Dog 4-6, give us everything you've got!" Brooks' voice, higher in pitch and intensity than before, shouted through the radio's tinny speaker. We relayed our fire orders to the mortar pits and the crews began to snap off rounds every fifteen seconds or so, pausing only to swab the tube after every tenth or twelfth round. Brooks was radioing us again when we heard heavy gun fire and then lost contact. I told Moreno to pour everything we could onto the last targets Brooks had identified and I grabbed the radio and attempted to regain contact. Nothing.

We were firing as fast as we could. The Japanese on the ridge responded in kind and began lobbing shells in our direction. The first several fell short, impacting near the fox holes from which our platoons had started their attacks. As the morning brightened, the rounds came closer and closer, and began falling among our mortar positions, spewing hot shrapnel, mud and rocks like an angry volcano spits lava. So far, none of our men had been hit, but the Japanese fire was quickly zeroing in on our tubes.

Something in the corner of my eye grabbed my attention and I glanced between the sandbags covering the front of our little command hole. The lanky form of Oliver Cameron was stumbling toward us through the smoke. He had lost his hat and had blood on the side of his face, but his camera was still held fast to his hand by its leather strap and his canvas bag was still slung across his shoulder. A shell impacted to Cameron's left and he slumped to one knee. Before I realized what I was doing, I was scrambling out of the hole. Moreno lunged to pull me back, but his hand slipped off of my muddy boot as I pushed off the rim of the hole.

"Frank!" Moreno screamed, his voice immediately drowned out by another impacting mortar round.

I sprinted toward Cameron who balanced on one knee, dazed, as if deciding whether he wanted to remain in that spot or stand back up. An explosion just behind me shoved me forward and sent sharp fragments of metal whistling past my head. The air rippled from the concussive effect of the exploding shells. Despite the tremendous noise of the shelling, deafness had overtaken me; I could hear nothing except my racing heartbeat.

I reached Cameron, who was bleeding from a gash on his forehead, and stuck out my right hand to steady him. Cameron disappeared in a flash of blinding light, I was catapulted backward and my world faded to black.

Chapter 2

Fuzzy, white overhead light assaulted my eyes when I finally had the strength to open them. They would blink open halfway, absorb the brightness for a moment and then surrender again to oblivion. I don't know how long I teetered between sleep and wakefulness, but when I could finally keep my eyes open for more than a few seconds, I noticed that the world which I inhabited was completely different from the one I remembered. Everything seemed white: the light, the ceiling, the sheets on the bed, the pillow, the nurses' uniforms, the enamel metal bed pan and the pitcher of water on the small table beside my bed.

I pushed myself up on my elbows and the room began to spin like a Bing Crosby record. "Easy, lieutenant," a pleasant voice warned from over my shoulder. As I carefully settled my head back on the pillow, the nurse came into view. "How're you feeling?" she asked. She had large brown eyes and brown hair, was a little on the stocky side, and her friendly smile was comforting.

"Never better," I squeaked, my voice struggling to escape my desert-dry mouth. "Can I have some water?"

"Sure you can!" the nice nurse replied, pouring some from the pitcher, which I now noted was strategically placed just beyond my reach.

"Here." She held a paper cup out toward me. "Think you can hold it?"

Did I think I could hold it? What kind of question was that? I was an officer in the United States Army for Pete's sake—a combat veteran! Of course I could hold it! "Sure," I said with a voice that grated like the hinges of a rusty screen door, pushing myself up again and reaching for the cup with my right hand. A moment later, the nurse was toweling me off. She refilled the cup, and this time, she held it to my lips as I took tiny sips.

"There," she announced once I had emptied the cup, "that's it!" She smiled and gave me a wink. "Glad to see you're feeling better." She picked up a clipboard hanging at the foot of my bed and scratched a note on it.

"What day is it?" I asked.

"Saturday," she answered without diverting her attention from the clipboard.

"Which Saturday?"

"June the ninth."

I attempted some quick calculations, the kind most people—even Marines—can perform with little effort, but my mind was still working at a diminished capacity. "How long have I been here?"

"About two weeks. You're lucky. They got you to a field hospital pretty quickly and got you stabilized."

"I'd have been a whole lot luckier not to have been hit in the first place." I tried to grin. It hurt my face.

The nurse laughed. "Well, you're in good hands now."

Again I pushed myself up on my elbows, this time with less dizziness. "What's wrong with me? I don't feel too bad."

She chuckled again. "I reckon you don't. You're on morphine. Now that you're awake, the doctor will probably start weaning you off. But, to answer your question, you had a severe concussion, a broken fibula—that's one of the bones in your leg," she reached over and rapped her knuckles on a plaster cast on my right leg, "a ruptured spleen and numerous lacerations and contusions consistent with shrapnel wounds. You've had three surgeries, one on your spleen, one on your leg and one to get at some stubborn shrapnel." She smiled again and I was beginning to like her. "Plus you got a Purple Heart. A colonel was in here last week touring the ward and handing out decorations."

"How long do I have to stay in here?"

"As long as the doctor says so. He'll come around again later this afternoon. In the meantime, if you need anything, just let me know. I'm Alice," she stepped in a little closer and extended a firm hand, "Alice Ramsay."

"Frank Russell," I managed to say as a new wave of fatigue washed over me. I gave her hand a weak shake and then eased myself back down on the pillow. "Nice to meet you," I muttered before I drifted off to sleep.

My cast came off the last week of July. By then, I was off the pain medication, eating solid food, and spending as much time in the sun as I could. The doctors and nurses were pleased with the rate of my recovery and even hinted that I might be released for limited duty within a couple of weeks. Even though my leg was now freed from its plaster prison, I was still limited to walking with crutches and worked as much as I could to rebuild the muscle tone.

The *Stars And Stripes* was delivered daily to the hospital and I read it cover-to-cover, paying close attention to any mention of the 77th Division. The fighting on Okinawa had been the costliest and most bitter of the Pacific war and I wondered if Lieutenant Brooks and Sergeant Moreno had survived and, if so, where they would be now. According to the paper, the Army, Marines and Navy were now marshalling forces for the next big operation, the invasion of mainland Japan. In the meantime, the Army Air Force was conducting raids with huge formations of B-29 bombers in an effort to burn Japan's major cities to the ground.

Under the circumstances, limited duty didn't sound so bad. I thought I could handle duty on a regimental staff or an administrative headquarters somewhere. Maybe General MacArthur needed a combat-tested aide.

Major Mills, the orthopedic surgeon who had set my leg bone to heal, was strolling through the hospital courtyard with me on the first Monday in August, a sunny, warm morning. I was still required to wear pajamas and a robe, but at least the slippers the hospital provided were comfortable.

"You seem to be maneuvering pretty well, Frank," Dr. Mills observed.

"Yes sir. I think I'm ready to go back to work."

Mills chuckled and that's when I noticed a nurse hurrying toward us—well, actually him. "Colonel Parilli is asking for the staff to assemble," she said, a concerned look on her face.

"Be right there," Mills replied. As she scurried away to find the next doctor, Mills said, "Keep walking, Frank. I'll come back as soon as possible and we'll discuss getting you back to work. Whatever this is shouldn't take long; we don't have any meetings scheduled for this morning."

I had worked up a light sweat by the time Mills returned. I was walking with assistance from my cane, and felt I had an even chance at getting him to set a release date.

"So, what' da'ya say, Doc?" I asked hopefully. "Do I get to check out of the Ritz here and go back to work?"

Mills shook his head. "Sorry, Frank. I think we're going to keep you here for a few more days." Then he broke into a broad smile.

Based on what we read about the atom bomb and what we heard over the radio, I never could figure out why it took the Japanese nine more days—not to mention a second bombing—to surrender. Dr. Mills, a career Army doctor, had been smart enough to keep me in the hospital. As it turned out, that hastened my return trip to the States. If I'd been released back to duty status, no telling how long it would have taken me to earn enough points to rotate home. But, as a combat veteran recovering from wounds, I was assigned to an east-bound transport faster than you could say Fiorello La Guardia.

"Say, lieutenant," the pimply-faced, red-headed sailor asked as he helped me up the ramp onto the USS *President Adams*, "got any souvenirs you'd be willing to sell?"

I guess he figured that because I was still using my cane I had seen some combat—a correct assumption. Unfortunately for him, my time on the front lines had been only slightly longer than the running time of *Gone with the Wind.* He looked a little crestfallen when I explained my situation, but as he was helping me with my heavy duffle bag, I thought the least I could do was show some interest in his enterprise.

"What are you looking for?"

"Oh, just about anything: officers' swords are pretty valuable, Jap flags, pistols, helmets. I can get you top dollar for stuff in good condition."

"There's a pretty good market for the stuff?" I asked.

"Oh, yes sir," he smiled as we reached the top of the gang plank. "Most of our officers have never come closer than a kamikaze to a real Jap. Not much chance to collect a souvenir to impress the missus back home. Now that the fighting is over, a lot of these guys, excuse me sir, gentlemen, understand that the chance to obtain a suitable memento is fading pretty fast. Guys who've been in the real fighting can make quite a bundle of cash."

"If I'd only known," I sighed. Of course if I had known it wouldn't have made any difference. During those few hours I'd been on the front lines, survival had shoved souvenirs completely from my mind. We reached my stateroom, a tiny, gray space I would share for the next two weeks with three other lieutenants. "Thanks for the help," I said, hanging the crook of my cane over my left forearm and shaking the sailor's hand. I was a little winded by climbing the ramp and then threading my way through the crowded passageways of the troopship. My leg was aching a little too. Most of my previous recuperation had consisted of lazy walks on flat ground. "I wish I could do some business with you, but I'm just lucky to be here myself." A small fan was whirring in the upper corner of the tiny cabin but it wasn't enough to cool the space and I wiped the sweat from my brow with the back of my hand.

"Well, if you come across anybody with some Jap gear, let me know," the sailor said. "I'll cut you in for a piece of the action. My name's Chandler and I work the fore deck in first division."

"I'll keep a look out, Chandler. I wish I had some stuff myself, but I don't."

I would soon discover how wrong I was.

My cabin mates were chivalrous enough to let me claim one of the lower bunks since my mobility was still noticeably less than a hundred percent. Like me, their remaining possessions were crammed into duffel bags that now looked like fat, olive-colored sausages. In my case, someone else had done the packing. Once I was wounded, my gear had been returned to company headquarters, then on to battalion and finally to the 77th Division's

G-1, or personnel officer. He, or more likely one of his sergeants, had made sure all my belongings—and believe me, there weren't many—caught up with me before I left the hospital for what I hoped would be a leisurely cruise home.

I was sitting on the side of my bunk sweating in a pair of boxer shorts and a tee shirt, digging through my bag for a clean set of khakis. I was eager, despite the lazy roll of the ship, to get out of my cabin and on to the open deck. The sea breeze and sunshine would be far more pleasant than the stifling heat and stale air down below. While there had been a noticeable relaxation among the Army personnel now sailing east toward their own personnel liberations, we were still aboard an active naval vessel and still subject to military regulations, including proper uniform. The ranking Army officer on board, a lieutenant colonel, had ordered all officers to be in Class C khakis when outside of their assigned quarters.

My cabin mates had deserted me. Ben was probably in a chow line somewhere, JC playing poker with a couple of guys from his old outfit, and Knox roaming the deck with his sketch pad and pencil. I had already pulled from the bag some underwear, socks, and a scuffed pair of dress shoes when my fingers brushed against something hard with a ragged edge. I didn't remember what it might be, but then there were a lot of things I didn't remember from the last couple of months. I felt around carefully in the bowels of the bag and pulled out a film canister that had been ripped open along one edge as though it was a can of beans that had lost a fight with a hatchet. Based on what I knew about photography and film, I was pretty sure the film inside was worthless, having been exposed to the light. I tossed the canister on my bunk and reached back inside.

My fingers felt the rough texture of heavy canvas and closed around what felt like a strap. I tugged on it and worked its cumbersome, heavy bulk from the bag. No wonder the duffel had seemed so heavy! As soon as I got it out into the light of the cabin, I recognized the canvas bag that Cameron, the Australian camera man, had carried. The bag had been ripped along one side leaving a five-inch tear. The shredded canister had probably arrested the momentum of a piece of shrapnel and that had likely saved the other canisters in the bag from a similar fate.

Cameron's wind-up camera was in the bag too, dented, the strap torn away. I didn't know anything about movie cameras and couldn't tell if this one was salvageable or not. The bag was dirty and blood-stained. I remembered just enough about my last few moments on the battlefield to accept the fact that I was holding the possessions of a dead man. I turned the bag over in my hands. "Pacific

Pictures Newsreels, Hollywood, California, USA" was stenciled in faded black ink along the shoulder strap. As I turned the bag back over, the barrel of the Japanese officer's pistol poked through the tear. I remembered that Cameron had laughed when I asked him if it was loaded. I checked it and found that the magazine had been removed and that there was no bullet in the chamber. I thought of Chandler and wondered how much he'd pay for a Japanese pistol---but only for a second.

I emptied the rest of the duffel out on my bunk, flattening my khaki pants as best as I could without the benefit of an iron, and then quickly repacked the duffel. I put Cameron's bag on the very bottom, where it would be safe—and undiscovered.

Chapter 3

"How about a shine for those shoes, lieutenant?"

I had taken the street car down Hollywood Boulevard and was slowly strolling down Vine Street, trying to put as much weight as possible on my leg while leaning as little as possible on my cane. Cameron's bag, minus the pistol which I had left in my hotel room, was over my shoulder and I was wearing my khaki uniform with the overseas cap tilted at what I supposed was a jaunty angle.

A week after arriving in San Francisco, I'd received travel orders to my home of record, Los Angeles. Although it was a struggle to heft the heavy duffel bag, I'd managed with occasional help from sympathetic strangers to clamber aboard a bus to the Oakland train station and then had used my travel orders to requisition a seat on the first train to Bakersfield. From there, I'd hopped a bus to Hollywood. As you might imagine, the trains, buses and stations were crowded with soon-to-be-former servicemen heading home to pick up their lives. Some of us were a little the worse for wear, but all of us were happy to be going home.

I had no family left in Los Angeles; my parents had both passed on during the war. Nonetheless, I considered the city my home. Arriving rather late on a pleasant October evening, I booked a small room at a hotel off Highland Avenue. My plan was to visit Pacific Pictures Studios' newsreel department and hand over Cameron's gear and film, then head into the city and find out if any of the aircraft manufacturers were looking for production supervisors. With the fighting over, I feared that aircraft production was going to be dramatically reduced with a corresponding reduction in available jobs.

The sun was shining, the air pleasantly cool as I turned west on Sunset Boulevard. That's where the shoe shine boy accosted me. "How about it? You don't want to go to your meeting with those scruffy-looking shoes now, do you?" he asked, a wide grin splitting his face. Before I could answer, he spoke again, pointing toward the blue patch on my shoulder. "Say, you with the Liberty Division?" The 77th Division's unit patch was a gold Statue of Liberty against a blue field.

I figured a guy who worked that hard to get to shine a pair of shoes deserved a response, so I stopped and smiled. "Yep, I was with the 77th on Okinawa."

"That where you got your limp?" My inquisitor was a young black man, about my height, wearing a white t-shirt and a faded pair of dungarees.

"Yep," I nodded. "How about you? Where'd you get it?" He wasn't the only one who could be observant. His right hand was missing most of its thumb and forefinger. He smiled again, a knowing smile as though he and I shared a bond due to our wounds.

"Out in the deep blue somewhere. I never was really sure where we were. I spent most of my time down in the galley dishing slop. Then one day when we were all at battle stations, there's a big crash and things just turn to hell in a second. Fire and smoke all over the place and I'm scrambling around trying to help fight the fire and I go to turn on the hose and I ain't got no way to turn the handle. I look down at my hand and I'm missing some pieces!" With that, he laughed, and although I wasn't sure why it was funny, I joined him.

I stuck out my hand and said, "I'm Frank Russell."

Still smiling, he said, "I'm Marcus Shreves. Pardon me for not shaking your hand, but I expect you don't want to go to your meeting with shoe polish all over you."

I was really intrigued now, so I placed my right shoe on the angled top of Marcus' shoe shine box and said, "You're right, Marcus. These dogs need to look a little better before I go inside." He smiled again and whipped out a can of brown polish and a multi-colored rag and dropped down on his knees. I watched as Marcus worked quickly, wiping off my shoes with the rag and then applying polish with his hand. "How'd you know I'm going to a meeting?" I asked.

"Well, Frank," he said without looking up, "you seemed to be moving with a purpose, even if you are moving a little slow with your cane and all. And I know that bag you're carrying ain't Army issue. And I see the name Pacific Pictures stenciled on it and I figure you're headed to the gate over there for a meeting or appointment or something." He nodded toward the main gate to the studio, which was about a hundred feet beyond the northwest corner of Sunset and Vine where I was now standing getting a shoe shine.

"I'm pretty impressed," I said, and I was. "I ended up with some stuff that seems to belong to the newsreel department."

Marcus continued to work, now moving to my left shoe. "You're in the right place, Frank. Just go up to the gate there and tell them you'd like to see Mr. Burke. He's head of newsreels."

I chuckled. "Is there anything you don't know, Marcus?"

"Not much," he laughed as he began to buff my shoes with a clean cloth. "You being in uniform and all, I don't think you'll have any trouble with those picketers, but if I was you I wouldn't speak to them."

Until that moment, I hadn't even noticed the dozen or so men walking back and forth in front of the studio gate holding signs that said "ON STRIKE."

"What are they striking about?"

"Well, see," Marcus snapped his buffing cloth one last time across the toes of my shoes and stood up, a smirk on his face, "they ain't never been at battle stations and they don't know how good they got it."

"How much I owe you?"

"Two bits, please."

I gave him thirty cents and said, "Keep the change. And thanks for the information, Marcus."

"Thank you, Frank. Now any time you need a shine just hop on down to Sunset and Vine!"

Just as Marcus predicted, the picketers saw my uniform and gave me a free pass. In fact, they seemed to be giving everybody a pass. A large, black Chrysler sedan pulled up to the gate and the picketers parted like the Red Sea to let it through, some of them even doffing their caps. The main entrance to Pacific Pictures Studios was comprised of an inbound lane and an outbound lane between which sat a guardhouse. From here, three uniformed, but unarmed, gentlemen raised and lowered whitewashed barricade poles to control traffic. There were sidewalks on either side of the driveways and it was one of these that I used.

After waving the Chrysler through the raised barricade, one of the guards noticed me. "Help you, sir?" he asked, taking in my uniform, which was a marked contrast to his own. His was pulled tightly across an expansive stomach that showed no effect of wartime rationing.

"I'm here to see Mr. Burke in the newsreel department," I said as though I'd been there a hundred times before. Of course I hadn't, and if this fellow was a regular on the gate he'd know that. He reached into the guardhouse and picked up a clipboard holding several yellow sheets of paper.

"Have an appointment, sir?"

"No, but I'm sure he'll see me. I'm returning some equipment and film that was shot at Okinawa." This little revelation got the guard's attention and he straightened up a bit.

"May I have your name?" he asked before ducking back into the guardhouse and picking up a telephone. I could hear his muffled voice, but the sound of the mockingbirds singing in the pepper trees that lined the perimeter of the studio grounds was far more appealing. In a moment, the guard was back. "Please step this way, Lieutenant Russell," he said, leading me around the barricade and along the sidewalk to a small patio with a couple of benches. The whole area around the studio gate was landscaped with manicured bushes and colorful flowers. The message I got was that the movie business hadn't suffered too much due to the war. "Someone will be right out," the guard said, gesturing toward the benches and tipping his cap before turning and heading back to his post.

I took a seat, happy to give my leg a rest, and enjoyed the cool air and the warm sunshine. For the first time in over two years, I was the only guy in sight wearing a military uniform.

"Lieutenant Russell?" I looked up to see an older man walking toward me. He was lean with very short gray hair and black-rimmed glasses. He wore a gray tweed jacket with dark slacks, a white shirt and a dark blue tie. "I'm George Burke," he smiled, extending his hand.

I pushed myself up from the bench. "Frank Russell," I replied with a smile. "I think I have some things that belong to you."

"Yes," Burke answered, "that's what Pete said over the phone." I gathered Pete was the guard.

I pivoted back toward the bench and picked up Oliver Cameron's bag. "This ended up in my personal effects when I left Okinawa," I began, handing the bag over to Burke. "Oliver Cameron was with our company when he was killed. I'm not sure how I ended up with this stuff, but it belongs to you."

The weight of the bag caused Burke's arm to sag a bit as he took hold of it. He looked from the bag back to me and then noticed my cane. "Lieutenant Russell, do you have a few minutes to come inside?"

"As you might surmise, our department is not a money maker for Pacific Pictures," George Burke explained as I took a seat in front of his cluttered desk. "Abe Baum, Pacific's founder, decided years ago that the studio would produce newsreels as a public service, but I suspect the whole truth is that movie-goers expect to see the news when they go to the theater and that Abe understood that." Burke was pouring two cups of coffee from the baked enamel pot on the hot plate on the corner of his desk. "At any rate, what budget we get goes into production, not accommodations," he said with a nod toward the block walls of his Spartan office. "How do you take it?"

"Black is fine."

"So tell me, Lieutenant Russell, how did you come to be in possession of this gear?" he gestured with his coffee cup to Cameron's bag as he handed me the other.

"Please, call me Frank," I replied. "To tell you the truth, I have no idea. Like I said, Mr. Cameron had joined our company just the day before. The next morning, he was killed and I was wounded, and somehow I ended up with that shoulder bag and the stuff inside it." I neglected to mention the pistol, but then again, that didn't really belong to Pacific Pictures anyway. "I didn't even discover I had it until I got out of the hospital and was on the ship headed back to the States."

Burke took a seat behind his desk and examined the bag, running his fingers reflectively along the rip and the brown stains. Then he unfastened the clasps holding it closed. Carefully, he removed eight film canisters, segregating them into two piles—one of five and one of three. Then he pulled out the camera itself. "Would you look at that," he said softly, his eyes fixed on the camera while slowly shaking his head in wonder. "Quite a rugged piece of gear." His right hand gently wiped dust and dirt from the housing. "It's got a couple of nicks and dents on it," he said as he wound the key, "but there's tension in the spring and the lenses look to be in serviceable condition. I guess we can't say the same for Oliver." He pressed his lips together and looked back at me. "Well, Oliver knew what he was getting into. He'd been on Iwo Jima and the Philippines so he was well aware of the risks involved in what he was doing."

"Did you assign him to those places?" I asked.

"Heavens no! All our combat photographers were volunteers. They went because they wanted to be part of the action and bring back the story." Burke reached over his coffee cup and flipped the switch on his intercom box. "Stan, can you come in here, please." Turning his attention back to me he asked, "Do you have plans for the rest of the morning, Frank?" I shook my head no.

There was a tap on Burke's open office door and I turned to see another guy stick his head in. He was younger than Burke, but not by a whole lot. "You rang, master?"

"Stan, meet Frank Russell," Burke nodded toward me and Stan offered his hand.

"Nice to meet you, Frank," he smiled.

"Frank's just back from the Pacific. He brought back some of Oliver's gear."

"Oh." Stan's smile faded.

Burke stacked up the canisters in the larger pile and handed them to Stan. "Run these over to the lab and put them in the front of the queue. It's the least we can do for Oliver."

"On it right now," Stan replied and hustled back out of the office.

"Stan's our chief cutter," Burke explained after his colleague departed.

"Cutter?" I asked.

"Film editor. He takes all the footage and matches sequences up with the cameraman's notes." He opened the canvas bag wider, peering inside and determined that it was now empty. "It doesn't look like Oliver's notes survived him."

"What are you going to do with the rest of that film?" I asked, pointing to the three canisters left on Burke's desk.

"This is unexposed. We'll have one of the lab boys check it and if it's still in good shape we'll use it to film another story. As Abe often reminds us, 'This isn't MGM.'" He laughed at that and I smiled, but I didn't really get the joke.

Although I was satisfied that my mission was complete, I accepted Burke's kind invitation for a tour of the studio. The morning had warmed up, the sun perched happily in a pristine blue sky. I didn't know it at the time, but it was the kind of day that had lured the motion picture industry to southern California in the first place. Back in the days before artificial lighting, the pioneer movie-makers like Jesse Lasky and Cecil B. DeMille had realized that the weather back east was too inconsistent to keep filming on schedule, especially in the winter, when weeks could pass without the bright sunlight needed to illuminate a set.

We started at another non-descript, white-washed block building, which turned out to be where Stan had taken Oliver Cameron's film. Burke walked me through the building and explained the step-by-step chemical processes involved in developing movie film. He was obviously fascinated by it, but I didn't really understand much—only that the film had to be kept in the dark until it was developed. Next door was a building of similar size and appearance. This is where the cutters, or editors, worked. Here there were spools of film all over the work tables and shelves, along with cardboard barrels modified by flimsy racks which spanned their diameters. On these racks, the cutters hung pieces of film until they were ready to splice them together to tell a story. Hand-cranked spindles were used during editing to move the film along as the newsreel was assembled scene-by-scene. A small room next to the editors' workroom had been converted into a tiny theater, a projection room with a six-foot screen on one wall and a movie projector surrounded by half a dozen mismatched folding chairs.

Leaving the newsreel buildings, we stepped back out into the pleasant morning. "Now that you've seen the slums," Burke smiled, "let me show you how the other half lives." We walked toward three huge structures that would have looked at home on an airfield. "These are the heart of the studio," Burke explained, "the sound stages where all of our interior production shots are staged. Even when we go up to the San Fernando Valley for on-location shooting, the interior scenes are filmed here. See that red light over the door?" he pointed to a slowly revolving red light above the door of one of the buildings. "That means the stage is in production. Open that door right now and the wrath of the entire production team, director, producer, technicians, even actors, will come crashing down on you." The red lights were shining on two of the buildings, but the third was off and Burke escorted me inside. "Watch your step," he cautioned, pointing to a collection of cables snaking across the floor.

"Big," I said, which no doubt must have made Burke wonder why he was wasting his time on me. "And empty."

He laughed. "Sure, now. But you should see this place when they start filming. I've seen it go from an ocean to a desert to Berlin under an air raid and New York during Prohibition. It's amazing to see it transform. This, Frank, is where the magic happens!"

I asked a couple of questions just to show I was interested. It was endearing to see Burke's face light up as he answered. I could tell he was passionate about the movie business, even if he was relegated to the newsreel department. To me, the soundstage looked like a giant, empty warehouse, but as we were leaving, Burke pointed out a large wooden sign affixed to the outer wall. On it were listed the movies that had been filmed inside. The list was long and I recognized several, including the

Kit Justice serials and *The Brookridge Girls*, which had come out just before the war.

Just below the list of pictures was a small bronze plague. I moved in closer to look at it. "That's a memorial to Candy Cain," Burke said from over my shoulder. "She was going to be a big star for us."

"What happened to her?"

"She was killed on a war bond trip to England. She was visiting Army bases over there and her plane crashed. She worked on this soundstage often. She was a real sweetheart too, not like some of the young actresses on the lot these days."

We stepped around the corner of the soundstage and I thought for a moment I'd taken a wrong turn. Suddenly, I was staring at the New York skyline, complete with the distinctive Empire State Building and other skyscrapers I couldn't name. Burke just chuckled. "Pretty realistic, isn't it? Come on," he tugged me by the sleeve. "It's all about perspective, see?" From where we stood, the buildings looked real, but as we walked a few paces down the "New York" street, the façade quickly shrank into nothing more than an elaborate backdrop. Burke led me behind the skyline and showed me the nothingness behind it. Then, turning around, I found myself in the middle of the dirt street of an old western town. Hitching posts stood empty in front of the wooden boardwalk spanning the fronts of a saloon and general store.

"Amazing," I mumbled, which brought another chuckle from Burke. "So all those movies I saw were really made here, not out in the old Wild West somewhere?"

"All the Pacific Pictures westerns anyway. We rarely film on location. Only the projects that have the biggest box office potential film away from the studio. It's a lot easier and cheaper to film here on the back lot and in the soundstages than to go on location and have to feed and house all the crew for several weeks."

My leg was starting to ache a little, but Burke carried on as if he had nothing in the world to do but entertain me. He led me to the technical area and we stuck our heads inside the carpentry, paint and electrical shops. The latter was stuffed full of various kinds of spotlights, wheeled tripods and seemingly miles of heavy, black cables. Pick-up trucks and motorized carts were parked helter-skelter around these smaller buildings, most of them partially loaded with equipment and supplies destined, I guessed, for one of the soundstages.

The clear, cool morning had turned to a warm mid-day by the time we approached Pacific Pictures Studios' main building. "Now this," Burke the tireless tour guide continued, "is the nerve center for the entire enterprise—the Aaronson

Building. Here reside the offices of Mr. Abe Baum, president of Pacific Pictures, along with his key staff members in finance, accounting, personnel, publicity and so forth. Abe and his partner Morty Aaronson started the studio back in 1919 and we've been cranking out pictures ever since. Of course, Aaronson is long gone, it's just Abe now." The building was three stories tall, a pale yellow U-shaped stucco structure with a central courtyard filled with roses and other flowers which obviously received daily attention from a team of gardeners. As we entered the garden through the open end of the U, I noticed people moving toward a set of double doors on the ground floor of the building. Some were in office attire, some in work clothes and a few in costumes, as though they'd just stepped out of one of the soundstages.

"Come on," Burke nodded toward the double doors. "Let me buy you lunch as a small token of Pacific Pictures' appreciation for the return of Oliver's camera and film." I followed Burke through the doors, removing my overseas cap and tucking it under my belt. We turned to our left and joined a cafeteria-style line, picking up a nicked, wooden tray and sliding it along a wooden counter as the commissary staff ladled portions of food onto our plates. I got fried chicken, macaroni and cheese, green beans, whipped potatoes with gravy, rolls and butter, and a piece of chocolate cake. A cooler filled with ice and bottles of pop sat at the end of the counter, just before the cash register. I pulled out a green bottle of Coca-Cola and used the opener, secured to the cooler by a light chain, to open it.

"Go ahead and find us a seat," Burke said from over my shoulder. "I'll settle up."

I balanced my cane and tray and stepped away from the serving line and toward the rows of wooden tables and chairs which were gradually filling up with midday diners. The dining room was open and airy with tall windows letting in the light from outside. The black and white tile floor reflected the scattered sounds of cutlery and dishes clacking against each other and the low mumble of two dozen conversations filling the hall. Oversized movie posters, some yellowed by years of exposure to the bright light streaming through the windows, decorated the walls.

I scanned the room for an appealing table and that's when I saw her for the first time. This may sound trite, but my heart did a little flip and I knew right then where I was going to sit! She was dressed in a blue gingham dress covered by a white apron. A matching bonnet was tied loosely around her neck, leaving her honey-colored hair to reflect the sunlight like a Madonna's halo. She had high cheeks that looked like they'd been brushed by roses. She was seated at a six-place table at the front of the long dining room. She was gabbing with a couple of others also in costume, but my brain disregarded her colleagues.

It was a reflection of my two years living mostly among men when I reached her table and asked with a dumb grin, "Hey, good looking. Where have you been hiding?"

She cocked her head and fixed me with a blue-eyed gaze that short-circuited every cell in my brain that was capable of rational thought. "Over on Soundstage 3 working my ass off for twelve hours a day." She stuffed a forkful of ham in her mouth without shifting her gaze and without smiling.

My lack of interaction with the fairer sex left me unable—or unwilling—to interpret the signals she was sending, so in true infantry fashion, I forged ahead. "Mind if I join you?" I asked as I pulled the chair out from under the table.

"You would do that for me?" she asked with raised eyebrows. "You would grace my humble existence with your magnificent masculinity?" She batted her eyelashes, her eyes the deep blue of the cool Pacific on a hot, sunny afternoon. I was so out of practice that her mocking tone barely registered.

Then, from over my shoulder a strong, deep voice snapped me out of my romantic trance. "That's my seat, pardner." I turned around ready to tell the guy to shove off, that I'd gotten there first, that I was enjoying the first blissful moments of the relationship which would define my remaining time on earth. But there in the flesh stood Saturday's hero, Kit Justice himself. He was dressed in his trademark light blue shirt, denim jeans protected by leather chaps, and black boots, with a dark blue kerchief knotted around his neck.

"Hey, Kit Justice, right?" The big man smiled. "Yeah, I was in the Army with your co-star, Pepe. Remember him?"

Kit Justice's smile vanished, replaced by a grimace. "That little scene-stealer?"

"He saved my life."

"Just as long as you didn't save his ..." Justice shouldered his way around me and set his tray on the table.

Before I could say something that would no doubt have resulted in intense embarrassment and a likely lifetime ban from Pacific Pictures' commissary, George Burke had snagged me by the arm and was leading me toward the other side of the room.

"Aww. Cheer up; life could always be worse!" the girl of my dreams said sarcastically as I stumbled away.

Despite my obvious discomfort, Burke was smiling. "We don't eat with the 'talent,'" he explained setting his tray on a four-seat table in the corner. "Here, sit."

I put my tray down, sat with my back to the girl's table and straightened my leg. "I think she really likes me. Who is that heavenly creature?" I inquired with eyes that were still a little star-struck.

Burke laughed and took a bite of fish. "That, my friend, is Vera Vance, star of the silver screen and 'heavenly' she is not. She's now appearing in *No Pause for Justice*, Pacific's first Kit Justice feature since the end of the war. That's Terry Thorpe, who plays Kit, that you just met. Encountered." He smiled again. He was clearly more amused than me.

"How about that?" I mused, shaking my head.

"What? Oh hey, there's somebody I want you to meet." Burke stood up and waved to someone behind me. "Come on over, Goz!" he called. "Frank, meet Larry Gosnell, director of publicity for Pacific Pictures."

I stood and shook hands with Gosnell, who had a fleshy but firm grip. "Pleased to meet you, Frank," he said sitting next to Burke and across the table from me. "What brings the Army's finest to our little world on such a lovely day?" Gosnell was heavyset, the buttons of his shirt threatening to pop loose from their assigned holes at any moment. His hair was well oiled and combed back from a round, friendly face. He had a broad forehead, blue eyes and a white, even smile. He was handsome enough to have been in the movies himself, maybe as a younger Judge Hardy.

"Frank came to do us a favor," Burke began and then related the circumstances of my visit. He shared my connection with Oliver Cameron and through him with Pacific Pictures. Before he could recount my all-too-brief encounter with the beautiful Miss Vance, I interrupted.

"Actually, I have one other connection with Pacific Pictures," I smiled, stabbing some macaroni noodles. "My platoon sergeant on Okinawa was Mickey Moreno." Burke and Gosnell glanced briefly at each other and then looked back at me.

"No kidding," Gosnell said. "Imagine that. A small world, as they say. And you were with Mickey on Okinawa?"

"Right!"

"What happened? To him, I mean."

I chased some more noodles around my plate and confessed, "I don't really know. I was on the line less than two days when I got wounded. I came to in an army hospital. I don't know what happened to Moreno."

"Well," Gosnell smiled, "it's not every day we get to have lunch with a hero, eh George? I hope you bought his lunch."

"Oh, Mr. Burke—" I began.

"George—" Burke corrected.

"—George has been a gracious host. He gave me a tour of the studio and bought me lunch and managed to rescue me even when I didn't realize I needed rescuing." George laughed out loud, briefly drawing attention from a couple of nearby tables.

Burke shared his version of my encounter with the "talent," which caused Gosnell to laugh too.

"What are your duties, Mr. Gosnell?"

"Please! That sounds way too formal. Around here people call me Goz." His smile and bright eyes were friendly and his genial manner put me at ease—unlike some of the other patrons in the dining room. "I'm in charge of publicity for the studio."

"Goz is the master of superlatives," Burke interjected. "Every picture is the 'best' or 'funniest' or 'most heart-warming' or 'most suspenseful.' I don't know how he does it. I would have run out years ago."

Goz's eyes twinkled. "My office works with each movie's producer to come up with a good publicity campaign. That includes everything from the trailer to the lobby posters, newspaper ads, premier showings and the star's personal appearances. On top of that, we work with our talent to keep them in the public eye between pictures."

"How many stars do you have?" I asked.

"Four that can headline a movie, well, five now that Thorpe is back. Plus we have a good roster of contract players, mostly character actors and actresses who fill supporting roles. And then we've got a few up and coming youngsters Abe is hoping to develop into stars, like Beverly Skardon and Miss Vance, for instance," he tipped his head toward the talent. I saw his eyes shift and his body tense. "Uh oh. How'd she get in here?" I turned to see a woman of about forty striding confidently toward our table. She was dressed in a bright yellow suit with matching heels and a hat that sported the remains of at least one plucked bird. Her white gloved hands held onto a purse out of which stuck a fountain pen and small note pad.

"Hello, Goz darling!" she sang out as she approached. "Jane told me I could find you here."

Goz was on his feet by now and George and I stood as well. Goz flashed his smile and greeted the woman. "Joan Roswell, Hollywood's favorite columnist! To what do we owe the pleasure of your company?"

"Just catching up with all the news from my favorite studio!"

"MGM's over in Culver City. You must have taken a wrong turn!"

Joan Roswell threw her head back and laughed, a shrill, tittering sound. By now, nearly everyone in the dining room was staring at her. She was no Vera Vance, but for a woman her age was still quite attractive. Her blonde hair was stylishly fixed, her green eyes heavily made-up. Her voice was high pitched, like an opera singer who'd wandered away from the stage. "Oh, Goz, you are so rich!" She glanced at George and me and then back to Goz. "Aren't you going to introduce me, dear?" she asked, showing off a beautiful smile.

"Of course," Goz grinned and turned toward George. "You remember George Burke, head of newsreels." George offered his hand.

"Oh yes! We both have the same mission," she batted her eyes at George, "keeping the movie-going public informed, though we have different means at our disposal." She shook his hand.

"And this strapping young man is Lieutenant Frank Russell," Goz said, sweeping his hand toward me. "Frank's just back from the war." I shook her hand.

"Charmed," she smiled. Then glancing back at Goz, she asked, "Aren't you going to invite me to join you?"

Goz blushed and laughed. "I've forgotten my manners today. Won't you sit with us, Joan?"

"Thank you, darling," she purred, and I pulled out the chair next to mine. I could smell her now, a mixture of rose-scented perfume and powder that was really quite pleasant and not at all what I was accustomed to.

"What can I get you to eat, Miss Roswell?" George asked.

"Oh, let's see, maybe some fruit and a little salad. With oil and vinegar. And a lemonade, George. Thank you." George headed toward the serving line and Goz and I sat back down. "Back from the war, Frank?"

"Yes ma'am."

"None of that! It's Joan, darling."

"Yes, Joan." That made her smile.

"You know, after those little Japanese bastards attacked Pearl Harbor there was a real fear that the west coast would be next. All the wags around town said Pacific Pictures would be the safest place to be in the event of an air raid."

"Why's that, Joan?" I asked.

"Because they hadn't had a hit in years!" Joan threw back her head and tittered again. Goz rolled his eyes.

"Why *are* you here, darling?"

Goz intercepted the question. "Frank was returning some exposed film shot by one of George's cameramen who was killed on Okinawa. Frank brought back the film and the camera. In return for this good deed, we thought we'd treat Frank to a free lunch. And now he's lucky enough to dine with a famous columnist to boot." I nodded.

"Okinawa you say?" Joan was eyeing me again. "Did you see a lot of action?"

"Yes and no," I laughed. "I wasn't there long, but the time I spent was pretty intense. I was wounded on my third day and the next thing I knew I was in a hospital."

"And now here you are back in the good old USA! How marvelous!" George returned and set a tray in front of Miss Roswell. "Thank you, George. You're such a dear!"

"Just out looking for a story, Joan, or is there something particular I can help you with?" Goz asked, leaning forward in his chair.

Joan carefully forked a dainty bite of her green salad between her bright red lips. "I'm interested in the studio's response to these picketers at the gate. You've only got a few here, but they're really causing Jack a problem over at Warner Brothers. They keep blocking his gates."

"Well look, Joan," Goz began, "we really don't want to get dragged into this fight. It's a union issue. CSU and IATSE are battling over who's going to do what jobs and who's going to represent which trades. The studios are sort of on the sidelines."

"Yet it's the studios that are being picketed?"

"Well, sure," Goz grinned. "On background, all right?"

Joan nodded. I was lost. I had no idea what CSU and IATSE and background meant. I felt as if I'd just blundered upon a cricket match: I knew both sides were playing a game with some rules, but had no idea what those rules—or their strategies—were.

Goz resumed, "CSU is picketing the studios because they won't get Joan Roswell or anybody else to pay attention if they picket another union's headquarters. You know better than anyone that the studios represent the glamour of Hollywood. They're here and at Warner's and Columbia and MGM and Paramount because that's what will get them noticed. But like I said, we're trying to keep out of it. It's a jurisdictional issue that the unions need to work out."

Joan chewed and stared at him for a moment. Then she smiled again. "Mind if I quote you?"

"Background, remember?"

"Oh, all right!" she snapped, but her annoyance seemed contrived to me, as though she was merely pretending to be put out. She set her fork down and looked Goz squarely in the eyes. "You know the story I'm really after."

"Can't help you with that one." Goz held her stare. After a few moments, Joan tittered again and dropped her stare.

"What a treat for me to dine with three handsome gents," she pushed back her chair and we all stood. "So nice to meet you Frank," she said, shaking my hand. "George, thank you for your hospitality. And Goz, please tell Jane I said 'thank you.' Now, dear, call me when you have news I can share with my readers. They love to hear about Pacific Pictures!"

"I'll do that," Goz said through a tense smile. "Let me walk you out."

"No need, dear! I can find my way. So long!"

Joan tossed smiles and waves as she made her way back through the dining room. "Finish your lunch," Goz said, watching her exit the main doors. "I'll be right back." Goz trailed behind Joan and disappeared through the doors.

"What was that all about?" I asked.

"Joan Roswell is an unofficial power broker. She doesn't own a studio or direct pictures or run a chain of theaters, but she can make or break a star or a picture or even a studio. When she's around, you're walking on egg shells. She can take a casual comment and turn it into two weeks' worth of news. Well, not news, but gossip and innuendo and that's worse. She's not as widely read as Hedda Hopper or Louella Parsons, but she works a lot harder. She's more aggressive too."

"She can be vindictive too," Goz added, returning to the table, "that's why we always treat her like a VIP. I wanted to make sure she left the lot. The last headache I need is her wandering around on her own and getting into trouble."

"Causing trouble," George corrected with a laugh. "You should tell your secretary not to let her off her leash."

"Jane didn't let her in here unescorted. My guess is that Joan sweet-talked her way past the gate and came straight here." Goz shook his head, then chuckled. "Oh well, another day in paradise, huh? Say, Frank, since you've gone to all this trouble on our behalf--" I wasn't sure if he meant fighting the Japanese or returning the film--"how about I take you upstairs and introduce you to Abe?"

We turned in our cafeteria trays and then Goz and I headed up to the third floor and Pacific Pictures president Abe Baum's office. Suite would have been a better description. From the third floor corridor, Goz pushed open the glass door leading into the reception area. A knock-out gorgeous woman wearing a blue dress with a plunging neckline was seated behind a desk, the top of which was clear of all clutter save a single note pad and a telephone.

"Hi, Goz!" she sang out as we entered.

"Hello, Betty! How's my girl?" Goz took her offered hand and lifted it to kiss. She positively glowed at his attention and I could tell that Goz was pretty good at making people feel appreciated. "The chief in?"

"He's in the dining room," she cooed. "Want me to buzz him?" Great, I thought. We'd just come up from the dining room and now we'd get to go all the way back down. Just shows how little I knew about the ways of the movie business.

"Naw, that's all right. We're just going to poke our heads in to say 'hello.' Oh, what am I thinking!" Goz slapped his forehead. "Betty, meet Frank Russell, just back from the war." Betty stood and I discovered that she had a figure to match her face.

"Very nice to meet you, Frank!" she flashed a radiant smile at me.

"Nice to meet you, too," I replied working hard to focus on her pretty blue eyes.

Betty stepped around the desk and said, "Follow me." Watching her walk was a rare pleasure and I began to wonder if all the women at Pacific Pictures were so lovely. Betty led us down a darkly-paneled hallway lined with framed movie posters. The carpet we walked on was so thick we left footprints. We reached the end of the corridor and Betty knocked twice on a heavy wooden door, then pushed it open and stepped aside. Goz walked right in and so I followed.

"Abe, have you got just a minute?" he said to the well-dressed man sitting at the head of an otherwise empty, expensive looking six-place dining table made from a solid piece of some dark, heavy wood. The chairs were made of matching wood with wine-colored, cushioned leather seats. A sheaf of papers was sitting on a corner of the table next to an unfinished salad. The private dining room included not only the table and chairs, all very expensive looking, but also a seating area dominated by a stone fire place, sofa and arm chairs upholstered in matching wine-colored leather.

Abe Baum wiped his narrow lips with a linen napkin, pushed back from the table and stood. He wore his gray hair so closely trimmed that he might have been bald. His light brown suit fit impeccably and the handkerchief in its front pocket matched his red and gold tie.

"Abe, allow me to introduce Frank Russell," Goz said, sweeping his beefy hand toward me. Baum looked at me with a wrinkled brow, confusion in his brown eyes.

"What? We're not shooting any war picture right now."

Goz understood before I did. "No, we're not. Frank is not on our payroll. He's been in the Pacific Theater."

"Oh," Baum smiled, a note of relief in his voice. "The one over in Santa Monica?"

Now it was my turn to be confused. Again it was Goz to the rescue. "The war in the Pacific. Frank's been fighting the Japanese."

"Oh! Why didn't you say so?" He grabbed my hand and shook it. He was a small man, only about five feet six, but his hand was hard as a rock though his grip was surprisingly gentle. "Come sit down, sit down. Let me get Kevin to bring you some lunch."

"We ate downstairs, Abe," Goz explained and we remained standing. "I just wanted you to have a chance to meet Frank. He took the time to bring George Burke one of our cameras that had been lost in combat."

"Oh?" Baum said "Oh" a lot. "Well that's great, just great, because this isn't MGM you know. Thank you, Frank. Thank you very much."

"Happy to be of help, Mr. Baum."

"Abe, please! Everyone here calls me Abe." He was smiling and friendly and I wondered why he had been eating alone.

"It's ironic, Abe," I said, trying out his name.

"Oh? How's that?" he asked with a smile.

"Well, when I was sent up to the front lines on Okinawa, my platoon sergeant was Mickey Moreno. And here I am at Pacific Pictures."

Baum's smile froze and his eyes hardened, but just for a moment. "Well, that is a coincidence. And how is Mickey?"

"Unfortunately, sir, I don't know. I was wounded within two days and never saw him after that. I woke up a week or so later in a hospital, the war ended and I got shipped home."

"Well," Baum said, relaxing again, "thank you for your service to this great country of ours. And thank you for returning George's equipment. We're always on a tight budget. Every nickel counts."

"Anyway," Goz picked up the conversation, "I knew you'd want to have a chance to thank this young hero yourself, Abe." Then to me he added, "Abe has been a big benefactor of the USO and the Stage Door Canteen. The studio loaned a lot of talent to shows touring our bases both here and overseas, plus we did a lot of work on the war bond drives. We're all really grateful for all you boys did." Goz turned back to Abe. "Joan Roswell was on the lot. We bought her lunch."

"What'd she want?"

"A quote about the picketers. I stayed on background."

Abe nodded, but didn't speak. With that, Goz laid his big hand on my shoulder and with barely perceptible pressure nudged me toward the door.

"A pleasure to meet you, Abe," I nodded.

"Oh, same here. Thank you again for all you've done. Please let me know if we can ever help you out."

We were back out in the hallway when Goz said, "Abe's a great guy. Fierce temper, but he really cares about people. Very loyal."

I'd find out that Goz was right.

Goz ushered me out of the main building, shook hands with me again and then sent me back over to the newsreel department where George Burke was waiting.

"Frank," he began as I settled into the uncomfortable wooden chair in front of his desk, "you've been more than generous already, but I wonder if you'd let us impose on you just a little more?"

I was on terminal leave from the Army. In another week, I'd be out of the service completely. It wasn't like I had a lot of obligations. Plus, all the people I'd met so far at Pacific Pictures had treated me swell. Well, almost all of them. "How can I help?" I asked.

"Typically, when one of our cameramen sends in his film, it's accompanied by the notes he took. It usually takes the form of a log. He'll tell us that on roll one, scene one, we're seeing such and such a person doing such and such work. That helps us tell viewers what's happening on screen. Of course in the case of the film you brought back, we don't have Oliver's notes. Would you be willing to help us go through the footage and identify people and activities as much as you can? It won't take that long. You brought us five rolls of exposed film, so that's only about fifteen minutes of film that you'd have to watch. Could you help us with that?"

How could I not after the way he and Goz and even Abe Baum had treated me? "Sure," I answered, "it'd be my pleasure."

George smiled. "Great! How about tomorrow morning? I'll give Pete at the gate your name. Say, right after breakfast?"

George was all smiles as he walked with me through the early afternoon sunshine and to the studio gate. He shook my hand again and reiterated, "Right after breakfast." I should have thought to ask him what time he ate.

Chapter 4

I arrived the next morning just after 7 a.m. I was still accustomed to the Army routine, which was up early, eat early, work early and keep at it all day. I felt a little self-conscious dressed in civilian clothes, but I figured I might as well get used to it. I also decided it was time to get used to walking without the cane, so I'd left it in my hotel room. A green, slat-sided produce truck decorated with a giant picture of a pair of tomatoes and a head of lettuce, rumbled by but otherwise the streets were quiet. I turned the corner at Sunset and Vine and didn't see Marcus the shoe shine man. I guess he was still on Navy time and racked out somewhere. There also weren't any picketers this morning. I checked in at the gate, expecting to see Pete, but he wasn't on duty yet either, so another guard, Dennis, checked my name against the visitors list and passed me through. I headed to the western side of the lot toward the newsreel department office. It was empty, so I made myself at home. I rinsed out the coffee pot on George's desk and started a fresh one. Once the coffee was ready, I poured some into a heavy ceramic mug and stepped out into the cool morning sunshine. It was going to be another pretty day, sun shining, birds singing. But the sound coming from the direction of the studio gate wasn't birds, instead, it sounded like the crowd at a ball game: a low hum occasionally punctuated by cheers.

I strolled toward the gate and the buzz grew in volume. I heard shouts, angry shouts. Then, the big black Chrysler rolled through the gate and turned away from me and toward the main building. I spotted George Burke passing the barricade, looking over his shoulder. His bow tie was askew and as he straightened his jacket, I could see an exasperated look on his face. He'd taken a few steps in my direction when he saw me and gave me a wave, his lips pressed together in a grim smile.

"Quite a reception, huh?" he said, walking toward me along the raked pea gravel path.

"Reception?"

"Yes, all the picketers!"

"Ah. They weren't there when I arrived."

"Lucky for you. They're not as docile as yesterday. They were banging on Abe's car when he pulled up and then jostled me. Nothing dangerous, but clearly intimidating. What time did you get here?"

"Right at seven," I replied.

"Here," George said, sweeping his arm toward the gate and the street beyond, "come have a look."

As we approached the gate from the studio side, more and more men came into view, nearly all of them dressed in workmen's clothes and many of them carrying signs. "STUDIOS UNFAIR!" one sign proclaimed in bold red letters. Whereas the previous day there had been only a handful of marchers, today there were dozens.

I sipped from my mug and asked, "What are they after? More money?"

"Not exactly. In fact, I don't really understand the whole thing. It's sort of an argument between two of the union groups over who gets to represent the studios' carpenters."

"Studio carpenters are unionized?"

"All the trades are unionized."

"What union are you in?" I asked naively.

George laughed. "I'm in management. The real issue here is if the other trades decide to honor the carpenters' picket line—which they haven't so far. But if they do, that would put a serious crimp on production and that means a financial impact."

"So what does Mr. Baum do in a situation like this?"

"Abe and Mayer and Warner and the other studio heads are trying to stay out of the fray. They're encouraging the unions to work it out. We'll see what happens," he continued taking me by the elbow and turning me back toward his office. "Stan's got Oliver's film ready for us to look at today. I'm hopeful you can explain to us what's going on and maybe even identify some of the people in the frames."

I poured George a mug of coffee while he buzzed over to Stan's office. "No answer," he reported. "He's usually in by now." I glanced at the clock on the wall: eight-thirty. As if on cue, the phone on George's desk jangled and he lifted the handset to his ear.

"George Burke. Ah, we were just talking about you." George winked at me and mouthed "Stan." "You picked a bad day to sleep in; Frank has been here two hours already," he exaggerated. "What d'ya mean you can't get here? Blocked off? The whole street?" He covered the mouthpiece and looked at me. "Stan says there must be a hundred guys out there and that they're redirecting cars off of Sunset. He can't even approach the gate." He removed his hand and addressed Stan again, "We need you here. I want to get Frank to go through Oliver's footage with you."

"Where's he now?" I asked.

"Have you tried the delivery gate? Oh. Where are you now?" He listened and then turned back to me. "He says studio security has locked down all gates now, won't let anybody in—or out. What?" he spoke back to the phone. "Thrifty Drugs at Hollywood and Ivar." George looked back at me, "That's only a block away."

"I got an idea," I said. "Ask him to wait there for me." George did as I asked and then hung up the phone.

"What's your plan, Frank? If security has the gates closed, you can't get out and you sure as the dickens can't get back in. If the picketers don't stop you, the guards will."

"George, let's go over to the prop warehouse and take inventory. I need a flashlight, a piece of chalk and two clothespins." I also needed two pairs of high-topped boots if my scheme was going to work.

Thirty minutes later, I walked into the Thrifty Drugs store on Hollywood Boulevard, making the little bell at the top of the door tinkle. I'd parked the boots outside, but I was pretty sure nobody would mess with them. Stan was drinking a cup of coffee at the lunch counter. He stood and smiled when he saw me.

"Well, you made it! I was thinking maybe I'd be here all day." A confused look chased away his grin. "Do you smell something?" he asked.

"Believe me," I replied with a grimace, "I can't smell anything right now." I led Stan back out to the sidewalk and picked up my boots. "The clean pair is for you," I nodded.

"Boots?"

"Yep. Pick 'em up and come along."

"I'm not sure I like the looks of this," Stan said, worry creeping into his voice.

"You're not going to like the smell of it either." The clothespin idea had seemed smart at the time, but it pinched my nose so tightly that I had removed it before I got halfway. We reached the corner and turned south on Ivar Street then walked halfway down the block. Ivar wasn't one of Hollywood's main thoroughfares, nonetheless a fair amount of traffic traveled this north-south running street. "See that manhole?" I pointed to the heavy cover lying in the middle of the street.

"Sure."

"All right. We're walking right out to it. You direct traffic while I lift it up. Once I get the cover off, we drop down the rungs and into the sewer system. You go first and when you get to the bottom, don't move. I'll replace the cover and then guide you back to the studio. Got it?"

"That's what the boots are for?" Comprehension was creeping up on Stan like Charlie Chan closing in on the culprit.

"Right. Put them on and let's go." Stan pulled off his shoes, tied the strings together and hung them around his neck. I slapped Stan on the shoulder and stepped off the curb. A Ford coupe sped past and then I trotted to the center of the street, squatted down and heaved the heavy cover off the manhole. My leg was beginning to throb as

Stan waved a couple of cars around us. I tapped him on the leg and pointed into the dark hole. "After you!" Stan climbed down the rungs built into the side of the shaft. Once his head disappeared, I followed, pausing just long enough to shift the cover back over the hole. In the dark, I felt my way down the ladder as a car drove over the manhole causing the cover to shift and clang. At the bottom, with my hands free, I dug into my jacket pocket, removed the flashlight and switched it on.

"These boots don't fit very well," Stan complained.

"Just be careful the muck down here doesn't suck them off your feet. It gets pretty thick in spots."

"How do you know your way?"

"We're just going to follow the chalk marks I made. Stay right behind me and watch your step." Within fifteen minutes, we were crawling up the ladder of an open manhole right outside Soundstage 3. George Burke was standing there smiling broadly. "Nicely done, Frank!" He shook my hand as Stan and I blinked in the bright morning sunshine. Stan and I gingerly removed our stinking, muck-covered boots and I massaged my sore leg.

We moved from the darkness of the sewer to the darkness of the newsreel department's simple projection room with just a few brief moments in the sunlight. I sat next to George while Stan threaded Oliver Cameron's developed film through the projector.

"You just tell us what you see, Frank," George directed, a yellow pad on his knee. "I'll write it down."

The projector whirred and spit bright light onto the screen on the wall. A moment later, Sergeant Righetti's mortar team appeared. "That's Sergeant Righetti," I said, pointing at the screen. "He's from Philadelphia." I identified the other men and their hometowns as best I could and described what was happening on the screen while George scribbled furiously. After the scenes with Righetti's crew ended, there was a shot of two guys sitting on the edge of a hole eating from their ration cans. It was me and Moreno! I never knew Cameron had filmed us.

"Yeah," George thought out loud, pencil to his lips, "we'll have to figure out what to do with that one."

Most of the footage showed Dog Company soldiers in and around their fighting positions preparing for their next mission. The last three minutes of film must have been filmed on the day Cameron died, for these were scenes of battle. I saw Lieutenant Brooks shouting into the handset of his radio and wondered if he'd been calling for mortar support. An explosion nearby shook Cameron, causing the images to jerk violently. White smoke began to obscure the camera's view. And then it was over.

"I guess that's when Cameron came back down the hill."

"And then he got killed?" George asked, laying the pencil on his notepad. I nodded. Stan rewound the film, ran it through a second time and I added what details I could. But it was combat; when you're in it, everything is confused and chaotic. You can't tell what's going on from moment to moment. Watching from a distance of several months and several thousand miles didn't add any clarity. By the end of the second showing, I knew no more about the fate of Righetti, Moreno and Brooks than I'd known the day I was carried off on a stretcher.

"Listen, I've got to head over to the main building for the weekly production meeting," George told me. "If you can hang around for an hour or so, I'll buy your lunch. It seems a small reward for all the help you've given us. But remember, we're not MGM," he chuckled.

I had nothing else planned for the day except to start thinking about my post-Army life, so I quickly agreed to hang around. I figured I might get another chance to see Miss Vance and it was unlikely I could get out of the studio anyway—unless I was willing to go underground again.

When George arrived back at his office about twelve-fifteen, he was wearing a grin along with his striped bow tie. My stomach had been pressing the "feed me" button for an hour already, so I stood up, eager to head to lunch.

"Change of plans, Frank," he said.

"Don't tell me you're not taking me to lunch."

"I'm not taking you to lunch." He laughed, but I didn't think it was funny. "Actually, I am, but not in the commissary."

"Oh?"

"Nope, you've been invited to lunch with Abe Baum, and if we leave right now, we'll get there just in time."

George escorted me back to the Aaronson building and up to the third floor, where Betty was as beautiful and happy to see us as she had been the previous day. "Right this way, gentlemen," she said, leading us down the corridor to Abe's dining room. I was beginning to like this place.

The door to the dining room was open and I could see Abe and Goz standing in the sunlight streaming through the room's large windows. Four places had been set and a waiter in a white jacket and black neck tie was standing off to the side.

"Oh, here he is!" Abe's face lit up as we entered the room. From his place at the head of the table, he gestured to the chair to his right. "Come and sit by me, Frank." I noticed again his meticulous attire, from his starched white collar and tasteful, patterned tie to his glossy black shoes.

"Thanks, Mr. Baum," I said.

"Oh, no, no," he wagged his finger at me. "It's Abe. Always."

"Thanks, Abe," I corrected myself.

The waiter pulled out Abe's chair and he settled in, unfolding his napkin and placing it in his lap. Goz, George and I followed suit. It felt good to sit and give my sore leg a rest. The waiter poured ice-cold water from a silver pitcher and placed small tossed salads at each place. I noticed the letters "PP" stamped into the silver ware and embossed in gold on the china. Each plate sat on a fine navy-colored linen placemat. The rest of us waited until Abe took a bite, then we started eating.

"What did you do before the war, Frank?" Abe asked, beginning our conversation.

"I supervised an assembly line up at Lockheed. We were making the P-38 fighter."

"The Lightning?" Goz's eyes brightened with recognition.

"That's right. We were working at a limited pace until after the Japanese attacked Pearl Harbor. After that, of course, we were pushing to produce as many aircraft as fast as we could. We really concentrated on becoming more efficient without compromising our quality control. The last thing we wanted to do was put one of our pilots in an unreliable aircraft. My job was to fine-tune our production procedures to meet our new quotas."

"Efficiency is important, Frank," Abe observed, shaking his head. "We have lots of efficiency meetings around here. Sometimes I feel like all I do is go from one meeting to the next. We have finance meetings, accounting meetings. Goz makes me sit through publicity meeting. Then there are story meetings and I have to meet with stars and their agents. Those are the worst meetings of all." Goz chuckled. "But once a week," Abe looked over at me between bites of something leafy, "we have the most important meeting of all. Do you know what that is?"

"No sir."

"It's the producers' meeting, Frank. Every Tuesday morning at ten-thirty sharp I meet with all of the studio's producers to review the status of all projects. That includes our feature films, serials, shorts and newsreels." Abe's brown eyes fixed me with an intense gaze as though he was taking my measure. "The producers produce! They create product. Product drives our business, wouldn't you agree, Goz?"

"Absolutely, Abe."

"They're the geniuses who turn books, plays, magazine articles, short stories or what-have-you into motion pictures. So every week I invite them to tell me how they're doing." He stopped talking for a moment and speared some avocado. I noticed that Goz had already cleaned his salad plate and that George was almost finished as well. "And do you know what they told me this morning, Frank?"

"No sir," I replied since I really had no idea—about the answer he'd gotten or the direction of this whole conversation.

"No, of course you don't. Kevin," he said to the waiter and nodded. Kevin cleared away the salad plates and refilled everyone's water glasses while Abe continued. "This morning, Frank, as I went around the table calling on each producer for an update, I received a disturbingly consistent response, which was, 'We're at a standstill! We can't get our crews onto the lot! Picketers have blocked the gate!' I got that same answer over and over, right, Goz?"

"Right, Abe."

"I tell you, Frank, these unions! The rank-and-file are good, hard-working, salt-of-the-earth Americans, but their leadership!" he raised both hands in frustration. "A bunch of Communists! So anyway, nobody's getting any work done today. Nobody, that is, until …" Abe raised his right index finger as if to accentuate a point, "until I came to George here. I'm not sure how much you know about the picture business—"

"Hardly anything," I admitted.

"Oh. Newsreels aren't money-makers Frank. They're more of a public service really, but audiences like to feel that they are well-informed and I've always felt a well-informed public makes for better customers. At any rate, Pacific Pictures newsreel division is not driven purely by profit motive. Far from it." I glanced over at George as Kevin placed plates of broiled fish, asparagus and whipped potatoes in front of each of us. George glanced back at me and suppressed a smile. Abe continued, "Anyway, George usually reports last, for the reasons just mentioned. And so I came to George and asked for his report and you know what he tells me?"

"No sir."

"George tells me that the newsreel department is on schedule. Now Frank, all the other producers, producers with big budgets, full crews, generous resources and motivated by profit have just whined to me like children denied an ice cream cone that they can't maintain their shooting and production schedules. Yet George, with the fewest resources, without profit motive, is on schedule. I threw up my hands." To demonstrate, he threw up his hands. "'How can this be, George?' I asked. And George launches into this amazing story. Amazing, don't you think, Goz?"

"I do, Abe."

"This amazing story about a young man who snaps his fingers and outsmarts all the rest of us, not to mention the unions, and finds a way to keep newsreels on track. This same young man, mind you, who goes to all the trouble to bring back some valuable equipment and film stock that he could just as easily have dumped overboard in the Pacific Ocean. This same young man who is willing to spend half a day of his time helping us sort out some footage that one of our most experienced photographers gave his life to shoot. So George tells us this remarkable story and I look at the rest of my producers and I just shake my head, Frank. I just shake my head."

He took a bite of fish. "Here we have the executives of a multi-million dollar, highly creative and artistic business and we're all stymied by our lack of imagination. And here you come and bail us out." He put his fork down and leaned toward me. I leaned in toward him. "You're a go-getter, Frank. We need that 'get-the-job-done-no-matter-the-obstacles' attitude around here. Am I right?"

Three voices echoed, "Yes sir!"

"I'm a pretty fair judge of people, so Frank, I wanted to have lunch with you so we could offer you a position."

"A position?" I repeated.

"Right. You know, like a job. Unless you have something else lined up already." Abe again fixed me with his clear brown eyes. "What do you say, Frank? How'd you like to be Pacific Pictures' newest production assistant?"

I didn't have to think more than the time it took Charlie Chaplin to twitch his moustache. "I'd like that very much, Abe," I smiled.

"Excellent!" Abe smiled back. Goz and George were both smiling too. "How soon can you start?"

"How about right now?" Everybody laughed. Even Kevin smiled.

Chapter 5

The next two weeks were sort of a blur. Every day was something different. Larry Gosnell, at Abe's direction, had taken me on as his personal project. Each day, following a cup of coffee and a short visit during which I would relate what I'd learned the previous day, Goz would escort me to another of Pacific Pictures' departments. He would turn me over to the department head and I would spend the rest of the day learning just how much I didn't know.

In my rotation through the various offices, I learned the difference between a gaffer and best boy; how to calculate the amount of paint needed to cover a flat or back drop; why it's important for two men to carry any piece of lumber over six feet in length; where to get the best hot dogs for lunch; why the writers were confined to one floor of the main building; which producers were the biggest jerks; what happened when a soundstage door was opened during a take; where the cute girls auditioned for parts; which stars had assigned dressing rooms (Miss Vance did); and, why there were two phones on Larry Gosnell's desk.

This last lesson came at the end of a long, but interesting day in the publicity office. I'd been following Goz around all day as he supervised the studio's still photographer. The photographer had been taking shots on sets that would later show up on movie posters, newspaper ads and so forth. "Jimmy's been around the block," Goz explained as we walked from Soundstage 1 back to his office in the Aaronson building. "He knows what to do without me telling him, but I always want him to know that I care about his work. When you give a man a chance to take pride in his work, he will." I nodded as though I understood. I was having fun, don't get me wrong, but I was ready for the day to be over so I could get something to eat—and rest my leg. I was also eager to move my few belongings out of the Princeton Arms Hotel and into the one-bedroom apartment I'd found above a garage just off of Lexington Avenue. It was nearly six o'clock by the time we walked back into Goz's office.

In addition to shadowing the photographer, we had also reviewed some ad layouts and an outline of the premiere festivities planned for *Master of the Grenadines*, a swashbuckler starring one of the studio's male leads, Donovan Keegan. The film was already "in the can," according to Goz and the premiere, scheduled for the Chinese Theater over on Hollywood Boulevard, was just two weeks away.

We returned to Goz's office, which resembled a Pacific Pictures museum as much as a workplace. Every inch of wall space was covered by the autographed picture of a movie star, a scene from a movie set or a framed poster signed by the film's cast and crew. "Tomorrow, I'll introduce you to Beeker Douglas," Goz began as he plopped into his chair and scooted it under his desk. "He's about to start production on a picture, a good chance for you to see the production cycle start to finish."

"So 'musical departments' is over?" I inquired with a smile.

"Yep. Now you're going to have to start earning your keep! Beek is talented, no doubt about that. He's very good at planning and organizing and keeping the director and crew on schedule." Goz paused and picked up a folder lying on the top of his desk next to his two squat telephones, one black, one white. "He's got a thirty-day shooting schedule planned. You'll work for him until the picture is completed, all the way through. Good experience," he smiled as the phone on his desk rang. The white phone. I'd never seen a white telephone before and hadn't thought to ask why Goz needed two telephones.

"Uh oh," Goz muttered as he reached for the jangling telephone. "Larry Gosnell. Hey Tomás! Good to hear from you." He listened to the voice on the other end of the line. "Just now? Police been called? Well, stall that would you, Tomás? I'm on my way right now." Hanging up the phone,

Goz opened the top drawer of his desk, pulled out a roll of twenty-dollar bills, nodded at me and said, "Let's go."

The picketers had long since moved onto other studios, Columbia, Warner Brothers, even RKO, so we had no trouble leaving the studio in Goz's gray Chevrolet. "So, what's this all about?" I asked. "What makes the white phone so important?"

Goz snorted. "It's not the phone, believe me. It's the guys on the other end of the phone and what they do to keep us out of the papers."

"I thought we wanted publicity," I replied, intrigued.

"We want good publicity, yes. We don't want bad publicity. You've never seen Abe get worked up, never been the focus of his anger. And you don't want to. Just let one of our stars get into trouble the week before one of his or her pictures is about to open and the you-know-what hits the fan."

"So who was on the phone?" I asked as the car traveled south crossing Melrose.

"Tomás, the maître d' at Perino's over on Wilshire. Every maître d' and bartender in Los Angeles County—and some outside the county—has the number to the white phone. Remind me to give it to you too. When one of our people gets in trouble, they call that number, day or night. And it's usually night." Goz glanced at his watch. "Six is a little early to get a call, but it seems that young Mr. Evers has run his automobile into that of another patron."

Tom Evers was one of the studio's rising stars. He'd gotten a couple of good reviews and was being groomed as a leading man. We passed the Wilshire Country Club on the right and Goz said, "I can't decide if Tom is an actor with a drinking problem or a drinker with an acting problem, but as long as his pictures make money it doesn't really matter. One of the things you have to keep in mind, Frank, is that box office is what runs our business. Big star? Great. But if you don't pull the audiences in, you don't stay a big star. The public expects movie stars to live the high life, to enjoy the freedom to behave the way they want without worrying about the limits a nine-to-five job places on the rest of us. But still, we can't let knuckleheads like Tom Evers kill the golden goose for the rest of us."

"Who besides Tom causes trouble?" I asked, hoping my question wasn't out of line.

"Tom drinks too much too often, then always falls asleep. When he's not swashbuckling, Keegan chases anything in a skirt and too often they want to be caught. Some, whom I shall not name, have questionable sexual tastes. Nobody's perfect, Frank. Just keep that in mind. Take Terry Thorpe for instance. Terry's generally a nice guy, easy going, always cooperative. But on the rare occasions when he drinks, he turns into Bob Mitchum. Then he'll take a swing at whoever gets in his way."

Goz turned left on Wilshire Boulevard, saying, "Perino's is just up here on the left." We passed the restaurant and sure enough, there was Tom Evers sitting on the fender of his car while a man in a tuxedo, whom I took to be Tomás, talked to an older gentleman in a suit. Goz wheeled the Chevy onto Norton Avenue and parked on the curb. "Come on. Let's see if we can take care of this."

I trailed after Goz, content to let him handle things and, as I'd been doing for the past two weeks, learn what I could. A look of relief washed over Tomás' face as Goz approached. Goz shook hands with Tomás and the other man, whose name I didn't get. I glanced over at Evers, who continued to sit on his fender, a cigarette dangling from his lips, his eyes glazed. He didn't seem too concerned. The driver's side fender and headlight of the other car, a pre-war Cadillac Fleetwood, had been bashed in. Goz and its owner were now taking a closer look. I had no idea what kind of car Tom was sitting on. I'd never seen one like it before. It was a big, expensive-looking, baby blue convertible with wide, whitewall tires and no headlights. Its right rear taillight was broken and its small bumper mangled, but it was certainly still drivable.

By now, Goz was peeling bills off a roll of money and handing them over to the Cadillac man, who nodded his head as each bill found a home in his outstretched palm. "Well, that should more than make up for the damage, Mr. Davis. Again, our apologies for your inconvenience and our thanks for your understanding."

"And two tickets, right?" Mr. Davis smiled, pointing at Goz.

"And two tickets!" Goz laughed. "Plus we'll make sure Mrs. Davis gets to meet Tom in person." With that, they shook hands and Mr. Davis climbed into his Cadillac. Goz waved as Davis drove off down Wilshire. "Thank you, my friend," he turned to Tomás. "As always." He peeled two twenties from his roll of money and slipped them into Tomás's hand. "Any time you need me," Goz said, staring into the maître d's eyes, "please do exactly as you did this evening." Again Goz shook hands. Tomás disappeared back into the restaurant, which I imagined would soon start to fill up with evening customers.

Goz walked over to Evers. "All right, Tom?"

Evers nodded and smiled cluelessly. "Never better," he slurred.

Goz smiled back. "Excellent. Now let's get you home." Evers stood and reached for the handle of the driver's door. "No, no!" Goz exclaimed with a friendly but firm smile. "You come ride with me, Tom. We'll have Frank here drive your car."

"Oh, I'm sure that's not necessary, Goz. I can handle it."

The smile slipped away from Goz's face. I've mentioned before that Goz was a hefty fellow; hearty and gentle, but also big and strong. He placed his hand on Tom's shoulder, gave a gentle squeeze and repeated, "You ride with me."

"Sure, Goz, sure." Tom tossed his keys to me. "You sure he can handle it, pal?"

Goz laughed again and I could tell he was relieved that Tom had agreed to his plan. "Why, Tom, our friend Frank here is a combat veteran. There's nothing he can't handle." I was flattered and only wish Goz had been correct.

My first problem was that I couldn't find the stick shift—or the headlights— and it was getting dark. Tom, instead of being concerned that I might add to the damage already inflicted on his vehicle, found my ignorance funny. Ah, to be rich and drunk! He explained with a silly grin that the headlights were recessed within the front fenders and showed me where the switch was. He then gave me a lesson on the car's semi-automatic, electrical gear selection. After this quick tutorial, I climbed behind the wheel of his Cord 810. It was unlike any automobile I'd ever seen and had sold for more than $2,500 when it rolled off the assembly line in 1937. Apparently, there weren't enough ridiculously rich buyers like Tom Evers, and the company quit making them not long after.

"I'll lead and you follow," Goz directed. "We'll head up Western. Tom's got a place just below the hills on Chula Vista. If you have a problem, just flash your lights."

"Sure," I said, but I was thinking, How?

I was fairly certain that if that car had wings, it could have flown home. All I had to do was tap the gas and it leapt forward. After a twenty-minute ride in the light evening traffic, I pulled the Cord into Tom Evers' garage. I reluctantly climbed out, closed the garage's double wooden doors and walked to the front of the house. Tom had fallen asleep on the ride home and Goz was half-leading, half-carrying him to his front door.

"Now, Tom," Goz was saying, "you're in for the night, understand?"

"Sure, Goz, sure. I'm hitting the sack. Thanks for helping me out. I wouldn't want to have embarrassed the Old Man."

"Happy to help, Tom. You call me anytime, okay?" With that, Tom nodded and disappeared through his front door.

We heard the dead bolt slide in place and then turned and headed to Goz's car, which he'd parked at the curb. Rather than go all the way back to the studio, Goz offered to take me home, which due to the advancing hour would have to be the Princeton Arms for at least one more night.

"Tom's a good guy, he just doesn't have any self-discipline," Goz said as he drove. "These guys have more money than they can spend, more women than they can count and too much idle time. And there's not usually anybody around to look out for them. Too many of them are like big kids cut loose in the candy store; they're going to eat chocolate until they get sick. Hopefully, when that happens, Tomás or someone like him will call the white phone."

"You were going to give me that number," I reminded him.

"AX 6728. Write it down if you need to, but make sure you remember it. We have an ambulance crew on standby, a doctor, even a couple of policemen. We do what it takes to protect our stars. Car crash? We help out, like tonight; unless of course someone gets killed. Then, our hands are pretty much tied and the police and the press take over. Domestic situations? We can help out. Somebody needs to get married? We can help out."

"Why would somebody need to get married?"

Goz glanced over at me with a patronizing look.

"Oh."

"Somebody needs medical services, to dry out or kick a bad habit, we can help with that too. Remember, our whole business is built on illusion, Frank: illusion that there is a 'happily ever after,' that life's problems can be solved in two hours, that movie stars don't have the same problems ordinary people suffer from. We have to protect that illusion. Sometimes that means protecting the public from the failings of their idols. The public will tolerate a lot, but not to excess. If you don't believe me, ask Fatty Arbuckle."

"Who?"

"Here we are," Goz announced as he pulled up in front of my tired hotel. "How much longer you going to be stuck in here? I thought with the generous compensation Abe had offered you'd have made a down payment on a place up in the Hills," he chuckled.

In truth, I'd been happy to get forty dollars a week. It was a couple of bucks more than my Army pay, but of course the studio didn't supply me with a foxhole so I had to pay for my own housing.

"I'm hoping to move out tomorrow," I said, taking an exaggerated look at my watch, "assuming I don't get stuck working until seven-thirty again!"

Goz laughed. "Oh, I think your 'short' work days are about to come to an end!"

My pleasant ones too.

Chapter 6

In *Back of the Yards*, a Prohibition-era love story set around the Chicago stockyards, a young Irish immigrant played by Tom Evers falls for a Polish-American girl and runs afoul of her father, who just happens to be the ward's hard-nosed boss. After spending two weeks getting oriented to the studio and the many phases of the business of making movies, I was finally going to actually work on one.

My boss for the next two months would be Beeker Douglas, a fifty-four-year-old producer making his fifteenth film for Pacific Pictures. Goz had told me that Douglas was very organized and well-respected for his ability to deliver pictures on schedule and on budget.

Goz had escorted me to the producers' floor of the main building. In a nod to fiscal restraint, two producers shared a secretary. Her desk sat in an area that doubled as a waiting room and was located between the two producers' offices. Doris was a pleasant, middle-aged woman, with a round face, stocky build, and an organized desk. Like Douglas, she was highly efficient. We'd not even had a chance to sit down before she was ushering us into the producer's office.

"Pleased to meet you, Frank," Douglas nodded, though his expression hinted otherwise. He was a little on the heavy side, a light sheen of perspiration on his forehead. His wardrobe was monochrome: gray slacks, gray tie, gray jacket. Only his shoes, black, and his shirt, white, provided contrast. Goz had introduced me and then we'd made small talk for a few minutes before Goz felt his duty was done. As soon as he departed, Douglas took two steps over and closed his office door. He turned and stared at me, his brow wrinkled, a cigarette burning between the first two fingers of his right hand. "Listen kid: I'm a company man. Abe Baum tells me to take you under my wing and teach you the movie business, then that's what I do. But don't expect me to explain every move and don't expect me to babysit you, because that I won't do. You can watch what I do, but it's up to you to learn. And when I tell you to do something, you do it without hesitation and without question. Understand?"

"Yes sir," I answered, a little surprised at his tone. Douglas was the first person I'd encountered at Pacific, outside of the commissary of course, who wasn't friendly.

"Get me a cup of coffee. Black. When you come back, we'll get down to business."

Douglas showed me the shooting schedule, a tight twenty-five days set to begin the following morning. There would be no on-location filming—

everything would take place in Soundstage 5 or one of the adaptable street scenes on the backlot. Douglas shared a copy of the storyboard, a series of sketches that showed—more or less—how each scene in the movie would be filmed. Every close-up, every set-up, every critical image needed to tell the story was depicted by these sketches.

"Peter Shaw's the director. He worked the scenes first with the screenwriter, Hopkins Morton, and then brought his shooting schedule to me. A picture isn't made sequentially," Douglas explained as he flipped through the storyboard sketches. "We shoot all the scenes on a given set at one time, regardless of when they occur in the story. That way we aren't moving from place to place as much and we don't have to duplicate work. You'll see when we start filming."

"When do we start?"

"Tomorrow morning. Crew on set at seven-thirty, actors on set at nine. That way, when the talent shows up, we should be ready to go. I've worked with Peter before and I like him because he sticks to the schedule and he does good work. He's got a good eye."

"What do you want my role to be?" I asked cautiously. I'd gotten the impression that Douglas would have been happier if I had no role at all, but I wanted him to know I was ready to contribute.

"You're going to be my assistant. That means a lot of running around, carrying messages, getting coffee, whatever. It also means a lot of standing around. You'll be surprised at how little seems to get done during a day of work. Remember, this is art. The creative process takes time. Here," he said handing me a piece of paper. "This is the cast list. Make sure you know them all by sight. If you don't, go down to the publicity office and match their names up with their pictures. If I tell you to go get Doyle Burton out of the bathroom, I don't want you coming back with Wallace Beery." Burton, the studio's versatile character actor, was the male lead in our picture. He played Marik Wojciehowicz, the tough boss of a Polish neighborhood just south of Chicago's stockyards. Tom Evers, whom Goz and I had assisted the night before, was Danny Shea, his employee and, more importantly, the suitor of his daughter Irene. She was played by none other than Vera Vance! This assignment was starting to look better.

I wanted to learn as much as I could as fast as I could. I also figured it would help to have good relations with the people working on the picture, not just the director and cast, but the crew members also. I followed Douglas' directions and matched the cast list to their publicity photos. Of course I wouldn't have any trouble recognizing Miss Vance or Tom Evers, but the other members of the cast I didn't really know. Goz's secretary, Jane, let me borrow a still of each of the cast members. I pasted them into a notebook I planned to keep with me on the set.

My next stop was the commissary. The commissary's big meal was lunch, when the studio was full of workers: technical staff, actors and actresses, executives and administrative employees. After lunch, things slowed down, but a skeleton presence was maintained from 6 a.m. to midnight to serve sandwiches and coffee to those on night shoots or just working late. I wandered into the kitchen and found the evening supervisor, Ray, and introduced myself. Ray listened to my request and nodded.

"Can do, Frank. Just understand that it will hit your production budget. You sure Douglas'll be okay with that? He's pretty tight about spending money."

"I'll cover it with Douglas," I replied with more confidence than was warranted. "See you at seven?" I extended my hand to seal the deal.

Ray shook my hand and laughed. "Nope, I'll be sound asleep in my warm little bed. Phil's got the morning shift. He'll be in about five-thirty and that'll give him plenty of time to fill your order."

Eager to make a good impression on my first day on the set, I arrived early. By seven, I had already stopped by the commissary kitchen and was headed to Soundstage 5. I was carrying four dozen doughnuts. Phil from the commissary was walking beside me toting a large urn of coffee. We were the first to arrive at the soundstage, as had been the plan. We set up our goodies on a table out of the way and Phil plugged in the urn to keep the coffee hot.

Beeker Douglas and Peter Shaw arrived together about seven-fifteen. Douglas introduced me to Shaw, a rail-thin man wearing a blue sweater over a white shirt and gold tie, a contrast to the plump Douglas' gray wardrobe. "Now that we're into production, this is Peter's show," Douglas explained as he chewed a sugar-glazed doughnut. "I'm here to help solve problems but his is the creative hand that will guide things. In addition to doing whatever I tell you, Peter will also give you errands to run."

As though they had scripted this encounter, Peter took over. "Frank, I'd like you to help with the operations on the set. I'll give you instructions and you relay them to the crew. That will free me up to focus on the actors and the flow of the scene. Got it?"

"Got it."

The first shot this morning was scheduled to be a street scene, shot inside where lighting and sound could be more easily controlled. It was an intricate shot in which each of the main players would appear as their paths crossed one another's, though they wouldn't be together in the scene for more than a moment. It involved a lot of movement, both by the cast and the camera crew, and therefore took a good bit of planning. Beginning at about eight-thirty, the camera operator and his assistants had been practicing dry runs, pushing the camera along a track laid out by the grips.

At eight-fifty-five, Tom Evers pushed through the soundstage door. I checked his name off of the list I kept in my notebook and offered him a cup of coffee.

"Thanks!" he smiled, looking at me through red-rimmed eyes. "Have we met?"

"No, not formally at least," I replied. It occurred to me that I was actually better acquainted with his car. "I'm Frank, production assistant. You need anything, just let me know," I smiled.

"Thanks, Frank." He turned away from me pretending to be examining the set, but as he did a small silver flask appeared from his coat pocket and he poured something into his mug of coffee. It wasn't cream.

Just after nine o'clock, Vera Vance and Doyle Burton arrived together. Burton was a handsome sixty-year-old, with silver hair, twinkling blue eyes and a stocky build. He had been around Hollywood for twenty-five years and had appeared in dozens of films. He'd had a run as a leading man in lower budget "B" movies, but over the past few years had earned a reputation as one of the industry's great character actors. He was friendly and seemed happy to be back on a movie set. He called most of the crew members by their first names and even sought me out to introduce himself. I liked him right away.

Vera strode purposefully to where Douglas and Shaw were standing and shook hands formally with both. Then she sat in a canvas-backed chair with her name stenciled across the back and lit up a cigarette. I seized this opportunity to bring her a cup of coffee.

"Good morning, Miss Vance," I said, holding a mug of coffee out to her. "It's nice to see you again."

"We've met before?" she asked barely glancing in my direction as she took hold of the mug.

"Sure. We bumped into each other in the commissary a couple of weeks ago." She looked at my face, but hers was unmarked by any sign of recognition, which was probably to my advantage.

"I'm Frank Russell, production assistant. Please let me know if you need anything."

"You'll be the first person I call," she said, her expression as cold as the coffee was hot.

"Ladies and gentlemen," Peter Shaw stood in the middle of the make-believe street and addressed the cast and crew. "I'm delighted to have this opportunity to work with such a gifted team of artists on what I believe will be a marvelous picture. *Back of the Yards* combines action, drama and romance with a compelling setting to tell a wonderful story of the enduring power of love to overcome all obstacles." As I listened, I thought of Goz and how he should have recorded Shaw's little speech to help promote the finished picture. "Beeker Douglas and I have planned a twenty-five day shooting schedule that will give us ample time to make a first-class picture. We are counting on each of you to be prepared for each scene and to cooperate with one another to ensure a smooth and also pleasant shoot."

"Now, this morning, we are beginning with perhaps the most complicated shot of the entire picture, which coincidentally is scene one. There is a lot of movement by the characters and the camera. I don't expect to get this done in one take," he joked and the cast and crew acknowledged him with a chuckle, "but I do believe we can finish this today and stick to our schedule. I anticipate a wonderful experience working with you. And now," Shaw nodded at me, "everyone, please take your places for shot One-A."

"Places, please, everyone!" I echoed and the members of the crew scurried to their positions as the cast stepped to their starting marks.

Shaw settled into his director's chair, Douglas, the ever-present perspiration dampening his forehead, standing at his elbow and me standing behind Douglas. Rusty, the soundstage manager, closed the outer door and flipped the switch activating the red, revolving light, which alerted everyone on the outside that the set inside was active.

"Quiet, please!" I shouted and a telephone-like bell signaled all on the set that we were getting down to business.

"Lights!" Shaw called out and the set brightened as though someone had awakened the sun.

The camera operator announced, "Speed!" and his assistant stepped in front of the camera with a slate board marked in chalk. "Scene One-A, take one!" he snapped the clapboard together.

"Action!" Shaw called and the cast and camera began the first choreographed movements that would eventually result in a feature film.

After each day's shooting wrapped up, I would join the director, producer, key members of their production team and the lead actors in one of the studio's projection rooms to review the dailies, or rushes, from the previous day's filming. The dailies were the first positive prints of the film shot the day before. The production team reviewed the dailies to make sure that performances were hitting the right tone and that the various technical aspects of the film were satisfactory. These might include everything from how a set looked on film, to how a scene was lighted, and whether a cup and saucer that appeared in take one were still in the same spot on take four. It was important to see the dailies as soon as possible, because sets could not be torn down until the producer and director were certain they would no longer be needed, that no reshooting would be required.

By the end of the first week of filming, the crew had become accustomed to starting the day with a sweet snack. I was confident that the reason we'd enjoyed such a productive and harmonious first week was due to the high morale sustained in part by daily doughnuts. Peter Shaw also deserved some credit for the skillful way in which he managed the delicate and at times mercurial egos of the actors. Unfortunately, I had neglected to inform Beeker Douglas that our sweet morning luxury was being charged to his production account at the rate of four dollars per day. I was about to get a lesson in business.

Every Monday afternoon, each producer received a reconciliation of costs for each project under his supervision. The accounting department would submit these cost reports so the producers would have them to review prior to their Tuesday production conference.

Beeker Douglas was absent from the set on Tuesday morning, as were all Pacific Pictures' producers. They were all sequestered with Abe Baum in the executive conference room on the third floor of the Aaronson building. I, on the other hand, was hard at work. The day's shooting schedule centered on a pivotal scene between Tom's character Danny Shea and Doyle's character Marik Wojciehowicz. At the very end of the scene, Irene, played by Miss Vance, bursts into the office where the two men are meeting. That meant that although she didn't have a lot to do, Miss Vance had to be on the set all day. Clearly, this was a golden opportunity for me.

"Must be a pretty boring day for you," I said, coming up from behind her chair. "Another cup of coffee?"

She looked up from the issue of *Variety* in her lap and said, "Sure," staring right through me but taking the mug from my hand. "I hate Tuesdays."

"All Tuesdays or just this particular one?"

She removed the cigarette from her mouth and took a sip. "All of them," she answered without elaboration. This was our first sustained conversation. I could tell she liked me. She couldn't tell yet, but I could.

"Why's that?"

"We shoot all day and then it's 'date night.'"

"Date night?"

Her blue eyes locked onto mine and she sighed. "Date night. Tuesday's are slow news days so Goz assigns us dates and we go out so we can be seen, hopefully by Parsons, Roswell or Hopper or their stringers. We get mentioned in the columns and ticket sales get a little bounce."

"What's so bad about that?" I inquired as I reminded myself to register with Goz as an escort.

"Half the time you go out with an asshole," she explained, waving her cigarette in the air, "and you never get home before 11 p.m. and you have to be back in makeup by seven the next morning." I chuckled. "What's funny about that?" she sneered. For someone so beautiful, she didn't smile nearly enough.

"Well," I confessed, leaning in a little closer and smelling her perfume, "I was in the Army during the war and we'd have killed for those hours!" I probably should have phrased that differently.

"Oh," she squeaked as though she'd been rebuked. "Didn't know you were in the Army."

"What? You thought a handsome, virile, All-American boy like me wouldn't have served his country?"

The barest trace of a smile threatened to convert her face into a glorious vision. "Well," she leaned toward me conspiratorially, "a hell of a lot of the hotshots around here didn't and most of them are as able-bodied as you."

"Ha! Not by a long shot!" I said and she really did smile. I was enjoying this conversation and hoped to extend it, but at that moment, Beeker Douglas appeared with a face as dark as a theater before the opening credits.

"See you a minute, Frank?" he asked and then squeezing my upper arm in a vise-like grip made me understand it wasn't a request. His face was flushed. Given my keen powers of observation, I recognized this immediately as a sign of trouble. We walked some distance away from the set, into the vast, unlit regions of the soundstage. "What the hell do you think you're doing spending my money on doughnuts and coffee?"

"I'm sorry, Beeker," I stammered and I truly was, not for spending the money necessarily, but for failing to inform him.

"Do you think you have financial authority over this picture?"

"No sir."

"Do you think you can do anything you please around here because Abe Baum has taken a liking to you?"

"Of course not, Beeker, I—"

"Let me be frank with you, Frank," his eyes and his manner were as cold as a foxhole on a rainy night. "You've got a lot of ability. You learn fast. People like you. But if you pull another stunt like this, even if it's for a penny piece of bubble gum, I'll run your ass right off this picture. If you don't like it, you can go take it up with Abe. I'm now twenty-eight dollars over budget after just one week. That may not seem like a lot in the grand scheme of things, but you never know what else is going to come up. Twenty-eight dollars!" he shook his head in frustration. "This isn't MGM, you know."

I started to apologize, but he cut me off. "Hustle your ass over to the commissary and cancel all future doughnut and coffee orders. Go now." I did as directed, my leg throbbing a little. I wasn't sure if it was from the humid weather or from the ass-kicking I'd just gotten from Beeker.

It was two-thirty by the time I got back to the set. Shaw and Douglas were conferring off to one side while the rest of the crew awaited instructions. Vera was in her chair.

"So, who's your date tonight?" I asked.

"What? Oh, it's you." The phantom smile tugged at her lips. "Terry Thorpe. The studio thinks a romance with him will do me some good."

"What do you think?"

"Maybe. It can't hurt to be seen with the studio's top box office star. Who knows, maybe that will make my star a little brighter! Anyway, it's just part of the job. When the studio wants you to have a private life, they give you one."

"Where will you go?"

"What's it to you?"

"Just curious," I laughed. "I want to make sure our leading lady is being properly taken care of. You're working on my picture, after all."

"Funny," she smiled, piercing me with her cool blue eyes. "I thought you were working on mine."

Chapter 7

The following morning we were scheduled to shoot a scene between Tom and Doyle set in a meat locker in one of the packing houses. Large sides of beef hung by hooks inside a refrigerated room, ice forming in the corners. Of course the beef wasn't real and neither was the ice. Our artists had created these props using papier mâché. When I reached the set, I could already tell that the crew was unhappy about something. Instead of smiles and banter, there were frowns and sullenness in evidence—and we hadn't even started to work yet.

When Beeker arrived, he shot me a look that would have scared Joe Louis. I wasn't sure what the issue was this time, so I kept my head down and concentrated on my responsibilities. I didn't want to get crossways with Beeker for a second day in a row. Plus, I wanted to be caught up enough to visit with Vera Vance when she arrived.

Right on schedule at nine o'clock, Vera walked through the open door of the soundstage. She looked around as she walked toward the camera, where Peter and Beeker were reviewing the day's plan. "Where the hell are the doughnuts?" she demanded. I wasn't sure whether to laugh or cry, but decided I'd settle for a kiss. Of course that wasn't an option. I kept my distance from the three of them. I figured getting caught up in a doughnut discussion wouldn't be my best career option at the moment.

While Peter worked with the gaffer to get the lighting just right, Vera sat in her chair and began leafing through a copy of *Photoplay*. "Good morning," I smiled as I walked toward her. "Hope your day is off to a good start!"

"It would be if I had one of those damn doughnuts," she snorted without looking up. She flipped a page in her magazine, clearly annoyed at the lack of pastry on the set.

"Sorry," I replied. "Cost cutting move. Beeker thought with all this beef on the set today we could do without doughnuts." Vera giggled and looked up. "How was date night?"

"Oh, all right, I guess." A small smile brightened her face. "Terry can be, oh, I don't know, kind of exciting I guess."

"Really?" I replied, trying to conceal my disappointment. I wanted Terry to be just another part of the job, a dullard who made each passing minute seem as long as the train ride from Chicago to L.A., not somebody Vera Vance found "kind of exciting."

"He was a fighter pilot in the war, you know." She was leaning toward me now, smile still in place. "He was an ace, a real hero, according to Goz." I reminded myself to check Thorpe's war record first chance.

"No kidding."

"Uh huh. You said you were in the war." I was encouraged that she remembered. "What'd you do?" she asked me and for the first time I felt she was seeing me as a real person, not just some studio flunky.

"Me? Oh, well I was in the infantry. I fought the Japanese at Okinawa."

"Were you a hero like Terry?"

I laughed. "Not exactly. About all I managed to do was get myself blown up! I've got the scars to prove it."

"Terry doesn't have any sc—" she caught herself and looked away. Even with her make up on, I could tell that she was blushing, that she wished she hadn't made that last comment. She looked back at me and any hint of familiarity had vanished from her face. "Why don't you get me some coffee, Fred?"

"Frank."

"Whatever."

When the crew broke for lunch, Beeker called me over. His face was flushed, a vein throbbing at his temple, the muscles of his jaw tight. He was clearly angry and I hoped it wasn't with me. It was. "I want doughnuts here tomorrow morning at seven-thirty and each shooting day thereafter. Understand?"

"Yes sir."

"And Frank?"

"Yes sir?"

"If I see so much as a smile on your face I'm going to hang you on one of those hooks alongside the other dead meat on this set. You follow?"

"Yes sir."

"If you were making a decent wage, I'd deduct the cost of doughnuts from your pay. Now get out of here before I lose my temper."

Too late, I thought.

"I don't know how you did it, Frank," Ray said when I placed the order for four dozen doughnuts. "We've never had a catering order from one of Beeker Douglas' pictures before. He's so tight I'll bet he has to lubricate his eyelids."

From the commissary, I wandered over to Goz's office. His secretary Jane was on the phone, but she waved me in.

"Well, the working man returns!" Goz laughed when I stuck my head in his office. "Come on in. I thought you'd forgotten about us."

I dropped into the upholstered chair across from his desk. "Say, I was talking with Vera this morning," I began.

"Oh, it's 'Vera' now, is it?" Goz's eyebrows arched and a lascivious smile stretched his broad face.

"Yes," I replied with dignity. "We're developing quite the relationship. She now confides the intimate details of her private life to me. We've grown very close. She calls me 'Fred.'" Goz laughed. "By the way, where do I sign up to participate in date night? If Vera Vance thinks Terry Thorpe is exciting, imagine what she'd think of a real combat soldier who's gone toe-to-toe with the Japanese."

"Sorry, kid," Goz smiled, clearly enjoying himself. "You're on the wrong side of the camera for date night duties."

"Vera told me that you said Thorpe was some kind of flying ace." Goz smile again at my use of her first name. "Is that right?"

"He was a fighter pilot, in the Marines."

"How many planes did he shoot down?"

"One."

"That wouldn't make him an ace."

"Especially when it was one of ours." Goz gave me a stern look and added, "That doesn't leave this office, Frank."

I was startled by Goz's revelation and laughed out loud. "How did he manage to shoot down one of ours?"

"A training accident, from what I understand. Another plane was towing a target during gunnery training and apparently Thorpe attacked from the wrong angle. One of those one-in-a-million shots, I guess, and the tow plane catches on fire."

For some strange reason I felt vindicated, though I wasn't sure why. "Well, Goz," I said leaning back in the chair, "take this advice from a wily old pro: if you want that story to come out, just keep referring to Thorpe as an 'ace.' Hedda Hopper or Joan Roswell would string your boy up like a horse thief and you'd lose the goodwill of ten million veterans."

"Point taken," Goz nodded.

Chapter 8

I spent the weekend making my garage apartment more comfortable. It was a two-room affair which included an indoor toilet, all situated above Mr. and Mrs. Smith's garage. The garage was located directly behind the Smith residence on Lexington Avenue just east of Van Ness and was connected to the house by a covered walkway. The door to the upstairs apartment was on the east-facing side of the structure and could only be accessed by an exterior set of stairs climbing up the right side of the garage. It cost me $8 a month. I felt fortunate to find a place that was relatively secluded, being set back from the street as it was, and also affordable. Because I was now a brisk thirty-minute walk from the studio, I had also acquired a second-hand car, a 1935 dark blue Ford coupe. Using my Army pay, for which I had had scant use while confined to the Pacific Theater, I paid $130 for the car, which the Smiths let me park on the curb in front of the house.

The apartment came furnished with a double bed and chest of drawers, a small kitchen with an ice box and two-burner gas stove, kitchen table with four wooden chairs, an old sofa upholstered in an ugly green paisley and an old cane-bottomed rocking chair. I planned to buy a table-top radio the next time I got paid. All-in-all, it was comfortable and quite sufficient.

I continued to arrive early to the set each morning. By now, most of the crew members knew me and would come to me with little problems with which they did not wish to bother Peter or Beeker. For example, if between takes the lighting or sound guys needed to move some gear from one spot to another, they'd let me know and I'd make sure Peter and Beeker knew what they were doing. That part of the job was easy. Thawing out Vera Vance wasn't. I had purposefully avoided her for about a week, hoping she would forget our embarrassing little conversation about her date with the "ace."

All the members of the cast had, so far at least, been very professional. They'd been on time, had responded well to Peter Shaw's direction and had cooperated with each other and the crew. At least until Monday morning of the third week.

On this morning, the shooting schedule called for the climactic love scene between Tom's character, Danny, and Vera's character, Irene. They would be seated in a booth in the back of a dim, smoky speakeasy. The only trouble was that by nine-thirty, Tom still hadn't arrived. Beeker and Peter huddled together and called me over.

"We can start by shooting Vera's close-ups," Peter was saying as I joined them. "When

Tom gets here, we plug him in and do the wider shots."

Beeker nodded and then turned to me. "You know where Tom Evers lives?" He was surprised when I said I did. "Good. Go find him and bring him here yourself. The dollar meter is running and I don't want to waste a day. Take off."

I trotted from the soundstage to the main gate, using the route I thought Tom would be most likely to take if he was running late. Of course I didn't see him, so I checked in with Pete at the gate to see if Tom had come in this morning. Again, no luck. I hopped in my car, passed through the studio gate and turned left onto Sunset. Another left on Gower and I was headed north toward the foothills. By ten o'clock, I was parking my car in front of Tom Evers' house on Chula Vista. I strode up the sidewalk and knocked on his door. No answer. I tried again. Nothing. I walked around the side of the house and pulled open the doors to the garage. There sat the beautiful blue Cord. That made it likely that Tom was inside. I closed the doors and walked up the three steps to the back door. To my surprise, it was unlocked.

The kitchen was a mess, with dirty dishes stacked on the counter, dried food crusted on their edges. Three whiskey bottles, all empty, decorated the kitchen table while a nearby trash can was overflowing with Schlitz cans. I wandered through the rest of the house. Finding no Tom, I headed upstairs. At the top of the stairs was a bathroom, the door open. It was slightly neater than the kitchen in that there were no dirty dishes up here. A short hallway running in front of the bathroom connected two bedrooms. The door to the one on the left was open. The door to the room on the right was closed. I pushed it open and there was Tom, clad only in an undershirt and boxer shorts, stretched diagonally atop disheveled sheets and snoring lightly. An overturned alarm clock rested on the floor beside the bed.

I retreated to the bathroom, grabbed a blue-striped towel and ran some cold water over it, wrung it out and then went back to Sleeping Beauty. "Good morning, Tom," I said softly, not wanting to frighten him. He continued to snore and I realized it would take something like an artillery shell to shatter his blissful rest. I shook him by the shoulder and more loudly repeated, "Good morning, Tom!" I wiped the damp towel across his forehead. He stirred and so I continued to talk loudly. "We were all missing you down at the studio, Tom!" The bedroom curtains were drawn, so I opened them to let in extra light. I folded the towel and placed it on his head, the sunlight assaulting his sense of sight, while I continued my attack on his auditory nerves. The multi-pronged approach worked; Tom rolled over and smacked his dry lips. Using his unsteady hands, he pried open his eyelids.

"Oh, hey," he smiled sleepily. "Did I leave a wake-up call?"

"Apparently not. You're overdue at the studio, so they sent me to find you."

He sat up, wobbling like a pin that had been grazed by a bowling ball. "That's very nice of you," he said. "Let's have a drink."

"After your shower. Come on," I said, pulling him by the arm, "let's get you into a nice warm shower and then we'll get that drink." Tom stood, rocked back and forth and then when the room stopped spinning, took one step toward the bedroom door. "That's it. One step at a time," I encouraged him. We reached the bathroom and I leaned Tom against the door jamb while I turned on the hot water. "Okay, buddy, in you go!"

"Are you coming too?"

"No, I'm going downstairs to get those drinks ready."

"Great idea," Tom replied as he peeled off his undershirt and dropped his boxer shorts. I lent him a steady hand as he stepped over the side of the tub and then pulled the shower curtain behind him. I went back downstairs and searched the messy kitchen until I found some coffee and a pot and put it on the stove. Then I ran back upstairs taking the steps two at a time. I could hear Tom moving around in the shower and so I went into his bedroom and pulled a freshly laundered shirt and suit from his closet. There was no point in selecting a tie, since he'd have to go straight to wardrobe once he reached the studio. The only shoes I could find were a pair of black brogans with a crusty yellow residue on them that I took for vomit. I grabbed the wet towel off the bed and did the best I could with them. I opened drawers in his dresser until I found a dark pair of socks, a clean undershirt and boxer shorts. These I carried into the now-steamy bathroom.

"How you doing, Tom?"

"Okey-dokey. You're Frank, right?"

"Yep. I've set some underwear out for you and I've laid out a shirt and suit for you on your bed. Finish up and get dressed and then hustle downstairs for that drink, okay buddy?"

Fifteen minutes later, Tom Evers walked unsteadily into the kitchen. His eyes were puffy and his dark hair wet. Except for his shoes, which looked like they'd been shined with a Hershey bar, he looked presentable, if still a little wobbly. "Here," I said, handing him a cup of hot coffee. "I hope you like it black."

"Thanks, you're a pal. Now if you were a *real* pal, you'd give me something to put in it."

"Cream, sugar, both?" I asked, but I knew that's not what Tom intended.

"Something a little stronger," he smiled and reached for the cabinet. His smile faded when the cabinet revealed no bottles of alcohol. I had used the time while he showered to collect up all the remaining alcohol in the house—there wasn't much—and hide it in the clothes washer, a machine I was fairly certain he could not identify.

"Hey," I said as though I'd just had a revelation, "I know where we can get something to go with that coffee!"

"Yeah?"

"Yeah! Come on, my car's right out front."

At eleven-twenty, I pulled the car to a stop near the corner of Sunset and Vine. I jiggled Tom awake. "One quick stop before we get that drink. Hop out." I ran around the car and helped Tom out and then lent him a steadying arm. "Marcus!" I called out and Marcus Shreves flashed his 100-watt smile.

"Good morning Frank! Who's that you've got with you?"

"Marcus, I'd like you meet Tom Evers. Tom, this is Marcus."

Tom looked puzzled, but was nonetheless polite. "How do you do?"

"Marcus, we need your best work, but we need it fast! We're already a little behind schedule and Tom's shoes are in poor shape."

Marcus grinned, "That they are, but nothing ol' Marcus can't rec-ti-fy!" Marcus dropped his shine box on the sidewalk and gently placed Tom's right foot on top of it. I helped steady Tom while he balanced on one leg. In no more than five minutes, Marcus had restored the shine to both shoes. I gave him fifty cents for the rush job and hustled Tom back into the car. I waved to Marcus, pulled back into the street, turned right on Sunset and then into the studio lot.

"You promised me something to go with this coffee," Tom reminded me as we walked into Soundstage 5. I grabbed the last doughnut off the table and handed it to him.

"Here."

The crew was standing around and it was clear they were between shots. Beeker and Peter looked our way and I could see both of them relax for just a moment: the day wouldn't be a total loss. "Gentlemen," I announced as we reached them, "Tom Evers reporting for duty."

"We were worried about you, Tom," Peter Shaw said gently.

"You've cost us half a day," Beeker Douglas snapped. "Get to wardrobe and make up and then get back over here. We're going to break early for lunch. You be ready to work by the time the crew gets back," Beeker's face was flushed again, "or so help me I will dock your pay for every minute we get behind. Do you follow?"

"Sure, Beek, sure," Tom smiled. He patted me on the shoulder and then turned to go to wardrobe. Over his shoulder he said, "I'll be ready for my close-ups when you get back from lunch."

"I don't do close-ups with actors who are late!" Beeker snorted. He turned to Peter. "I hope he's sober by the time he gets back. He looks like hell."

Shaw nodded. "Yeah, but his shoes look nice."

"Oh, Danny," Irene moaned breathlessly, "just be careful! Papa's angry and I don't know what I'd do without you!"

"Don't worry, doll," Danny replied confidently. "I know how to take care of myself." He leaned in, took Irene in his arms and kissed her.

Irene took Danny's hands in hers and said, "Just promise me you'll be careful!"

"Sure, kid, sure." Danny pecked her on the cheek and slid out of the booth.

"Cut!" Peter Shaw shouted and the bell sounded marking the end of the take. "All right, that should do it for today." Shaw stood and walked to the middle of the set, then turned to face the cast and crew. "I'd like to thank you all for the extra measure of cooperation today. We got off to a bit of a rocky start, but due to your good efforts we managed to make up lost ground. Thank you all, have a pleasant evening and I look forward to seeing you tomorrow." As the crew began to tidy up from the day's shooting, Peter nodded toward Beeker and then turned to Tom Evers. "See you a minute over here, Tom?" Guiding Tom by the elbow, the three men retreated out of earshot. I kept my distance, but judging from Beeker's red face and Peter's occasional nods, I figured Tom was getting his comeuppance for missing the morning's call time.

"Wouldn't want to be in his shoes," Vera Vance said from over my shoulder.

"Me neither," I said, turning toward her.

"You got a stick of gum or something?" she asked. "Kissing that lush over and over has just about pickled my lips. I hope nobody lights a match around him. He's liable to combust."

I laughed and dug in my pockets for chewing gum, but of course I didn't have any. "No gum," I explained, "but I'll go find some."

"No," she smiled. "That's all right. You've already had a busy day." She turned and walked toward the soundstage door, my eyes trailing behind her. I was afraid I had let her down by not anticipating her request for gum. Regardless, I was encouraged that Vera had initiated a conversation with me. She was beginning to come around.

I was checking the schedule for the next day when I felt a hand on my shoulder. "Thanks for the help this morning, Frank," Tom Evers said, the relaxed, ever-present grin on his face. "You kept me from getting into big trouble." He gave my shoulder a squeeze and followed Vera out the door.

"Frank!" It was Beeker, with Peter at his side. "You earned your pay today. Your new assignment is to make sure Tom's here on time every day—starting tomorrow. You follow?"

"Can do," I replied, wondering what I'd gotten myself into.

I trotted after Tom. Since I'd delivered him to the studio that morning, I knew he didn't have his car on the lot. To get home, he'd most likely catch a cab from the gate. "I need your phone number, Tom," I said, catching up with him.

"Sure, sure," he smiled. "HO 7753. The phone's at the foot of the stairs, so sometimes it takes me a few rings to answer. You can call me any time, Frank. We can grab dinner some night."

"I was thinking about breakfast," I explained. For some reason, Tom's smile widened and his eyes brightened.

"That would be great! Are you taking me home then?"

"No. I can't tonight," I explained. "I've got some other things to take care of here." Tom greeted that news with a fleeting frown, but within seconds his grin had returned. "I was thinking I could pick you up in the morning about eight and we could grab a bite to eat before coming in to the studio."

"Make it seven-thirty," he suggested. "That will give us some extra time." Based on what I'd seen of his condition that morning, a little extra time seemed like good insurance. Sometimes I'm slow to catch on.

After seeing Tom into his cab, I headed back toward the commissary where I made a five-cent purchase. My assignment with Tom had given me a great idea that I planned to take advantage of right away. The dressing rooms were situated just to the north of the Aaronson building so Abe could keep his eyes on them from his third floor suite.

Vera Vance's dressing room was No. 8, two-thirds of the way along the ground floor. Not every actress had an assigned dressing room, but Vera's star was ascending and as a nod to her growing box office appeal, she'd been granted the key to her own private sanctum on the Pacific Pictures lot.

I knew better than to knock on the door, so I stood outside as the late afternoon surrendered to evening. After about ten minutes, Vera appeared, her honey-colored hair covered by a red, silk scarf. She was wearing dark slacks and a loose-fitting sweater and she carried a pair of dark glasses in her hand.

"I need to get your phone number," I blurted, causing her to jump.

"You startled me!" she said and then began walking toward the adjacent parking lot. I fell in beside her.

"Here," I said holding out a pack of Wrigley's Spearmint gum. She smiled, taking the pack and peeling the wrapper back. "After the fiasco with Tom this morning, I really do have to get phone numbers from all the actors."

"I'll bet you don't have Doyle's number," she challenged, but her smile was still in place.

"He's next." I held her gaze. She stopped walking and stared at me as though she was deciding whether she was going to actually part with this small piece of her private life.

"Okay," she finally relented. "CB 9922."

"Got it," I smiled.

"Aren't you going to write it down?" she asked.

"It's etched in my soul."

"Oh, you should be a writer. Thanks for the gum." She popped a stick in her mouth, gave me a flirty wave and headed to her car.

Chapter 9

At seven-thirty on Tuesday morning, I got out of my car and walked up to the door of Tom Evers' house. I knocked loudly, hoping he'd be able to hear me from upstairs. To my pleasant surprise, an apparently sober Tom opened the door almost immediately. He was wearing a heavy, navy blue robe, his dark hair wet from a shower.

"Hi, Frank," he greeted me with a broad smile. "Come on in. I've got coffee on. Have a seat and I'll go get us a couple of mugs." He nodded toward the front parlor, just to the right of the front door and then headed back to the kitchen, which was in the back of the house. I took a seat on an upholstered sofa facing the room's twin windows and surveyed the reading material on the low table in front of me. *Variety*, that morning's *Times* and *Life* magazine were my choices. Since I expected Tom to take a few minutes getting dressed, I picked up the newspaper and scanned the headlines, then flipped over to find Joan Roswell's column. "TRAGEDY AT RKO!" screamed her headline. A picture of a pretty girl stared back at me. According to Roswell, a young actress named Mary Ellery had overdosed on sleeping pills. Apparently, RKO had dropped her option during the studio strikes and she'd been despondent over her inability to get parts. "It's long past time for the unions to set aside their petty squabbles and find a common ground! Isn't that what unions are all about in the first place: common ground for the common good?" Roswell's last line made it clear whom she considered the villain of the story.

I was surprised when Tom quickly reappeared with two mugs of coffee and even more surprised when he plopped down next to me. My surprise gave way to panicked comprehension when he placed his hand on my knee.

"Why didn't you tell me about Tom Evers?" It was after 7 p.m. on an already long Tuesday. I was standing in front of Larry Gosnell's desk blowing off steam.

Tom and I had come to a quick meeting of the minds after I batted his hand away, jumped up and spilled coffee on my pants. Tom had been almost as embarrassed as me, but had apologized and smiled and pleaded for my understanding—and discretion. Even after the shock of Tom's unwelcome advance, it was hard for me to remain angry with him. He was a gentle soul and despite the discomfort I felt, it was hard to stay mad at him for long. By eight-thirty, Tom was in makeup and by nine o'clock he was on set and waiting to begin his work day.

"Tell you what? You've seen Tom in action. You know he drinks like a sailor on shore leave."

"That's not what I mean, Goz, and you know it!" My voice was rising in volume.

"Easy, Frank," he responded, patting the air with his hands in an effort to settle me down. He walked over and closed the door connecting his private office to the reception area where Jane sat. He crossed back behind his desk and dropped into his chair. "I didn't tell you because you didn't need to know. It's that simple. I'm sorry you found out the way you did, but now that you know, I expect you to protect the studio. Do you have a problem with that?"

Goz met my stare with one of his own. I exhaled and glanced away. "No."

"Good. Sit down," he motioned to the chair opposite his desk and I sat. "Tom Evers is harmless. Audiences like him and he's developing a following at the box office. So what if his tastes are a little different than yours or mine? This is business. We make business decisions. Can you handle that?"

"Yes," I snapped. "I just don't like surprises."

"Well, Frank, this business is full of them. Get used to it and learn to think on your feet."

"Anything else I need to know?" I asked, my annoyance still evident.

Goz chuckled. "Yes. Peter Shaw thinks you're doing a good job and Beeker told Abe at the meeting this morning that you'd saved a whole day of production last week by getting Tom to the studio. I might add that Beeker is not one to hand out unearned compliments. That ought to make you feel better." Goz's intercom buzzed and he leaned over and flipped a switch. "Yes, Jane."

Jane's tinny voice sounded through the small speaker, "You're wanted upstairs."

"Thanks." Goz switched off the intercom, glanced at his watch and looked back at me. "We okay now?"

"Sure. I'll be fine. I just need to cool off a little."

Goz gathered up three slim manila folders and headed toward the door. "We're reviewing publicity plans for some pictures now shooting. Want to come along? You could sit in. I'm sure Abe wouldn't mind."

"Thanks, but it's already been a long day and I could use a beer."

"I completely understand. If I'd known we were going to be starting this meeting at seven-thirty, I'd have taken an afternoon nap." He slapped me on the shoulder as he exited his office and said, "Think about me when you're enjoying that beer!"

I wouldn't get a chance to.

I lingered for a few minutes after Goz departed. I just needed to relax a little. I'd been in a hurry all day: in a hurry to get to Tom's; in a hurry to get away from Tom's; in a hurry to forget Tom's advance; and in a hurry to complain about Tom to Goz. I finally calmed down and was standing up to leave when the phone on Goz's desk rang. The white phone.

I grabbed it on the second ring before it rang through to the studio's main switchboard. "Hello," I answered, my relaxed mood chased away by the jangling bell.

"Hello, is Goz there?"

"No, this is Frank, his associate. How can I help you?" I wasn't really sure what to say, so I was trying to follow Goz's advice and think on my feet.

"This is Michael at the Café Trocadero. You might want to send somebody down here pronto."

"Can you give me any details, Michael?"

"Look, I've got customers to take care of. Just get somebody down here. We don't want to get crossways with Mr. Baum."

I got Michael to give me the address and hung up the phone. The Trocadero was just over three miles west on Sunset Boulevard. At this time of day, traffic would be pretty thin once I cleared La Brea. As I reached Goz's door, I stopped in my tracks. I had a total of four dollars in my pocket. I returned to the desk and jerked open the top drawer. There was a two-inch roll of bills, the top one a twenty. I grabbed it and stuffed it in the pocket of my jacket. Jane had left for the day and the outer office was empty.

I jogged to the parking lot, climbed into my Ford and was on my way within about two minutes. I caught a couple of traffic signals, but still managed to reach the Trocadero within ten minutes. I pulled up out front and handed the valet my keys.

"Just watch it for me," I directed, handing him one of my own dollars. "I won't be but a minute."

I trotted under the green-and-white striped awning, pushed through the door and strode briskly to the maître d's stand. "Michael?" I addressed a middle-aged guy in a black tuxedo. "I'm Frank from Pacific Pictures." I extended my hand and Michael shook it. "What happened?" A low hum and the muted clatter of utensils on plates drifted out from the dining room to Michael's rear. The lights were dim and a small band was playing while several couples waltzed their way around the central dance floor.

"A couple of your people were dining in the main room. I gave them a good table. I always give your people a good table, right by the dancing, you know, so they can be seen." I nodded, trying to hurry him along. "Your guy, the big guy, he'd had a couple too many and before I know it they're yelling at each other and wham—he pops her."

"Where is he?" I asked, uncertain who "he" was.

"When he realized what he'd done, he threw a C-note on the table and beat feet for the door. She, on the other hand, I stashed back in the kitchen." He jerked his head to the back of the dining room.

"Any press here tonight? Anybody see what happened?"

"I don't know about press, but the dining room was half full. I mean, you couldn't miss it."

I peeled two twenty-dollar bills off of Goz's roll and placed them in Michael's hand. "Thanks, Michael. You say she's in the kitchen?"

"Follow me," he said. Michael led me around the dance floor, through the dim dining room. A small combo imported from Nashville was in the middle of *The Tennessee Waltz*, the attention of the diners focused on the music, not on Michael or me. Whatever had happened in the dining room had already been cleaned up. We reached the black, swinging door that separated the kitchen from the dining room and Michael pushed it open for me. "To the left," he directed. The kitchen was far brighter, noisier and more aromatic than the dining room had been. I blinked my eyes in the bright light. Men in white t-shirts and aprons were chopping vegetables, stirring pots, grilling meat, washing dishes. I could smell onions and chicken and a variety of other aromas that I couldn't distinguish, but I wasn't there to indulge my sense of smell.

The kitchen workers moved purposefully, each action bringing a meal one step closer to its eventual consumer. I side-stepped to let a tuxedo-clad waiter remove plated food for delivery to his diners. It was warmer in the back and I noticed that the kitchen's screen door was propped open by a cinder block. I scanned the work area and there she sat on a crate of lettuce. She was wearing a modestly-cut, wine-colored dress with long sleeves. The right sleeve was split at the elbow. She was trembling and sucking so hard on her cigarette I thought she was going to swallow her lips. I pulled my coat off as I walked toward her and draped it over her shoulders. The left side of her face was red, her eye swollen shut. Vera Vance looked up at me and began to cry.

"Shhh, it's going to be all right now," I whispered as I helped her to her feet. I guided her through the cluttered kitchen, past an acne-faced teenager peeling potatoes. When we reached the back door, I placed my hands on her shoulders and turned her toward me. "Listen," I began, but she was in a daze. I lifted her chin with my left hand and she flinched. "Hey," I tried again, "it's Frank, remember me?" I stared into her right eye. It was red from her tears, but she began to focus on me. "I'm going to get you out of here, okay? I want you to wait right here for me. I'm parked out front. I'm going to go get the car. I'm going to drive around back. Then I'm going to put you in the car, okay?" I kept my sentences and directions short. "You stay right here, okay?" An almost imperceptible nod. I smiled to reassure her and gently patted her shoulders. "Be right back."

I passed through the dining room as briskly as I could without drawing attention. I thanked Michael again and slipped him another twenty. Sure enough, the valet had allowed my car to sit out front. He also got one of Goz's twenties. I drove my Ford into the alley leading around the side of the building and pulled up to the delivery entrance.

Vera was still standing by the door where I'd left her. I hopped out of the car, leaving the engine running and the headlights on. I ran around to the passenger side and opened the door, then took

Vera by the elbow and settled her into the front seat. I pulled out of the alley and turned left on Sunset, happy to see the Trocadero receding into the darkness. Vera still hadn't uttered a word.

"Tell me where you live and I'll take you home." A sob escaped her throat and she shook her head with a pained grimace. "It's all right," I assured her, "I'll get you home and you'll be safe there."

"I can't go there," she choked.

"That seems like the best place. We can take a look at your eye, get you fixed up." I was trying to come across as gently as possible.

"I can't go there!" she snapped, crying harder now.

"Why not?" I was in unchartered waters, confused and also a bit annoyed at her reluctance to take what seemed to me to be the most obvious course of action.

"Because Terry has a key!" she cried, burying her face in her hands.

A host of unwelcome images paraded through my mind. Intellectually, I knew my romance with Vera had to this point been painfully one-sided, but the thought of her and Terry Thorpe together wounded me as surely as one of Cupid's arrows shot through the heart. Still, at this moment I had a job to do and I needed to concentrate on our options. I could take her to the studio, but Terry

Thorpe, who I figured was the cause of the evening's troubles and Vera's smashing new look, might decide to head there if she didn't show up at her house—that is if he even cared at all. A hotel, even a discreet one, was out of the question. We, the studio that is, couldn't risk a hungry bellhop swapping such a juicy morsel of gossip for a quick payday. I was left with only one viable option at that tense moment: my place.

Under other circumstances, this might have seemed like a heaven-sent opportunity, but with Vera in such obvious physical and emotional pain, my objective was simply to get her some place safe where she could begin her recovery. By safe, I meant somewhere away from Thorpe, the public and the scavenging eyes of the gossip columnists.

Vera still had her face in her hands, although the sobs that had racked her body had slowed. "Hey, Vera," I said, glancing over at her, "I've got a plan. I'm going to stop and buy some things, then I'll take you someplace safe. You with me?"

"Yes," she answered meekly without looking up.

We passed NBC Studios on the left and I pulled in to Stanley's Food Market. "Stay here. Keep your head down and I'll be back in five minutes." I bought a bottle of orange juice, carton of eggs, some bacon and a loaf of bread. I also made a selection from the meat case.

It wasn't until I turned south on Van Ness and then left on Lexington that Vera looked up again. I slowed down and turned into the Smith's driveway.

"You live here?" she asked, a note of respectful surprise in her question.

"What? No," I chuckled for the first time since I had answered the white phone. "No, in fact I don't even have driveway privileges, so I'm going to pull up and let you out. I'll park back out on the street." I parked the car as close as I could to the stairs, got out and helped Vera from the car. Taking her by her arm, I helped her up the steps. She was a little unsteady and I wondered if her injuries were more than merely cosmetic. Unlocking the door, I turned on a lamp and eased her onto the sofa. "I'll be right back."

I parked the car in my customary spot along the curb in front of the house, grabbed the bag of groceries and jogged back to the garage. Vera hadn't moved. I put the groceries away except for the beefsteak. I had picked the cheapest cut of meat in the display case because I didn't plan on eating it.

"Here," I held the steak out to Vera.

"What the hell? You think I'm going to cook for you?"

"It's not for me, it's for you."

"Well, I'm not hungry!" she barked.

I was getting pretty exasperated with her. I'd galloped my white horse to her rescue and she was treating me like the cause of her problems. Choking back my annoyance I explained, "It's for your eye. Just hold it on like this," she flinched as I gingerly placed the cold steak against the side of her face, "and it will help with the swelling." She was sobbing again now, but she did as I suggested and kept the steak over her left eye.

"I'll let you have the bedroom and I'll sleep on the sofa."

"I'm not sleeping on your dirty sheets!" she snapped.

My chivalry was about to reach its limits. With a less fair-haired damsel in less distress, I think I would have already thrown in the towel, but this was, after all, Vera Vance!

"Of course you won't," I smiled in what I hoped would come across as a reassuring gesture. I left her on the sofa and went into the bedroom. I stripped the sheets, took the spare set from the top shelf of the closet and hurriedly remade the bed. I carried the dirty sheets to the sofa where I would shortly put them to good use. "Come on," I offered her my hand. "I'll show you the bedroom." I led her into the room, the small bedside lamp casting an anemic yellow glow over the bed and not much else. "That's the bathroom," I pointed. "The light is over the medicine cabinet. There's soap in the shower and the towel on the rack is clean."

"I need something to sleep in," she sniffed, wiping her nose on the torn sleeve of her dress.

"Got just the thing," I replied. I opened a drawer and pulled out a clean pair of pajamas. "Only the best for you," I smiled, hoping to get her to relax a bit.

"My head's about to bust open. Got any aspirin?" I stepped into the bathroom and found a couple of pouches of headache powder.

"Here," I handed them to her. "I'll get you a glass of water."

"I don't have a toothbrush."

The chivalry-limit alarm clanged inside my head. "Make do," I said sternly, staring into her one good eye. I walked out of the room, pulling the door closed behind me.

I was happy to sit down at the kitchen table for a while and rest my leg. One of the drawbacks to living above the Smith's garage was having to climb the stairs on a still-gimpy leg. I spent the next hour and a half reworking the shooting schedule. This wasn't my responsibility of course, but at this point neither Beeker Douglas nor Peter Shaw knew what I knew: Vera Vance wasn't going to be ready to appear in public or on camera for several days. Beeker and Peter weren't going to find out this rather pertinent information until the next morning, by which time it would be much too late to salvage a productive day. To minimize the time lost due to her injuries, I planned to offer Beeker and Peter an amended schedule. My plan was to shuffle the schedule and spend the next few days filming the remaining scenes which didn't involve Vera. Once she was healed enough to shoot close-ups, we would come back and finish filming her scenes. It was an imperfect plan which, this late in the production schedule, would mean some down time for the crew. I wasn't sure how Beeker would respond, but I also didn't see that the circumstances left many options. By the time I finally fell asleep sometime after midnight, I was mentally, emotionally and physically exhausted.

Chapter 10

I was used to waking up early, but it was nearly seven o'clock before a noise from the kitchen jerked me from my slumber. I wiped the sleep from my eyes and tried to piece together the events that had led me to stay up so late and then sleep on the sofa. The sizzle of bacon hitting a hot pan splashed over my brain like a bucket of ice water. I jumped up off the sofa and there in my kitchen, at my stove, was Vera Vance frying bacon.

"Good morning," I stammered, wondering how I must look.

"Morning," she replied without turning around. "How do you like your eggs?"

"Any way you want to fix them." I left Vera in the kitchen and took the fastest shower since I'd gotten out of the Army. By the time I finished shaving and dressing, she was putting two plates of eggs, bacon and toast on the little table. "Orange juice?" I asked.

"Sure."

I got two glasses from the cupboard and filled them with juice and set them on the table. So far, she'd managed to keep me behind her or to her right side. When she sat down across from me, my eyes must have betrayed me. "Is it that bad?" she groaned.

"Pretty bad," I nodded. The left side of her face was still puffy, but the red of last night had been replaced with a sickly looking yellow band forming a half-circle around a dark purple bruise above and below her eye. "Have you looked in the mirror?"

"I'm afraid to."

"Well, look at the bright side: if Universal ever does a remake of *Bride of Frankenstein,* you're a shoo-in."

"Funny," she replied, making it clear that my remark was not.

"I'm just trying to get you to smile. You had a rough night, but that's behind you. Things are going to be okay. Try to relax a little."

"Listen, Frank," Vera replied, staring down at her plate and pushing her eggs around with her fork. "I'm sorry I was such a witch last night. I'm afraid I wasn't very gracious to you for all you did for me." She looked up, a tear rolling down her right cheek. "Thanks for helping me."

"It was my pleasure," I said truthfully. With that, the glimmer of a smile flickered across her lips. "I need to make a telephone call," I explained pushing back from the table. The phone was on the end table by the sofa. Tom Evers answered on the second ring. He sounded wide-awake and on track to get to the studio on time. "All right, Tom. I'll see you there," I said and hung up.

"Sorry," I said, resuming my seat. "One of my duties is to make sure Tom gets to work on time. No repeat of last week's performance."

"He likes you," the one-eyed beauty replied.

"Don't I know it!"

"Not like that," she said. "Tom's a sweet guy. He doesn't have a mean bone in his body. He appreciated what you did for him last week and that you don't hold a grudge. He's like that."

"But I do hold a grudge," I replied.

"You do?"

"Yep. Right now I'm holding a very big grudge against Terry Thorpe." At the mention of his name she looked down again. "Tell me what happened last night."

"I had one too many drinks and asked one too many questions."

"Don't tell me you think *that*," I pointed to her black eye, "was your fault."

"Not entirely," she answered. "But I could have prevented it."

"What happened?"

"You remember that day we were talking about Terry and what he did in the war?" I nodded. "I told you Goz had called him an 'ace.' So I asked him how many Japanese planes he'd shot down. He says 'none.' So I say, 'Then how can you be an ace?' And he says, 'I'm not an ace. I only shot down one plane and it was one of ours.'" She paused and wiped her mouth with a paper napkin. "And that's when I started laughing. I guess I'd had too much to drink because I couldn't stop. Terry thought I was laughing at him, but I wasn't really. I just got tickled. I couldn't stop. So he whacks me. Next thing I know, I'm on the floor looking up at him and he calls me a 'bitch' and stomps out of the place. My head is throbbing and I'm seeing little stars, just like in the cartoons. I don't know what happened after that. I vaguely remember you talking to me in the kitchen and then we were here and you slammed the bedroom door. That's when I figured I hadn't been too grateful. I've watched you, Frank. You don't get angry over nothing."

"Well, don't worry about that. What we've got to do is get you healed up." I checked my watch. It was about twenty minutes until eight. I hoped that Rusty had noticed my tardiness and picked up the doughnuts. I explained to Vera the approach I planned to take with Beeker. I also made her promise that she wouldn't leave my apartment. The last thing any of us needed was for her to be recognized in public in her present condition.

"How long do you think this will take to heal?" she asked.

"I don't think it'll take too long. I'll get Goz to send one of the doctors over today. You can let him in, but if anybody else shows up, don't answer the door unless you know them. Don't go out. And call me later," I said, standing up and brushing the toast crumbs off my pants. "Let me know what you need and I'll pick it up on the way home."

Vera stood up and came around the table. She placed her right hand on my chin and kissed me gently on the cheek. "Thank you, Frank," she whispered.

"Make sure you have the kitchen cleaned up by the time I get back," I winked. She threw a piece of toast at me, but she was smiling.

Technically, I was late. The crew call was seven-thirty each morning and I was technically part of the crew. I walked into the soundstage about 8:05 and was relieved to see the doughnuts had been picked up. I quickly scanned the set and made a beeline to Beeker.

"You're late! Don't tell me Tom's bad habits have rubbed off on you."

"I need to talk to you and Peter. Right now."

"What?! Who do you think you are?" he followed me. "You don't give me orders!"

But on this particular morning, I was holding the cards. "You've got a big problem, Beeker," I replied calmly, "a problem not of my making. I'd like to offer you and Peter a solution." I could see the wheels turning inside his mind, but they weren't gaining any traction. "Now, Beeker," I repeated.

"Peter!" he shouted over his shoulder. Beeker's face was now crimson, the vein in his temple wiggling like a belly dancer. Alarmed by the volume and tone of his summons, Peter trotted over to us. "Frank here tells me we've got a problem and that he's going to solve it for us. Won't you please elaborate, Frank," he said sarcastically.

I explained the problem as succinctly as I could, leaving out as many details as I could, including the name of Terry Thorpe—I was saving that detail for Goz. "The bottom line is that she's not fit to be seen on camera for several days, maybe even a week. In fact, she's not fit to be seen at all."

"What about makeup?" Beeker, ever the businessman, asked.

"Right now, the swelling still hasn't gone all the way down. The bruises are too vivid to cover."

"We'll just shoot her from her good side, what was it, the right? Just keep her in profile. Peter?" Beeker looked to the director for concurrence.

Before he could reply, I spoke again, "For heaven's sake Beeker, she's unsteady on her feet. She's having headaches. She looks terrible. You really want her on the lot where any of two hundred people would be left to draw their own conclusions about what happened to her? I can see the headlines now: 'Struck Starlet Steals into Studio; Babbles About Battle!' I don't think that would help your picture very much! Is that what you really want?"

"What I want," Beeker shouted, "is for you to stop playing producer!"

Peter stepped in between us, placing a hand on both of our arms. "This really isn't helping, gentlemen. Frank, you said you had a proposal and right now," he glanced at Beeker, "I'd welcome one from any quarter."

I took a deep breath and tried to calm down. "I'm no doctor, but Vera's going to be out several days at least." I pulled the shooting schedule out of my coat pocket and handed it to Beeker. It was covered with arrow marks and notes. "This isn't perfect, I know, but it will keep us from sitting around."

Beeker looked at the sheets of paper, a frown on his face. He flipped a page, his finger running from scene to scene. "This will work, Frank. We'll have to get with the property office to reschedule the exterior shot. We may have to incur some overtime to get the fire scene ready sooner than we anticipated, but this will work. Nicely done, Frank," he added grudgingly.

"Now, gentlemen," I resumed, "I've got to go see Goz. We've still got to control the fall-out from this very public event and we've got to get our star back on the set."

Goz and I arrived at his office at the same time. "Good morning, Frank! How was that beer last night?"

"Never got to it. The white phone rang right after you left."

This got his attention. He hung his coat up and said, "Do tell." I pulled the money roll out of my pocket and tossed it to Goz. "How much did it cost us?" he inquired, staring at the roll as he weighed the bills in his hand.

"So far, about a hundred dollars. But I may file a claim for various incidental expenses." Goz was still standing by the coat rack, waiting for the proverbial other shoe to drop.

"So what happened?"

"Yours truly to the rescue." I sat down uninvited in the chair in front of his desk.

Goz slowly walked around the desk and asked, "Who was involved?"

"Terry Thorpe and Vera Vance." This brought a frown from Goz as he slumped into his chair. "It seems that Miss Vance laughed at Mr. Thorpe's war record and he slugged her for it."

Goz started. "He hit her? Geez! Damage?"

"Vera's got a shiner that would make Joe Louis proud. It's going to be at least a week before she can be seen in public, maybe longer. I gave Beeker and Peter Shaw a plan for shooting around her for the next few days."

"And Thorpe?"

"I have no knowledge of Mr. Thorpe and no interest in him. He ought to be booted off the lot. Big tough guy like that slugging a woman. What a phony!"

Goz leaned forward, picked up his phone and dialed three numbers. "Pete? Goz. Say, is Terry Thorpe on the lot this morning? Well, if he shows up, would you let me know? No, just give me a shout. Thanks, Pete." Goz looked back at me. "Any press? I didn't see anything in this morning's *Times*."

"None that I know of. But, Michael, the maître d', said it happened at a very visible table and that the dining room was half full, so who knows if this will get out."

"Where's Vera now?"

"She's safe, but she needs a doctor. She was a little wobbly last night, but she seems better this morning. Her head hurts but the swelling is down."

"I'll call the doctor right now. Is she at home?"

"No. It seems that in a moment of incredibly poor judgment, Miss Vance provided Mr. Thorpe with a key to her house. She is, under the circumstances, reluctant to return home. Understandably, I might add."

Goz shook his head and pressed his lips together in frustration. "You seem to be enjoying this way too much, Frank. This could be very bad for our business which, *I* might add, would be very bad for *your* livelihood. I've asked you twice where she is. Stop messing around!"

"She's at my place."

Goz thought for a minute and then nodded his head. "Good choice." He picked up his phone and dialed again. "Hi Doc, it's Goz. I need you to take a ride with Frank Russell. He's a production assistant working with Beeker Douglas. Shouldn't take more than an hour, two at the most. Great. I'll send Frank right over." He hung up and turned his attention back to me. "For now, you're on doctor detail. Doctor Sparks' office is straight across the courtyard. There's a red cross on the door. Go get him and drive him in your car. Stay with him and bring him back. When you get back, both of you come see me straight away. Any questions?"

"What about my day job? Beeker's already a little frosted with me."

"I'll handle Beeker and Peter. But I want to hear back from you and Sparks before I have to go handle Abe."

Dr. John Sparks was Pacific Pictures' resident physician, maintaining an office and examination room on the ground floor of the Aaronson building. He was a lean, tanned fifty-year-old with graying brown hair and a neatly-trimmed mustache. I introduced myself and waited while he replaced his white office smock with a sport coat. He placed his black doctor's bag on the front seat between us and I drove him to my apartment. On the way, he told me how he had come to work at the studio.

John Sparks had been a young doctor spending a pleasant Sunday on the Santa Monica Pier when he came upon an eight-year-old boy who had fallen and snapped his right wrist. Sparks had used a rolled up newspaper and the boy's belt to improvise a splint and had then helped the youngster locate his parents. The boy's name was David Baum and his father, Abe, offered the young doctor a unique type of practice on the lot of Pacific Pictures. As the studio's in-house doctor, Sparks had set broken bones, tended to burns, cuts and sprains, dealt with addictions, and provided the most confidential services of various kinds. In the process, he'd treated stars big and small and enjoyed the company of a long and continuing line of beautiful actresses.

Since it was mid-morning, I doubted Mr. Smith, a businessman, and Mrs. Smith, a school teacher, were at home. I pulled into the driveway and parked the car beside the garage at the foot of the stairs. Sparks and I climbed to the top of the stairs and I was pleased to find the door locked. We let ourselves in and found Vera stretched out on the sofa in my pajamas reading an old edition of *LIFE* magazine.

"How're you feeling?" I asked as she swung her legs over the side of the sofa and sat up. As she did, she immediately reached for the arm rest to steady herself.

"A lot better until just now. I think I sat up too fast. Hi ya, Doc."

"Miss Vance! What a pleasure to see you again," Sparks replied flashing a brilliant, white smile that would have seemed at home in the pages of *Photoplay*. "Mr. Russell, among others at the studio, thought it wise that I come out and visit with you."

I went and sat at the small kitchen table. True, it was in the same room, but it was behind the sofa so it offered the doctor and his patient at least the illusion of privacy. Besides, I had a vested interest in Vera and I didn't mind keeping an eye on things.

Sparks perched himself on the low table in front of the sofa and examined the multi-hued bruises on the side of Vera's face. He had one of those little lights that doctors use to spy inside your ears, throat and eyes and he used it to evaluate her left eye's responsiveness. He asked Vera to stand and lean from side-to-side. She had trouble doing so. He asked her about her headaches, which she said were mild as long as she didn't get into any bright light or move around too fast. After about fifteen minutes, he put his instruments back in his bag and snapped it shut.

"Now, Vera," he said, taking her hands in his, "I'm sure you're eager to get back to work as soon as you can, so I want you to understand what I'm about to tell you." Vera nodded. "You must rest for a few days. I suspect you've suffered a mild concussion. This is unlikely to result in serious long-term effects, unless you fail to give yourself time to heal. I'd like to take another look at you after the weekend. Between now and then, no activity. No work. No heavy reading. No nights on the town. No alcohol. No exercise. I want you to rest your brain, to be as bored as you can stand it for the next few days."

"What about these God-awful bruises, Doc? Can I do anything about them?"

"I'm afraid not, my dear. Time will take care of the bruises. While they may mar your loveliness at the moment, I can assure you they are only temporary."

"And the headaches?"

"Also temporary, I'm sure. Continue to take aspirin and drink plenty of water. If you notice any change of conditions, simply call me." He pulled a business card from his coat pocket and scribbled a number on the back. "This is my home number. The office number is on the front." Vera took the card and laid it on the table.

"Can you cook, Frank?" Dr. Sparks asked me on the drive back to the studio.

"I can open a can with the best of them, Doc. And I make a mean bowl of corn flakes."

He chuckled. "I had something a little more substantial in mind. Red meat, green vegetables and fresh fruit would be best. Can you manage that?"

"Yes sir."

"And no alcohol, not even a beer. Her brain needs to rest up. I'll check on her again on Monday. Bring her to the office first thing."

"Right."

I parked the car and walked with Dr. Sparks to Goz's office. He was eager to hear the good doctor's prognosis so he could brief Abe. I think, for my sake, he also wanted Beeker to hear from the doctor. When we got to Goz's office, Beeker and Peter had already arrived and were seated in the twin chairs facing his desk. I stood behind them, leaning against the window sill. Sparks stood at the corner of the desk and addressed the three executives.

"She almost certainly has, or has had, a concussion. In addition, she's suffered some severe contusions along the left side of her face."

"How long is she on the sidelines for?" Beeker interrupted.

"Until Monday at a minimum. I've asked Mr. Russell to bring her in first thing so I can evaluate her progress." Peter pulled the folded pages of the shooting schedule out of his pocket.

"So there's a chance she could work on Monday, right?" Beeker continued to push.

"A chance, yes. But I wouldn't put all my chips on that bet, Mr. Douglas. My best professional guess is that she could be back at work by the middle of next week. But," he held up a hand to intercept Beeker's objection, "that's still only a guess. It's hard to say with brain injuries. Sometimes they seem severe and they heal quickly. Sometimes they seem mild and they linger. Each patient is different."

Goz joined the conversation. "So for now, our best bet is next Wednesday, a week away?"

Sparks nodded, "For now."

"Thanks, Doc. Any other questions?" Goz looked from Beeker to Peter and then to me. He glanced to Sparks. "Confidential, right Doc?"

"As always," Sparks smiled. "Good day, gentlemen." He picked up his black bag and walked out.

"Now, let's get down to brass tacks," Goz resumed, addressing the three of us. "What do we tell Abe?"

At 3 p.m., the four of us trooped up to Abe's suite. The lovely Betty showed us into his private office where four handsome leather wingback chairs had been arranged in a semi-circle in front of Abe's desk. Behind the desk were an American flag and a California state flag. Unlike Goz, Abe had only one telephone, black, on the desk along with a picture of a pretty woman and a boy. I guessed this was the son whose broken wrist had brought Dr. Sparks to Pacific Pictures. A bookshelf behind the desk held leather-bound volumes, several plaques and other awards, and photographs of Abe with the studio's biggest stars. Autographed pictures of Doyle Burton, Donovan Keegan, Tom Evers, Vera Vance and a small galaxy of other stars beamed down at us. Abe stood up, removed his glasses and gestured toward the chairs. I took the one to the right, Peter the one on the left and Goz and Beeker landed in the two middle chairs. I figured they were going to be doing the most talking. I figured wrong.

"What brings such an august group to interrupt my work?" Abe smiled. He walked around to the front of the desk and leaned against it. I noticed the perfect creases in his trouser legs and the glossy shine of his brown wing-tip shoes.

Goz spoke first. "We had a little problem last night that we need to make you aware of. Fortunately, there's been no publicity about it so far, thanks to quick action by Frank here." Abe looked my way and cocked his head. "As part of our publicity efforts, we've been playing up a romance between Terry Thorpe and Vera Vance. Last night, we booked them a table at Café Trocadero. Frank was in my office when a call came in from there at about eight o'clock. When he got there, he found Vera with an eye swollen shut and—"

"How did that happen?" Abe barked. Goz looked over at me.

"Vera said that Thorpe socked her," I answered.

"What?" Abe's eyebrows arched, his eyes widened. "Terry Thorpe? What happened?"

I recounted the scene as best I could, including the help Michael had given us and his assessment of the number of people who witnessed the event.

"Goz," Abe interjected, "prepare a note with an appropriate appreciation for me to send to Michael."

"Yes sir."

"Continue, Frank," Abe directed. I relayed the whole story, from finding Vera in the kitchen to securing her in my apartment to delivering Dr. Sparks.

"And the good doctor's diagnosis?"

Goz picked up the narrative. "He says he'll examine her again on Monday morning. In the meantime, she can't work. He won't say when she can definitely return, but his best guess is a week from today."

Abe turned to Beeker. "How far along are you?"

"Today was our halfway mark, day thirteen out of twenty-five."

Abe looked thoughtful for a moment. "Lucky thirteen," he muttered to no one. "Are you idle because of her absence?"

"No sir," Peter answered. "Frank revised the shooting schedule. We're shooting around Vera right now." Abe's eyes flickered my way but were quickly diverted by Beeker.

"We'll be done with all but her scenes by the end of the week, Abe. We've got to get her back to work by Monday."

"There's no way Dr. Sparks is going to clear her to work again until after he examines her," I reminded the group, drawing a red-faced scowl from Beeker. Abe waved me to silence.

"How much will it cost us to idle production if she can't resume work?" he asked Beeker.

"Sixteen thousand a day."

"No location work on this picture, right?"

"Right, but we have a night fire scene scheduled for the back lot."

Abe chewed the earpiece of his glasses and rubbed his chin. "The doctor rules," he decided. "Miss Vance returns to work only when he says so. Work around her as best you can, Beeker. Peter," he turned to the director, "go back over that shooting list. Consider what scenes you could rework if the doctor releases her for some type of limited work, say shots in which she could sit still for example."

"Yes sir."

Abe slapped his hands on his thighs. "All right, gentlemen, thank you for bringing me up to the moment. Goz, you and Frank stay back for a minute." Peter and Beeker took that as their dismissal and filed out, closing the door behind them.

"Three issues," Abe said looking from Goz to me and back. By this point, my mind had been grappling with this situation every waking hour out of the last twenty. Abe, on the other hand, had known of the problem for fifteen minutes, yet he had quickly identified three matters which he needed to address. "One," he held up his right index finger, "Vera's health. Two, financial issues. Three, Terry Thorpe." He looked at me. "Emotionally, how's she feeling?"

"She's a lot better today. Last night she was pretty upset and frankly, a little bit out of it."

"So you've seen here today?"

"Yes sir. I drove Dr. Sparks to see her."

"She's at her house?"

"Not exactly, Abe," I hesitated.

Goz rescued me. "Frank thought pretty quickly last night, Abe. He determined that no one would be served by Vera being left alone at her house and he knew he couldn't take her to a hotel, so he hid her in his apartment. I think it was a pretty smart call." Abe crossed his arms over his chest and nodded at me.

"I want to see her as soon as possible." He looked at his watch. "I'm committed this evening. Pan Berman is having a showing of a new picture at his house and Mrs. Baum and I have been invited. I want to see her tomorrow morning. Goz, can we, should we move her?"

"We could, Abe, but based on what the doctor said and given that we don't want this to leak out, I think the best thing for tonight is to let her stay at Frank's. After you visit her tomorrow, we can reconsider."

Abe thought about this advice for a moment then nodded his head. "You're right. Call Romanoff's and have them prepare dinner for two for Frank to pick up at seven. Include a bottle of wine and dessert."

"The doctor said no alcohol," I reminded him.

"No wine then. Club soda. You can pretend it's champagne. Charge it to my office account. Draft a note for me to send with it."

"Yes sir," Goz replied, making a note on his pad.

Abe turned his attention back to me. "Beeker is extremely cost-conscious, but not always as flexible as he needs to be. Based on your observations, how damaging is Vera's absence going to be?"

I was surprised that Abe would ask this question of someone with so little experience. "I spent an hour and a half last night reworking the shooting schedule. If Vera can come back to work on Monday, we won't lose any time. If it's Wednesday, it could be two days. But we could have the crew take Tuesday and Wednesday as their 'weekend' and catch up by working Saturday and Sunday. I know we'd have to pay time-and-a-half for weekend work, but that'd cut the financial loss to the equivalent of one day instead of two."

"I like the way you think, Frank," Abe smiled. "We'll cross that bridge when we get to it. Now," he directed his question to Goz, "what do we do about Terry Thorpe?"

Goz made a show of checking some notes. "He's not in production this week. He's scheduled to begin two weeks from Monday with Sam Levin on *Pioneers on the Prairie*."

"You didn't answer my question."

"Slugging a girl? I think you should cancel his contract and kick him off your lot." I engaged my mouth before I put my mind in gear. The silence that greeted my comment wrapped around me like a python and threatened to squeeze the breath from me.

Abe snorted and smiled while Goz looked on wide-eyed. "If only it was so simple, young man. Terry Thorpe is this studio's single biggest box office attraction. MGM's got Clark Gable, Fox has Tyrone Power, Columbia has Cary Grant and we have Terry Thorpe. Firing him might make you feel good at the moment, but it wouldn't be in our best interest. No, I'd like some more realistic, less damaging options."

"You could dock him some pay; make him do some public appearances. You know how he hates that kind of thing."

"Maybe," Abe mused. "Remove him from your publicity efforts for the time being. If this thing blows over without further damage, we might reconsider, but for now, no more studio-sanctioned events. You said he's not filming this week or next. Is he in town?"

"I'll find out," Goz answered, making another note.

"He was last night," I reminded them.

"I want to see him as soon after tomorrow as possible." Abe stood up. "All right then, we've got our marching orders. Good work, Frank. You've helped contain the damage all around, both to our reputation and to our finances. Come by tomorrow at ten o'clock and pick me up. Traveling in your vehicle will be less conspicuous."

"Yes sir."

"Thank you both," Abe dismissed us with a wave and returned to his desk.

The finishing touch to our intimate dinner from Romanoff's was the candlelight. The restaurant had supplied the works, everything from fine linen napkins and candlesticks to silverware to an insulated basket in which to transport everything. They even included a book of matches with which to light the candles.

The candles cast a warm glow on Vera's face, her bruises fading under the yellow light. She had devoured a medium-rare porterhouse steak and I'd nagged her to eat some of the roasted Brussels sprouts the restaurant had provided. A crisp, mixed greens salad, buttery rolls and Lyonnaise potatoes had rounded out the meal. Now, as the candles burned lower, I picked at the skeletal remains of my apple pie as Vera read the note Abe had sent.

"What a sweetheart," she smiled looking up from the note, the candles' flames dancing in her eyes. "He's such an old softy. Please tell him how much I appreciate his thoughtfulness."

"You can tell him yourself. He's coming to see you in the morning."

"What? Here?" A panicked look flashed across her face.

"Yep," I pushed my dessert plate away. "He insisted that I bring him here to see you. I'm to pick him up at ten, so we should be here about ten-fifteen. Please have the place tidied up," I teased.

"He can't come here. I don't have any clothes or makeup!"

"You don't need any; makeup, that is."

"You don't understand! He can't see me like this! I must look hideous!"

"No, you don't," I said, reaching across the table and taking her hand. "You look like a beautiful woman who got slugged by a 200-pound movie star. And that's exactly what Abe needs to see. He also needs to hear you tell what happened. I hope you'll do that without trying to protect Thorpe."

"I shouldn't have laughed at him."

I stood and started clearing the table. "This isn't your fault, Vera. You didn't do anything to merit this."

She propped her elbows on the table and rested her chin in her hands. "I just want this to be over. I just want to go back to work. Beeker must be beside himself. He can be a real pain in the ass when he doesn't get his way."

"Tell me about it." I was scraping the remaining food into the trash can.

"Frank," she said looking up at me, "I'd like you to take me to the studio tomorrow. I can go to my dressing room and fix myself up a little before I meet Abe."

"No chance," I said, stopping my work and staring at her. "You heard what the doctor said, and what's more, Abe has heard what the doctor said."

"Whose side are you on?" she pouted.

I put the plate down and squatted by her side. "I had hoped that would be obvious by now." I stared into her deep blue eyes. She matched my gaze and then looked away.

"Oh, you're right, of course!" There was frustration in her voice. "Don't take this the wrong way; you've been very kind to let me disrupt your privacy. It's just that I want to go home and I want things to get back to normal."

"The quickest way back to normal is to follow the doctor's orders."

Chapter 11

At five minutes before ten on Thursday morning, I arrived at Abe's office. Goz was waiting in the reception area so I sat down next to him. I'd already put in an appearance on the soundstage where shooting continued according to the revised schedule I'd submitted the previous day. At ten o'clock sharp, lovely Betty ushered us back to Abe's private office.

"Good morning, gentlemen," he greeted us.

"Good morning, Abe," we replied in unison.

Goz spoke next. "I was on the phone last night with Ken Britten, Thorpe's agent. He says Terry is in Juarez and will be back Sunday. Shall I schedule something for you Sunday afternoon?"

"I'm obligated on Sundays," Abe said without elaboration. "Schedule him for first thing Monday, say nine o'clock. Let Betty know." Abe reached for his suit jacket.

"Yes sir."

"Ready to roll, Frank?" he asked as he shrugged his coat on.

"Ready," I replied.

Traffic was light, as most of those with jobs had already made it to work. We covered the few miles to Lexington Avenue without incident. I slowed as I reached the Smiths' and pulled into the driveway.

"Very nice," Abe said, surveying the house as we drove down its side. I pulled to a stop next to the stairs leading to my apartment above the garage. Abe seemed puzzled. I got out and came around and opened his door. Then I started up the steps. "You live above a garage?" he asked.

"You only pay me forty dollars a week, Abe." I knocked once on the door and then unlocked it and pushed it open. Vera was standing in front of the sofa, looking lovely in the morning light—as lovely as her puffy, bruised face and black eye would allow. She was barefoot and wearing one of my freshly laundered white dress shirts, the sleeves rolled up to her wrists, the tail hanging down to her knees. On her it looked like an elegant gown.

Abe stepped inside and strode directly over to her, taking her hands in his and kissing her lightly on her right cheek.

"Good morning, my dear," he said with the concern of a father. He stepped back and appraised her while I closed the door and took my seat at the kitchen table. "I am so sorry this has happened."

Vera's eyes began to tear up. I guess the fact that someone else was now witnessing her injuries made them seem more real, maybe more painful as well. "Let's sit down," Abe said, pointing to the sofa. "Now, tell me how you are feeling."

"I am so much better," Vera smiled. "Frank's been an angel from the very beginning. And you," she smiled, placing her hand on Abe's knee, "were so sweet and generous with that scrumptious dinner last night! I told Frank, I'm ready to go back to work."

"And we're ready to have you back, my dear," Abe raised his eyebrows and smiled, "particularly Beeker Douglas!" He covered her hand with his own. "But your health is our top concern. Dr. Sparks says that you should rest and so it shall be. Frank will bring you to him on Monday morning and we'll see how things work out from there. Frank has full authority to get you whatever you need from your home or from the studio and bring it to you here." Without saying so outright, Abe was making sure Vera understood she was not to go out in public. And I was to be her contact with the outside world. I rather fancied this new responsibility. "Now, I've heard Frank's report, but since neither he nor I was present when this unfortunate incident occurred Tuesday night, I would be grateful if you would tell me what happened."

Vera looked down at their joined hands and took a deep breath. She told her story matter-of-factly, her voice faltering only when she recalled the blow to the side of her head. To my satisfaction, she did not spare Thorpe his due. In her telling, she also made me out to be a minor hero. This also pleased me. When she finished, Abe spoke quietly, but there was a sharp edge to his words.

"I intend to meet with Terry on Monday morning. Based on our conversation, I will determine the proper steps. For starters, of course, there will be no more of these publicity dates for you and Terry."

Vera shot me a quick smile and then looked back to Abe. "Thanks. I think I can do a whole lot better on my own."

Abe chuckled. "I'm sure you can!" He stood, indicating the visit had reached its conclusion. Vera stood and kissed him on his cheek, while I came from the kitchen and waited by the door.

"Thank you, Abe," she smiled. "It was so thoughtful of you to take time out of your hectic schedule to check up on me."

"Your welfare, as I said earlier, is our utmost concern. Let Frank know of anything you need." Abe opened the door leading to the stairs. Vera winked at me and blew me a kiss.

I followed Abe down the stairs and held the car door open for him. He hesitated as he climbed in. "Forty dollars a week?"

After I dropped Abe off, I grabbed a quick sandwich in the commissary. By one o'clock, I was back to the soundstage. "You had a couple of calls this morning," Rusty, the soundstage manager said, as I entered. "I took a number for you," he added, handing me a piece of note paper.

"Who was it?"

"Didn't say. It was a dame, though."

"All right. Thanks, Rusty." I didn't know any "dames" other than Mrs. Smith and the females who worked on the lot. Rusty had a phone at his post by the door. It wasn't equipped with a bell like a normal phone, but instead used a flashing red light to alert that a call was coming in. "Borrow yours?" I gestured at the phone.

"Sure," Rusty nodded and then, gentleman that he was, he wandered off a ways to give me some privacy.

My call was answered on the second ring. "Joan Roswell." I was startled. Why would Joan Roswell have called me? "Hello?"

"Uh, hi, Joan? Frank Russell over at Pacific. I had a message from this number."

"Frank! Darling, how are you? I understand you're now a production assistant. Congratulations! I'm so pleased to see good things happen for our boys back from the war."

"That's right," I replied. "I'm working with Beeker Douglas on his new picture."

"*Back of the Yards*? Yes, I understand it's going to be marvelous." She paused for a second and then said, "Actually, Frank, that's what I wanted to talk to you about."

"Really?"

"Yes, I heard a rumor and I thought you could clear it up for me."

"A rumor?"

"Yes. I've heard your leading lady has missed the last two calls. Any truth to that, Frank?"

I had to think fast. I didn't know what she knew for a fact and what she was guessing, but since Vera had missed the last two days, I figured Joan might in fact know that. The last thing I wanted was to leak what had really happened to Vera. The next to last thing I wanted was to get caught in a lie and embarrass the studio.

"Frank? Are you still there, darling?"

"Yes. Sorry, Joan, we're in between takes over here and the crew is moving a lot of stuff around. It's kind of noisy. What was your question?"

"Vera Vance, dear. She's missed the last two days of filming. Why is that?"

"Oh, Miss Vance! Yes, she's been sick. Sinuses or something. From what I've been told, which isn't much," I chuckled to let her know that I was just a flunky, "she'll be back in a day or two. Nothing serious."

I could hear crackle and static over the line. After a moment, Joan spoke again. "Is that all, dear? Nothing more you can tell me?"

"That's what they're saying here on the set."

"They, dear?"

"Yes, Beeker, Mr. Douglas the producer." Silence again. I was starting to sweat.

"Thank you, Frank. I do hope darling Vera feels better soon. Do give her my best wishes, won't you?"

"Sure, Joan. I'll be happy to."

"So long."

The phone went dead and I breathed a sigh of relief. I wasn't sure what she knew, but she didn't really know any more now than before she called. My next call was to Goz. I replayed the conversation for him.

"She obviously knows something, but hopefully not much," Goz surmised.

"I think all she knows is that Vera isn't at work. I think she's grasping at straws."

Goz agreed. "Let's just hope she doesn't find any."

I told Vera about my conversation with Joan Roswell and that she had a sinus infection. I told the Smiths that Vera was a cousin visiting me from back east. I don't think they bought it, but at least that kept them from asking uncomfortable questions as she roamed their back yard over the weekend. I made a couple of trips up to her house to pick up clothes, toiletries and other items she requested. She pleaded to go with me, but I explained again why that was unwise. I also arranged for a locksmith to change all the door locks and brought Vera a new set of keys.

"I found your pistol," Vera said after I returned home. I kept Oliver Cameron's Nambu in the drawer of my bedside table, alongside a pad and pencil for recording brilliant ideas that occurred to me in the middle of the night. "I wasn't searching your apartment or anything, I just needed an ash tray. Did you get it in the war?"

"I did," I answered without providing any details.

"Is it loaded?"

"No, but there's a magazine in the same drawer. It's got five bullets left in it."

"That's good to know," she laughed, "in case I get into trouble and have to blast my way out."

"If you have to blast your way out, you better make sure you're close to your target. That thing is built for short range. Better yet," I smiled, "if you get into trouble, just call me."

Vera was up early on Monday, monopolizing the bathroom while she showered, fixed her hair, and worked on her makeup for sixteen hours. Okay, it was really only about eight hours—okay, two. I'd let Beeker know that I was under Abe's orders on Monday morning, though I still placed my wake-up call to Tom, and that my day would be occupied by escort duties.

A brightly colored, floral-patterned scarf covered Vera's head, dark glasses hid her eyes, as I drove with her through the Pacific Pictures Studios gate on Monday morning. I parked as close to the main building as I could and hustled around the car to help Vera out. We entered the building through the ground floor entrance on its south side, which was the one closest to Dr. Sparks' infirmary.

To the great relief of everyone at the studio, at least those of us in the know, the doctor released Vera to work beginning that day. She was all smiles and contagious enthusiasm as I walked with her to her dressing room. She called makeup and wardrobe to send people over and I let Goz know that she was back to work. Next, I reported the good news to Beeker and Peter.

"Thank God!" Beeker sighed. "Now we won't have to spend overtime prepping the fire scene!" Peter was still working off the revised shooting list that had my notes on it.

"We won't really need her today," he explained. "We'd planned on her not being available until Wednesday afternoon, but now that she's back, tell her to be ready for the market scene tomorrow. The boys can get that set ready this afternoon while we shoot the office scene."

"You mean after sitting on her can for five days she's going to have to wait until tomorrow to get back to work?" I asked, as disappointed as I expected Vera to be.

"Yes, I'm afraid so. We just didn't expect her so soon."

I trudged slowly back over to her dressing room, not eager to tell her that she'd have to get through one last day of idleness. To my surprise, Abe and Goz were standing in her doorway when I arrived.

"Frank!" Abe's eyes brightened when he saw me, "I was just telling Vera how glad we all are that she's back!" A casual look around revealed that no one from makeup or wardrobe had as yet arrived. "Goz told me the good news from Dr. Sparks and I wanted to come down myself and welcome Vera back." Abe reached out and took Vera's hand in his. "You probably don't realize what good hands you've been in these last difficult days," he said to her. She smiled at Abe and then at me. "Frank's a very able young man. He's got a bright future."

"He's certainly taken good care of me," Vera nodded in agreement.

Abe draped his other arm over my shoulder. "Thank you for restoring this star to the Pacific Pictures heavens," he said smiling at me. "And now, dear lady, please accept my welcome home. Let me or Frank know if there is anything you need." He leaned in and kissed her cheek, then released her hand. "Frank," he said, turning back toward the main building, "walk back with me." I completely forgot to tell Vera she wasn't needed today, but as we turned, she called after us.

"Frank, I'll need a ride home later. Can you take me?"

"You bet," I smiled.

People told me later that those who saw us walking around the west side of the Aaronson building stopped and stared. Abe's personality in public was cordial, but not overly familiar, yet here we were walking beneath the shade of the pepper trees with his arm across my shoulders, a broad smile across his face.

"Lockheed and the Army trained you well, Frank. For a young man you show admirable initiative, good judgment and confidence—that's the critical ingredient many otherwise intelligent men never exercise. In order to lead others, a man must exude confidence; he must make others believe that by following him everything will turn out all right."

"I don't think Beeker would agree with you."

Abe tilted his face up to enjoy the warmth of the sunshine. "I've spoken to Beeker Douglas about you, in fact." Uh oh, I thought. "Beeker is gruff and focused and is one of our more profitable producers. His pictures routinely make money, an achievement not to be taken lightly. But Beeker lacks the creative spark and his rough approach with people prevents him from making great pictures." I opened the door to the main building and we stepped into the ground floor corridor. "That's all well and good. Beeker and I both know his place here at the studio and it's a place that we will always need to fill. He's complimentary of you, by the way." Abe glanced at me and waved his hand dismissively as I started to object. "Oh, there are certain aspects of your personality that he finds grating, but on the whole, he says that you've made valuable contributions to both the morale and efficiency of the production." I gathered from this comment that Abe must have learned of Tom Evers' tardiness. I wondered how much of the story he knew. "I know Beeker's place in the scheme of things," Abe continued as we approached Abe's executive elevator. "What I'm struggling with Frank is *your* place in the scheme of things. What's become quite clear to me over the past few days is that it isn't as a forty dollar per week assistant."

"I won't take a pay cut," I said.

Abe laughed. The doors to the elevator opened and we stepped in. "Third floor please, Henry," Abe said to the uniformed operator. We rode up in silence. I wanted to believe good things were going to result from this conversation, but I didn't want to be disappointed if Abe carried the conversation in a different direction. We reached the top floor, exited the elevator and turned toward the executive suite. As we reached the double glass doors behind which Lovely Betty kept watch, we paused to allow two workmen from the props department to wheel a handsome desk and chair into the suite.

"Where do you want this, Betty?" the taller of the two asked.

Betty pointed down the hall toward Abe's private dining room and said, "First door on the left." Seeing Abe and me behind the workmen, she smiled.

Abe and I trailed the desk down the hallway. When the workmen stopped to wiggle the desk through the door of an empty office, Abe and I squeezed past them and continued on to the dining room. Two places had been set and Kevin was standing by waiting to serve. Abe took the seat at the head of the table and motioned for me to sit at his right. As Kevin set salads in front of us and then poured water from a silver pitcher into our glasses, Abe picked up the conversation.

"Frank, I know this may make you a little uncomfortable. In fact, I suspect it will stretch you quite a bit, but I consider myself a good judge of people, and you've got what it takes." I was trying without much success to follow along. "We're in the motion picture business. That's our product, that's what fuels the engine of our business. The pictures we put out every year determine our success and whether we'll stay in business. Yet I spend only about one to two hours per week monitoring production. The rest of the time I'm meeting with agents or bankers or publicists or columnists or visiting dignitaries. In the evenings, we're always going to a premiere or a private showing or a charity event. I need someone to supervise the studios' production effort and report directly to me. I'd like that someone to be you, Frank."

After a few seconds of thunderous silence, I realized Abe was staring at me, motionless as a coiled snake, though friendlier.

A wave of doubt rolled over my mind as Beeker's crimson face bobbed to the surface. Abe's offer had blindsided me. I wondered if his confidence in me was well-placed, if I'd have the maturity and judgment to nominally supervise men twice my age with skills developed over decades in a craft to which I'd been exposed for only weeks. "I'm flattered," I finally said, simply to break the silence.

"Then you accept?"

"You're sure this won't cause jealousy among the producers?"

"Of course it will! But I'm equally sure that you have the skills we need to produce motion pictures with greater efficiency. Your response to the unfortunate incident with Miss Vance showed your understanding of production—whether it's with airplanes or pictures. So, yes, there's bound to be a little grumbling, but I'm confident you will quickly develop relationships with these men that will further not only their interests, but those of our business as a whole."

Abe had done an excellent job of setting the hook. I wasn't yet smart enough to know what I didn't know, but I was smart enough to recognize a once-in-a-lifetime opportunity—and I wasn't going to let it slip away.

"I accept." Abe smiled and clapped his hands. "But not at forty dollars a week!" I added. He laughed louder and longer.

"Of course not! What do you say to $300 a week? A hefty increase, don't you agree?"

Abe liked me. I knew that and it mattered to me. But it was also important that he respect me. If I accepted his first offer, he would doubt my toughness and my ability to negotiate, an ability that we both knew would be critical to success. "A hefty increase, sure," I nodded, looking down and spearing a piece of lettuce.

"Of course, no one will know what you're being paid."

I fixed Abe with a stern stare. "Everyone will know." I paused. "That's why three hundred is a bad number." Abe met this statement with a look of confusion. "Two-fifty a week is a better number." I paused again, but not long enough for Abe to catch up. "What I propose Abe, would assure the producers that I'm on their side and the side of the studio as well."

"Go on."

"We're within a few weeks of the end of the year. The studio is on track to make a profit of what, $3 million?"

"Closer to 3.5," Abe corrected.

"Okay, 3.5. Suppose you pay me $250 a week so I can live a lifestyle that won't embarrass you or the studio and you offer me compensation based on our results."

Abe leaned back in his chair and waved Kevin in to remove his salad. "What do you have in mind?"

"One percent of the profits over $3.5 million for 1946. If you're happy with me at the end of next year, we renegotiate. This reduces your fixed cost and provides me with a strong incentive to increase profits."

"Too rich," Abe shook his head. "I could never get this past the board."

It was my turn to laugh. "Come on Abe; you *are* the board! It does whatever you tell it to."

"Half a percent," he countered.

"Deal!" I agreed. Abe laughed again and reached out his hand.

"I would have offered more," he said, shaking my hand firmly.

"I would have taken less." We laughed again.

My new title was director of production. The desk we'd seen moving into the executive suite was for me. Abe, confident as he was concerning the outcome of our luncheon, had engraved business cards waiting on my new desk, along with a nameplate showing my new title. He'd also informed Beeker Douglas that my work on *Back of the Yards* had come to an end.

I spent the rest of the afternoon putting my new office in order and meeting Gladys, who would become my secretary. Gladys was prim, proper and somewhere between 45 and 106 years old, I couldn't tell. An expressionless woman, she seemed to know more than I did about every aspect of Pacific Pictures.

A few minutes before five o'clock, I rapped on the frame of Abe's open door. "I'm Miss Vance's chauffeur this afternoon," I explained, "so I'm ducking out a little early."

"Oh, I'm sure we'll get our money's worth out of you!" Abe smiled. "I'll see you tomorrow morning."

On the way to get Vera, I stopped by the publicity office. Goz wasn't in, but Jane pulled two glossy photographs from the files and placed them in a folder for me.

Despite the good news from Dr. Sparks, Vera had had a disappointing day. Rather than jumping back into action, she'd sat on the soundstage all day watching others work. Sometimes sitting around being bored is the most tiring thing you can do and by the time I got to Vera's dressing room, she was ready to leave. Even so, when she saw me approach, her face broke into a radiant smile.

"Congratulations!" she exclaimed, pecking me on the cheek. "Abe told me he was going to make you a proposal." She linked her arm in mine and we started toward the car.

"What makes you think I accepted?" I stopped and faced her. A look of concern chased the smile from her face. Then she smiled again and cocked her head.

"I know you, Frank Russell. This business has gotten into your blood. You can't fool me."

"You're right," I confessed and we started walking again. "So what did Abe tell you?"

"He said you are very capable and that you have a good rapport with people."

"And you said?"

She glanced up at me, the late afternoon sun illuminating her eyes. "Oh, I always agree with Abe," she smiled.

Vera, because she was a bona fide movie star, could afford a house, and she had a nice one, tucked up in the hills above the city. It had gotten dark by the time we reached her house, which sat on the side of a steep hill just below Bryn Mawr Drive. I unloaded her clothes and the other things that had collected at my apartment. On the last trip from my car to the house, I also carried the folder I'd picked up from the publicity office.

"Before I go," I said, laying the folder on the counter and pulling a pen from my pocket, "would you mind autographing a picture for me? I want your picture to be the first one to go in my new office." I opened the folder to an eight-by-ten portrait of Vera and held the pen out to her.

She looked at the picture, then at me and smiled. "How sweet of you!" She seemed genuinely pleased that I'd asked. She signed her name with a flourish and then wrote in a bunch of Xs and Os beneath her signature. "There. You and Abe are the only two men at Pacific Pictures who got Xs and Os on my picture," she paused, "unless someone wrote them in himself!" She handed me the pen and I closed the folder. I had also gotten a photo of Tom I planned to ask him to sign.

It was time for me to leave, but I wanted to linger, to remain in Vera's presence as long as I could. "Listen, it's time for dinner. Would you like to go someplace nice and celebrate with me?" I asked, holding my breath.

"Actually," Vera replied, a sly smile forming on her lovely face, "I was rather hoping you'd stay for breakfast."

It had turned out to be the best day of my life.

Chapter 12

When I wasn't spending time with Vera—and I did whenever I could—I spent the last weeks of the year reading every new book, and some old ones, I could lay my hands on. Our story department already had eight properties lined up for 1946; Mary, our story editor, thought she needed just one more to round out our schedule for the year. Under my plan, we'd need seven more. I knew that in order to get to fifteen properties quickly enough to make an impact in 1946, I would have to find some good leads fast.

Over the holidays, I compiled a list of twenty possible properties: ten from new novels, two from plays that had recently debuted back east, three from short stories that had been carried in one of the national magazines and five from ideas I'd quickly sketched from newspaper articles. For instance, there had been a political scandal in Mississippi involving a state legislator accused of accepting bribes to steer state contracts to a Pascagoula ship-building company. My story idea was for a returning veteran to challenge the corruption of the state legislature and to prevail in his efforts to restore good government to the state. Of course, in my story, we wouldn't name the state!

Based on the top box office pictures of 1945, I figured we'd need some westerns, crime dramas, comedies, and romances. I was confident we could find or develop the right stories using our in-house writers. If they got overwhelmed, we'd hire outside help. The piece of the plan I couldn't put in place was the financing. Abe would have to agree to the risk and then convince the bank.

"Fifteen?" Abe asked with an incredulous look. "We only shot nine all of last year!"

It was the first Monday of the New Year and the studio was cranking back up after a two-week holiday break. I had just told Abe how many pictures Pacific was going to produce over the next twelve months. Abe was seated behind his desk and he was surprised, to put it mildly. "What makes you, when you've been in the movie business for all of three months, think that we can increase our output sixty percent like flipping on a light switch?"

"We ought to be able to shoot even more than that, Abe," I began, assuming my most reassuring tone. "This isn't about knowing the movie business. Everybody on this lot has more experience in movies than I do. But, the man at the top," I pointed at him, "told me to boost production. This is how we do it."

"We can't afford to produce fifteen pictures. You realize how much that would cost?"

"Based on last year's production costs, all things being equal, about ten to twelve million dollars. Last year, we filmed an average of forty-five days per picture—except for Beeker Douglas. He averaged twenty-five days on three pictures and never went over thirty. He may not be our most creative producer, Abe, but he is by far the most profitable." I paused for a moment to let this sink in, because this was the key to my whole plan. "To become more efficient, we've got to take advantage of the pieces of the puzzle that are already in place. If we get all our producers to follow Beeker's pattern, then we get three pictures from each one and we get them in a total of about seventy-five to ninety days."

Abe started to interrupt, but I pushed on, "Sure, I know there's post-production time that we have to build in, but the point is that we've got three soundstages that are used only part-time. They just sit empty half the days of the year! The producers are the key. We set guidelines for production, number of days, shooting schedules. We assign projects based on demonstrated ability. For example, Dawes does a good job on westerns. So we give him westerns. Simpson can do comedy, or if we get a musical, we give him that. Sure, we may have to add some staff, but as long as we make good pictures that the public wants to see, we'll be adding six new streams of income. That's six more pictures to help offset our fixed costs."

Abe's eyes weren't on me; they were focused on some distant point, a point I suspected had dollar signs in front of it. "I'd have to go to Harley at Security Trust. He won't loan us that much all at once."

"Of course not," I agreed. "He'll want to see some return on his risk. That's why we take our best stories and push them into production as quickly as we can. We show the bank the kind of return we're getting and they loan us a little more, then a little more and so on. Abe, look, I'm not a banker and I'm not a studio chief. I don't know that end of the game. I know how to tighten up our production cycle. What I know is if we make good pictures, we'll make money and if we make more good pictures, we'll make more money!" I waited for Abe to make the next move.

"All right," he said after a wait of several long seconds, "show me your plan."

I spread several sheets of paper out in front of Abe. One showed the number of days each soundstage had been in use and the percentage of available days these represented. Another showed our production cycle for our average picture and compared this average to the production cycle on Beeker's three pictures. Next was a sheet showing the work load of the studio's five contract producers. Beeker had been the most prolific, guiding three films to completion, while Max Hooper had produced just one.

Money would be the biggest issue once Abe bought into my plan. But, in order to make the bet payoff, he would have to make one other big—and difficult—decision.

"I'm seeing possibilities here, Frank," he said, his eyes scrutinizing each line on each page of paper. "This could work."

"It will work, Abe," I plunged ahead. "This is what you wanted when you offered me this job. I will report directly to you and will have profit and loss accountability for feature motion picture production. This is how we make Pacific Pictures into the company you want it to be."

Abe shook his head and smiled. "That's a lot or responsibility to give to a twenty-five-year-old who doesn't know this business."

"I'm twenty-six and these ideas are not unique to this business. I won't be making pictures, Abe, I'll be managing production. Production is production, whether you're making fighter airplanes or movies. Guys like Douglas and Hooper and Dawes, they'll still have their hands on the reins. The experts will still be in control."

Abe looked at me, clearly weighing his decision. He reached over and flipped his intercom switch. "Betty, get me Bill Harley at Security Trust Bank."

"Just once I'd like to play something other than a damsel-in-distress or the hero's love interest," Vera complained as we sat in a booth across from the bar in Romanoff's. Vera was between pictures, it was Friday evening and we'd driven over to Beverly Hills to begin what I hoped would be a fun night of dinner and dancing. Vera had ordered lamb chops and I'd devoured a filet. With appetizers, salads and drinks, we were probably looking at a tab of over twenty dollars. Even with my new salary, that was a lot of dough and we hadn't even started dancing yet.

"Well," I answered, "we've got *A Matter of Discretion* coming up in a few weeks. You want me to change the casting and put you in that?" I didn't actually think *Discretion* would play very well at the box office. It was what Abe called a "message" picture about a family with a mentally retarded child. The subject matter seemed a little depressing to me, but for some reason Abe was adamant that Pacific Pictures make the picture. He said that to be taken seriously in our business a studio had to occasionally make a film about socially important issues. That was all well and good, but my deal with Abe was to increase profits and I didn't see how *Discretion* was going to help.

"No, thanks," Vera said, exhaling smoke from her cigarette. "The mother's role is the only good female part and I'm too young for it."

"And also too beautiful," I added, tipping my glass in her direction.

"Keep that up and you'll be rewarded," she smiled. "Sam Levin's been after me to play Terry's sweetheart in his next western. Can you get me out of it?" she asked, tapping ashes onto her plate. "I don't want to work with that bastard."

"Who, Sam or Terry?" I teased.

"The latter. You know that son-of-a-bitch never even apologized for slugging me. And he wants me in his picture. Ha!"

"I thought you said Sam asked you."

"Sam only asked because Terry told him to. Terry's the big star. He gets first choice of scripts and co-stars." She reached across the table and laid her hand on top of mine. "You'll keep me out of it, won't you Frank? I can't even remember the name of it."

"*Streets of San Antonio*," I said. "Sure, I'll keep you out of it, if that's what you want. But it's likely to be one of our best box office pictures of the year; Terry Thorpe in a western. Who doesn't like that? It would keep you in demand."

Vera eyed me, smoke from her cigarette forming a thin veil between us. "Get me a good role, Frank. A really good role. Look what *Mildred*

Pierce has done for Joan Crawford. I'm twice the actress she is."

"Better looking too!"

Vera smiled again. "Oh, you *are* being good tonight!"

I spent a couple of hours at the office on Sunday afternoon. We'd had a great Friday night and Saturday at Vera's place, but she needed some quiet time to review some scripts the studio had asked her to consider, so I took my leave and decided to see what I could find to advance the career of my favorite movie star.

Our conversation at Romanoff's had gotten me thinking. Thorpe, as the studio's biggest star, had the informal privilege of reviewing any scripts we were thinking about producing. If he liked the script, he could and frequently did lobby to be cast in the starring role. The best story we had under rights at the moment was based on a *Saturday Evening Post* short story called "Midnight Shamus" by Jack Lafferty. I'd persuaded our story editor Mary Goldman to purchase the screen rights for $5,000 just before the end of the year. As the title suggested, it was the story of a hard-nosed private eye who solved the city's darkest crimes during the darkest hours between midnight and dawn. It was a role that I had all along imagined Terry Thorpe would claim. But the screen adaptation hadn't been written yet and Terry Thorpe wasn't my favorite movie star.

George Burke knocked on my open office door the following Monday. "Good morning, boss!" he smiled. "Just wanted to come by and say congratulations on your new gig."

I stood up and invited George in, shaking his hand and guiding him to one of the chairs in front of my desk. I took the other. He glanced around taking in the autographed portraits of Vera Vance and Tom Evers that sat on the dark wooden shelves behind my desk. Unlike Abe's shelves, which were filled with memorabilia, photos and awards, my shelves were cluttered with stacked books, script treatments and screenplay drafts. "Looks like you're really working in here," George chuckled and I remembered the Spartan accommodations over in the newsreel division. "Most of the guys up on this level," he teased me gently, "use their offices more for show than for work."

"Well, I don't know about that," I smiled, "but this one's seeing a lot of labor—if not a lot of results yet!"

"Listen, Frank," George leaned forward, a serious expression replacing his smile, "I suspect you'll get a little resistance from some of the older hands, but just stick to your guns. Most of them will come around."

"Most of them?"

"Yeah. You might have one or two who bitch a little and drag their feet, but you've got good instincts. Be consistent and let them know what to expect and they'll get on board."

"Anybody in particular I should look out for?"

George smiled again. "I wouldn't want to prejudice you. Review each producer's recent performance. That'll give you some good preparation for your first producers meeting tomorrow."

I knew Pacific Pictures' producers were the keys to my plan to boost feature motion picture production. Without their commitment, I'd be left spinning my wheels. I counted on George Burke being an ally. Beeker Douglas would be supportive too, as he was already doing what I'd be asking the others to do. I was most worried about Max Hooper, who through a lack of supervision had been coasting along completing just one picture a year. His life was going to change—one way or another.

Abe Baum was my heavy artillery. He had put me in this position, he had accepted my plan, and he was going to make the financial commitment. Even so, I was the one who had to deliver the results, and the time frame for doing so was rather short.

By the second Tuesday of the year, four of our producers were at work on their next projects. Max Hooper, as was his habit, was in no hurry to get started.

The weekly production meeting took place in the board room, part of the third floor executive suite. The board table seated ten, four on each side and one at each end. Comfortable, black leather swivel chairs lined the table which was a solid, heavy dark mahogany. A leather-trimmed blotter rested on the table in front of each participant. On each blotter lay an agenda and a closed folder.

On this cool, gray winter morning, when the production team gathered for its weekly meeting, Abe was not in his customary seat at the head of the conference table—I was. The cooler weather made my leg ache and I was gently kneading my calf while we waited for the meeting to begin. Abe took his seat at the foot of the table, next to Goz. Abe and I had agreed that after a very short introduction, he would turn the meeting over to me and then depart. He wanted to send a clear message that I had the authority to manage production.

The producers were arrayed on both sides of the table, their reports and notepads joining the other material on the blotters. I was grateful to see George's friendly face among them. "Let's get started," I announced, bringing the meeting to order. I nodded toward Abe.

"You're all aware that we've made a change in structure and that Frank here is going to be our production manager. I want you all to understand that you have my full confidence. You all know how to make good movies, pictures that are both high quality and profitable. I've known for a while that there needed to be more coordination in our production efforts and I finally figured out that one person who was not named Abe Baum should be in charge of this." A couple of the producers nodded their heads and chuckled. "As head of the studio, I simply don't have as much time as I used to and there is nothing more important than our feature films production. Now, Frank showed up here on an errand last fall. I've watched him handle some tough assignments and I have great confidence in his initiative and his judgment. You may wonder how a young kid like Frank can take on a job like this. But let me tell you, it's young kids like Frank who just saved the world for us older guys." Nods again. "So, I expect you to give Frank your full support because he has my full backing."

Abe stood. "Well, if you'll excuse me, I've got an early lunch date with a banker. I leave you gentlemen to it." He left the boardroom, pulling the door closed behind him.

I directed everyone's attention to the folders in front of them and for the next fifteen minutes, I outlined the plan that Abe had approved. I explained that our soundstages were in use only fifty percent of the time; that our days in production per film were too long; and that we were going to increase the number of pictures filmed annually. By the time I finished, Beeker was the only guy still nodding. Hooper's face was a mask of open hostility. When I asked for questions, he was the first to speak.

"So this is all about speed. We're not making widgets here, Frank. There's a strong artistic element involved in what we create. I'm hearing 'Faster, faster, faster' regardless of the impact on quality story-telling.'" It wasn't a question so much as a shot across my bow. Beeker rolled his eyes.

"Not at all, Max. Beeker here can tell you that I'm no film maker. I've never produced. I've never directed. Never written a script. But sound business practices still apply, even in an environment as creative as this. Most of the pictures we shoot can be completed on a schedule of twenty-five days or less. We're averaging forty-five. Conservatively, we could save $100,000 a picture by making our productions more efficient."

"Do you want quality or efficiency?" Hooper responded and it was clear where the resistance to my scheme would be coming from.

"Efficiency isn't a dirty word," I replied, keeping my voice as calm as possible. The last thing I wanted to do was swallow Hooper's bait and lose my cool. Actually, the last thing I wanted was to lose. "There's no reason efficiency can't be the escort of your creative efforts." I didn't want to get into a debate; didn't want these men to think my plan was optional, so I charged ahead. "Here's a list with a synopsis of the projects we have in the works for this year." I passed out a copy to each producer. The list was not quite complete, but they didn't need to know that. "If you're already assigned to one of these projects, you'll see your name typed in beside it. For example," I turned to James Lynn, "JJ is already working on *Downtown Division*, a police drama set here in Los Angeles. Beeker's working on *Jungle Command,* a war picture. I might come by and give you some technical advice," I smiled at Beeker and he laughed. "If the project is unassigned and you're interested in it, let me know and we'll talk about it."

The four producers with pictures underway updated me on their progress and their expenses to date. George gave a quick update on newsreel's plans for the next couple of weeks. I had to mediate a schedule conflict between Nestor Dawes and Chas Simpson. Dawes was producing *Streets of San Antonio*, the Terry Thorpe western Sam Levin was directing. Simpson's picture was a comedy, *Three's the Number*. Both had planned to film on Soundstage 5 on the same day. That issue was easily disposed of and the rest of the meeting ran routinely. Most of the guys seemed to have accepted the new ground rules; most, but not all. Hooper, after his initial comments, had remained noticeably silent.

The meeting broke up about twelve o'clock and the producers headed either to the offices downstairs or back to their soundstages. All except Hooper. He waited until the others had cleared the room and then stood up and closed the door. He turned to face me.

"What's in it for me? I've got a pretty good deal going here right now, Frank. Nobody imposed a quota on Da Vinci or Michelangelo. Why should I work twice as hard for no more reward?"

"Three times," I replied, hoping to sound cool and in control.

"Three times?"

"Yeah. You're going to work three times as hard because you're going to be making three pictures a year instead of one." I sat quietly while Hooper composed his reply.

"Why would I want to do that?" he asked, teeth gritted, a flush coloring his round face.

"Look, Max, everybody around here respects the quality of your pictures. But the days of one a year are over. Your quota is three."

"Well, maybe I don't want to do three." He picked up the list of projects I'd handed out.

"Maybe there aren't three on this list that I think are good enough." Hooper stepped right into my trap.

"Maybe not. I tell you what, Max, there's one project that I haven't put on the list yet. I think it's the best story we've got and it needs our most capable producer and most gifted director. If you'll get on board, I'd be happy to discuss it with you."

Since Abe was lunching with his banker, I'd made arrangements to use his dining room. I thought the effect of inviting Hooper into this executive sanctum might help solidify my authority and contribute toward winning him over.

Kevin served us salads with an entrée of baked ham, potatoes au gratin and green beans. It was the same food that was served in the dining room on the ground floor, but eating it in Abe's private room made it taste better.

"I'm listening," Hooper said as Kevin retreated into the adjoining kitchenette.

"We bought a story late last year about a private eye. The writing is first rate, by a guy named Lafferty. His main character works nights in a big city, sees the gritty side of life, but also has a sharp wit. The story is both dark and hilarious."

"Sounds interesting," Hooper said between bites. "I like the combination of dark and funny, but how is it different from *The Maltese Falcon*, for example?"

"Well Max, here's my idea and this is why I wanted to discuss it with you in private. We've bought the short story, but I haven't assigned a writer to work up a screen play yet. I didn't want to do that until I could bring a producer and, hopefully, a top director in. I agree with you that this is a creative endeavor and I want to make the most of this story. I think it's that good." Max continued to chew and nodded. "My other thought is that to make this thing really stand out, to make it both a critical and commercial success, we change the main character from a he to a she." He stopped chewing and stared at me.

"Let me guess: Vera Vance." A smile tugged at the corners of his mouth.

I nodded. "Yep. We call it *Redheaded Shamus*."

Max set down his fork and eyed me with a new respect. "I like it," he said. I was sure Vera would too.

Max Hooper also laid claim to *A Matter of Discretion*. No problem, I told him, but to get to *Discretion*, he'd first have to make *A Lovely Evening*, a romantic drama. That put him squarely on the hook for three films and I felt my biggest challenge had been resolved—at least for the time being. With Hooper on board, I did not anticipate any trouble from the other producers. By the end of

Wednesday, I had assigned all fifteen pictures, at least in my mind. Of course at this point, I hadn't publically committed anything beyond the pictures already in production. Before I took that step, I owed Abe a visit.

Lovely Betty worked me into Abe's schedule on Thursday morning, between a photo shoot with a visiting congressman and a lunch meeting with some distributors. Once again, I stood in front of Abe's massive wooden desk. It was covered with stacks of neat folders, each representing some issue requiring Abe's attention.

"How'd it go after I left the meeting?" he asked.

"As well as I could have expected. Max dug his heels in, but he and I met privately after the others broke up. Thanks for letting me use the dining room, by the way. That helped. Now, here's what I've come up with so far," I began, laying a single page in front of him. On it were listed the names of the projects, the proposed producers, suggested budgets and the tentative shooting dates.

Abe scanned the sheet quickly and glanced up. "You got Max to agree?"

"I did, but I had to give him the best stories. I think it's a good trade, though. And if he doesn't play ball by our rules, he won't make *Discretion*."

Abe looked up. "*Discretion* gets made Frank. No ifs, ands, or buts. Understand?"

"Yes sir, absolutely. But if Max doesn't adhere to the plan, it may be someone else making it. Are you comfortable with that? If you're not, I need to know now."

Abe waved his hand as though shooing away a pest. "Sure, sure. Why's the budget a million dollars on *Redheaded Shamus*? What is that, anyway? I haven't read a script."

"We don't have a script yet."

Abe looked up, his eyebrows arched. "No script and you want me to spend a million dollars?"

"It's the best property we've got. I want to film it in Technicolor."

"Why haven't I heard of this?"

"Mary bought the short story which is called 'Midnight Shamus.' "

"Oh, yeah," Abe recalled, his eyes straying toward the ceiling. "Yeah, this looks like a good picture for Thorpe."

"I want to change it, Abe. I want to make the main character a woman."

"Miss Vance?" he asked, his eyes reading my face.

"Yes. She's got the charisma to carry it off. We craft the story the right way and it'll appeal to men *and* to women. This has huge box office potential, Abe."

Abe shifted his eyes back to the sheet in front of him. Would he trust me or assert his right to overrule his inexperienced protégé? I held my breath. This was the moment of truth for me. Without looking up, Abe said, "She'll have to dye her hair."

"Dye my hair?" Vera had asked over shrimp cocktail. "Why would I need to do that?"

"Because we're going to be shooting in Technicolor and the title of the movie is *Redheaded Shamus*, so you can't be some honey-haired vixen!" She stopped in mid-bite and lowered her fork back to her plate. I'd waited until Friday at dinner to share the good news with her.

"Shamus?" she'd asked, confused.

"Yeah, as in 'Midnight Shamus,' only we dropped the 'Midnight' and replaced it with 'Redheaded.' In the short story, the shamus is a guy, but given my creative genius, nearly limitless authority, overwhelming affection and deep sense of loyalty to you, I thought, 'Why not change this into a star vehicle for Vera Vance, the woman I love?'"

Her eyes slowly registered what I was telling her and a grin broke across her lovely face. "You didn't?"

"Did. And guess who didn't even get a chance to review the script."

"Who?"

"I'll never tell, but his initials are Terry Thorpe."

Vera's eyes got even wider and she covered her mouth with her hand and began to laugh. After a moment, she regained her composure, looked me squarely in the eyes and said, "Pay the check and take me home!" Understanding that opportunities like this don't come around often and that when they do they can be fleeting, I did as I was told.

Vera was kissing me all over. She started at the top of my head and had worked her way down to my chest. We'd raced to her house from Perino's restaurant on Wilshire Boulevard where we had been enjoying our Friday evening dinner. Vera had dragged me, quite willingly, to her bedroom where she'd peeled me like a banana and we'd made passionate love. Now, I was catching my breath and reliving the delight with which she had received the news about her next picture.

Vera rolled off of me, her breasts brushing my chest. "So who's going to produce and direct?"

"Oh, that's it?" I teased. "Service Frank and then get down to business?" I rolled over onto her and playfully pinned her arms. I kissed her rapidly all along the curve of her neck until she started to giggle. Then, I rained my kisses down to her shoulders and across her breasts. By now she was so tickled that she was breathless.

"Stop!" she pleaded, wheezing.

"No! Not until you say that Frank Russell is the greatest lover of all time!"

"Okay, okay! Frank Russell is the greatest …" but she couldn't finish she was giggling so hard. I started laughing too and she took advantage of the moment to roll over again and pin me to the bed. "What do you say now, tough guy?" she laughed.

"I love you."

Her smile broke for the briefest moment but then she laughed again and began kissing me all over. I enjoyed the moment and considered the profound irony of the gratitude I felt toward Terry Thorpe.

Chapter 13

Things were going really well. Abe had approved the production plan; the producers, even Max Hooper, seemed to be on board; and my relationship with Vera was drowning me in wonder and contentment. But when I opened the paper a couple of mornings later, I got a reminder that good times don't always last. Joan Roswell's column included a pointed paragraph about a certain up-and-coming young studio executive to whom I felt very close.

"Pacific Pictures' Abe Baum has rolled the proverbial dice on an inexperienced and untested young war veteran as his new head of production. Frank Russell is only twenty-six years old, the same age as Irving Thalberg when he took over as MGM's production chief twenty years ago. Of course dear Irving amassed a record of achievement unlikely to ever be equaled before dying of overwork at age thirty-seven. We'll be watching to see how this gamble pays off; watching, but not betting."

Nothing like a spotlight to turn the heat up. I'd have to remember to send Joan some flowers and pretend she'd paid me a compliment. I was sure she'd pretend the same thing.

Working from Lafferty's short story, Hopkins Morton, one of the studio's best in-house writers, banged out a draft screen play of *Redheaded Shamus* in two weeks. Max had asked for Peter Shaw as the film's director and, together with Morton, they polished the script for two more weeks before handing it over to me in a mid-February meeting in my office.

"Thanks," I said accepting the folder containing the script and dropping it onto my desk.

"Aren't you going to read it?" Morton asked.

"Of course I am. But if you three think it's ready to go, I'm sure it's ready to go. I'll read it and if I think I have anything to contribute, I'll tell you. I'll give it to Abe too. He might want to make suggestions." Max nodded his agreement. "Now tell me, how soon until you have a shooting schedule?"

"This time next week," Max answered. So far so good, I thought.

"And casting?"

"Donovan Keegan as the male lead, Mr. Clifton, Janet Cantrell as his wife and Doyle Burton as Lieutenant Larson." It was my turn to nod. It was a good cast. Keegan had the looks to go along with his movie star status. Janet Cantrell was cute, a "girl next door" type who would be easy on the eyes but wouldn't detract attention from the far more glamorous Vera Vance. Burton could play practically any part and got along well with his cast and crewmates. I thought the cast would complement the star.

Max reviewed some of the preparatory work already underway and asked when I was available to meet with Goz to review the publicity plan. As the producer, Max was in charge of the picture from a business and logistics perspective. As the director, Peter had creative control. In truth, the two would work very closely throughout production. Hopkins Morton, the writer, would contribute only if requested from this point forward. With his talent, he would quickly be assigned another writing project. Some of the writers—okay, most of the writers—resented the lack of influence they had once the script left their typewriters, but that's just how the system worked.

We consulted the soundstage schedule and penciled in production of *Redheaded Shamus* to begin on Friday the 15th —the Ides of March.

I was spending as much time as possible in one of the projection rooms on the lot. The ultra-efficient, humorless Gladys scheduled a screening of one of Pacific's films for me each day as I tried to learn as much as I could as fast as I could. I'd started with the pictures Beeker Douglas had produced, further categorizing them by director. I was looking for trends, styles, techniques—

anything that would help me better understand the art and science of movie-making.

For example, Beeker's pictures, regardless of the director, had a certain economy to them. Beeker confined the action to fewer sets than in pictures produced by Nestor Dawes, for instance, who favored more exterior settings and who filmed more often on the studio's back lot. In addition, Gladys gave me a daily schedule of what dailies were being screened in which projection rooms and I attended as many of these as I could. It was important to get an interim look at the products we were turning out and it also helped me better understand what directors and producers were looking for in their final product.

At the end of February, I was invited to a different type of screening. It was customary for the studio heads to invite peers, colleagues and friends to their homes for pre-premiere showings of upcoming releases. On Thursday, the final day of the month, Abe and Ruth Baum opened their magnificent Bel Air home to a guest list of at least sixty. The event included a light supper and then a viewing—in the Baum's private home theater—of *Downtown Division*. As the picture had been made with the active cooperation of the City of Los Angeles, and in particular the police department, both the mayor and chief of police were included among the evening's guests. I escorted Vera, stunning in a bright red chiffon gown, which no doubt made me the envy of all the men present. Except maybe Tom Evers. My rented tux wasn't very comfortable, but I was too mesmerized by the pageantry of the evening to care.

The Baums' house sat atop one of the ridges north of Bel Air and was closer to a palace than a house. A concrete courtyard greeted visitors traveling up the winding driveway. Here, liveried attendants greeted guests and guided them inside while valets tended to their automobiles. In the high-ceilinged rotunda, Abe and Ruth personally welcomed all visitors before handing them off to an usher who would escort them to the bar and assure they knew their assigned seat for dinner. Ruth was even shorter than Abe, with a face that you'd describe as handsome rather than pretty. Her black gown was modestly cut, befitting her age and her position among the Hollywood elite. She had dark hair that was losing the battle against graying and dark eyes that crinkled when she smiled, which she seemed to do a lot. She was warm and cordial without being overly familiar.

Abe presided over the banquet table in the dining room where he and Ruth were joined by Louis and Margaret Mayer of MGM, Sam Goldwyn and his wife, Frances, Jack Warner accompanied by one of his studio's starlets, Terry Thorpe and his date, and Donovan Keegan and Janet Cantrell. Keegan was the star of *Downtown Division*, playing a detective who had helped crack a ring of anarchists planning to blow up city hall. His honor the mayor and his first lady and the police chief filled out the table.

Vera and I were invited to dine at one of the several round tables arranged in the great hall of the mansion. Joining us were producer JJ Lynn, the film's director Sam Levin, Goz and his wife, Pat, and Tom Evers and his date, Beverly Skardon, one of the studio's pretty contract players. Studio department heads, actors and actresses—some from rival studios—and friends of the Baums rounded out the guest list.

The meal had been billed as "light," but included a salad, salmon filets, asparagus, whipped potatoes and rolls, served with a white wine from a vineyard in which Abe was part-owner. I was enjoying myself, visiting with my tablemates and relaxing. I had no responsibilities for the evening other than escorting Vera, a task at which I excelled. Our table was closest to a stone walk-in fire place in which a fire popped and crackled. Vera was seated closest to the hearth.

"God, I'm burning up," she leaned over and whispered halfway through the meal. I glanced over to see a thin trickle of sweat pushing its way past her ear.

"You've always been a hot-blooded thing," I agreed.

She slapped me playfully on my forearm. "Oh you! You're just saying that because it's true." Her smile kicked me in the chest, making my heart beat a little faster and attracting the attention of certain other organs as well.

"Do you want to swap seats with me?" I asked more seriously.

"No, then I'd feel like he was watching every bite," she replied, jerking her head toward the life-size portrait that hung above the mantle. The painting was a realistic rendition of a young man, probably in his late teens or early twenties. I assumed he was the older version of the youth whose picture graced Abe's desk.

"Abe's son?" I asked, looking over her shoulder at the handsome young man hanging on the wall.

"Yeah."

"Where is he now? I've never met him."

"I don't know," she said, staring down at the half-eaten fish on her plate. I was about to dig for more information when an usher entered the room tapping out notes on a set of hand chimes, Abe and Ruth right behind him.

"Welcome again, everyone," Abe began as the other guests in the room fell silent. "Ruth and I are grateful for your friendship and pleased that you could join us for this special occasion. Because tomorrow is a work day for so many of you, and because we would never want to be the cause of your tardiness," this brought forth laughter, "we're going to adjourn now to the theater where dessert will be served along with a showing of Pacific Pictures' newest feature, *Downtown Division*! In addition to our many friends from Hollywood's motion picture industry, we're pleased to welcome Mayor and Mrs. Bowron and Chief Horrall of the Los Angeles Police Department. So, ladies and gentlemen, right this way!" Abe and Ruth, followed by the mayor, his wife and the chief, led the rest of us down a long, wide corridor.

Vera was on my right as we fell in, shuffling our way along with the rest of the crowd. Suddenly, a hand grasped my left elbow. I turned my head to find Joan Roswell linking her arm with mine. Joan was dressed to the nines, as usual, but this time her apparel was formal: a white gown with a plunging neckline, an ermine stole and bright red gloves that reached up past her elbows. In the rarefied company of Hollywood's royalty, her green eyes practically glowed with contentment.

"Hello, Frank darling!" Then looking over at Vera asked, "And how are your sinuses, my dear? Back to normal, I hope!"

"Yes, thank you, Joan. The doctor said it must have been a seasonal allergy."

"Oh?" Joan's eyes were wide with delight. "And what was blooming that would have triggered your discomfort?"

"Well, who knows," Vera laughed. "It's California. Something's always in season." The two women on my arms laughed as though sharing a private joke.

"Aren't you the envy of the evening, escorting the beautiful Miss Vance?" Joan said, turning back to me.

"Two beautiful ladies," I corrected and she smiled, her green eyes twinkling at the compliment.

"You know, Frank," she said lowering her voice and leaning her perfectly-coiffed head toward mine, "there's a mystery about Pacific Pictures that I've yet to resolve." She looked up at me with eyebrows raised. For a moment my ego led me to believe she was asking about how a guy like me had gotten a job like this, hobnobbing with studio fat cats and escorting movie stars to private showings. Joan quickly brought me back to earth. "The movies are a fascinating business, don't you think?"

"Sure," I agreed.

"But the story I really want is right here in this house."

"And what's that, Joan?"

"The story of David Baum." She said this quietly so that in the bustle of the crowd, my ears were the only ones who could hear.

I looked at her hungry cat's eyes, searching for some glimmer of mischief, but all I found was cold calculation. "So why are you asking me? I've never met him, don't know that I've ever even seen him."

"Yes," she said knowingly, "that's the mystery isn't it? Where is this boy? What's become of him? Why do you suppose Abe would be seeking a surrogate?" We'd reached the theater room and people were filing in. "A car crash. That much I've been able to piece together."

"I'm sure I don't know, Joan." I said this a little coolly, her questions inappropriate and discomforting in the Baum's own home. To tell the truth, I was glad I didn't know. Not knowing, I couldn't tell.

Joan just smiled. I got the feeling that rejection didn't deter her. "I guess I'm just a curious cat. It would make a great story, don't you think?"

"You'd be a better judge of that than me," I said, smiling and trying to make things a little lighter. I pivoted and swept my hand toward the theater. "After you."

Joan walked down the aisle. I held Vera back to let several other couples go in between us and Joan. I didn't want to end up sitting beside her. The theater was much nicer than the commercial theaters I was used to. For one thing, your feet didn't stick to the floor, plus every guest was handed a thick slice of chocolate cake on a china plate. Vera and I slid into seats on the back row.

After a brief introduction from JJ, which included words of thanks to the city and police department, the room went dark and a bright shaft of light burst forth from the projection booth. The Pacific Pictures logo, a crashing wave above the words *Ars Est Vita,* which with my rusty high school Latin I translated as "Art is Life," appeared on the screen followed by a fade to black and the sound of a police siren wailing in the distance. A tiny speck of light appeared in the lower right corner of the screen. The light grew bigger, the wailing siren louder and the picture was underway.

"So where's the son?" I whispered, leaning over and nuzzling Vera's ear.

"Shh!" she slapped my arm. "I don't know. Apparently he was in a car crash a few years back."

"Did it kill him?"

She shook her head. "No, but it ruined him."

"Ruined him?"

Vera turned to me and quietly growled, "Shut up and watch the picture!"

I was working hard every day to identify new stories we could turn into feature pictures. I was also continuing my study of the filmmaker's art and allocating resources for the four pictures under production at any given time while balancing the funds with which we had to work. Abe and I met almost daily. He was a good listener and offered wise advice which I ignored at my own peril. One day, a week after the private screening of *Downtown Division*, he asked, "You still living in the garage?"

"Above the garage; yes."

"You're the head of production for a major studio, for Pete's sake! When are you going to start living like it?" I couldn't tell if he was angry or just interested in my well-being.

"I am living like it," I shot back with a smile. "I'm dating a movie star!"

"Oh! And that's another thing," Abe replied, his eyes wide, wagging his finger at me. "You want to be real careful with that. These starlets got one thing on their minds and it's not true love! These kids'll do absolutely anything to make the big time."

"Vera's already made the big time," I protested."

"You just be careful, my boy. Don't let her use her feminine wiles to cloud your judgment."

I was a little offended at Abe's inference, not to mention the notion that having a love affair with me constituted "absolutely anything." I shot back, "If you think I shouldn't have built *Redheaded Shamus* around her it's a hell of a time to say so. We start shooting next week."

"I didn't say that!" Abe snapped, and now he was a little angry. "I just don't want to see you get hurt by her or anybody else, Frank." He was calming down. "Listen to me," he broke eye contact and waved a hand in the air. "I sound like an old man. Sure, you've got to live a little. Vera's a great gal, but she is what she is. Don't forget that. You two have fun together—that's all right. Just be careful. That's all I'm saying." He seemed wistful.

"Sure, Abe," I said and when he looked up again I smiled.

"But go buy a house or something!" he exclaimed. "We can't have you sleeping above a DeSoto every night!"

That conversation led me to begin a search for more permanent accommodations, a search that would result in the purchase of a bungalow on Taft Avenue the following month.

In the meantime, I was devoting a great deal of effort to ensuring *Redheaded Shamus* got off to a smooth—and timely—start. Hopkins Morton's screenplay had improved upon the original short story—and not only by turning the protagonist into a female. Although the script didn't include a love interest for the shamus, Brigid O'Dell, the banter between her and police Lieutenant Larson was so smart and quick that it would make Nick and Nora Charles sound like tongue-tied buffoons.

Max Hooper was dragging his feet, though. He and director Peter Shaw still hadn't turned in their shooting schedule and set construction was lagging behind. We'd come to an agreement with the studio's set builders and painters to adjust their work day so as not to interfere with the increased daytime use of the soundstages. This meant more evening and nighttime work, which meant higher wages. It also increased the cost of operating the commissary, which now had hot food available into the evening. That's why Hooper's delay was so concerning: to make our fifteen-picture program pay off, we had to get our films into theaters and generate the revenue to offset these increased costs.

I decided to pay a little visit to Mr. Hooper.

Max Hooper enjoyed his lifestyle. He had a nice home up in the hills overlooking the city, drove a Cadillac and belonged to an exclusive club. He also liked the pace of his work. When I knocked on his office door, he was sitting with his feet propped on the corner of his desk, a cigarette dangling from the corner of his mouth, reading *Variety*. A radio sitting by the window was playing a Dinah Shore song.

"Got a second, Max?"

"Frank!" I had intentionally startled him, expecting to find just this relaxed pace. He laid his paper on the desk, pulled his feet down and turned to face me, flicking ashes into the blue glass ash tray on the corner of his utilitarian beige metal desk. "Why didn't you just phone? No need for the head of production to inconvenience himself by coming all the way down to the lowly producers' floor." He said all this with a smirk on his face, but it fled when I closed the door behind me.

"I thought it would be better to have a face-to-face chat," I said, making a show of looking at the top of his clean desk. I sat in the cheap wooden chair in front of his desk without waiting for an invitation. "Where are you on *Redheaded Shamus*? The meter's running. We've got to get moving."

"Hammer," Max replied.

"I beg your pardon?"

"Hammer," he repeated. "That's what you are, Frank, a hammer. To you every problem looks like a nail. Your only strategy is speed; 'hurry up, go faster.' This business doesn't work like that. It takes time to make a great picture. You've got to think things through, work out a million details."

"That's what you were doing? Thinking things through?" I pointed to the *Variety* on his desk.

"Let me think of a way you might understand this," he began condescendingly. "You were in the Army, right?" I nodded. "Well, I'm sure you did a lot of physical training. They'd work you really hard for a while and then you'd rest for a spell, right? Same thing with the creative process. I work really hard, and then I rest. That offers me a time of reflection, gives me some perspective on the work we're doing. This isn't like running a race or playing a baseball game, Frank. You can't gauge our progress by seeing where we are on the track or looking at the scoreboard to see what inning it is. Creative work is different. Don't be a hammer."

I struggled to control my temper. I knew it wouldn't do me—or Pacific Pictures—any good to antagonize this pompous ass. After all, his project promised the greatest potential of any picture on our schedule. He was also Vera's boss until shooting finished. "Don't act like a nail," I forced myself to smile. "It looks like you're just sitting here waiting for a hammer to come along and help you get moving. How can we make this work to our mutual satisfaction?"

"Just give me the space I need to do my job, Frank."

"Just remember that your job is three pictures a year, Max."

"Duly noted," he smirked again. I thought back to what George Burke had told me. Be consistent and let them know what was expected. I felt I'd done that with Max. I'd let him make the next move—and hope that it would be the right one. If he continued to delay and as a result threw the rest of our schedule off the rails, I'd replace him.

Max must have gotten the message, because over the next two weeks, preparations for *Redheaded Shamus* picked up momentum. The shooting schedule was submitted and set construction caught up so that we were ready to begin production on our targeted date. Starting a picture on a Friday may have seemed a little strange. After all, why start something new and then immediately break for the weekend? But it was important to drive home the fact that every day mattered. Every day we used our soundstages to further production was one day closer to achieving our goal of fifteen feature pictures.

Doyle and Vera, the two highest paid members of the cast, had decided to go in together and provide doughnuts and coffee each morning on the set. I thought that was a pretty neat idea and wondered where they'd come up with it. Just kidding. In truth, it was a great morale builder. It was a great way to make two movie stars, each pulling down better than $2,000 a week, seem like "regular folks" to crew members who might be hauling in all of ninety dollars a week for their not-so-glamorous contributions.

Filming on *Redheaded Shamus* would be out of sequence to accommodate Doyle's schedule. He had been cast as a supporting player in *Streets of San Antonio,* which had an overlapping production schedule, so the first day's plan called for shooting a key scene between Vera's eponymous character and Doyle's Lieutenant Larson. When I arrived on the set at nine-thirty, Peter Shaw was coaching his actors for the upcoming scene.

"You're beseeching him, Vera," Peter explained, "using your considerable sex appeal to enlist his help in catching the thief. But you, Lieutenant Larson," Peter continued turning toward Doyle, "you are far too professional to fall for that tactic."

"No I'm not!" Doyle winked at Vera, causing the crew and director to chuckle.

Peter retreated from the set and took his seat beside the camera. The assistant director called out, "Places! Quiet, please!" The bell rang alerting all that shooting was set to begin.

"Lights up."

"Speed!" the camera operator called.

"Action!" Peter barked.

Brigid O'Dell perched on a corner of Lieutenant Larson's desk, leaning over toward him in an alluring pose. "Come on, Larson," she cooed, batting her eyelashes, "what have you got on this palooka? You can share it with me."

"What? And miss the pleasure of watching you finally solve a case!"

Brigid pouted and cocked her head. "Aw, why you want to be so rough on me?"

"Listen, Brigid, you ain't seen rough like you're going to get if you cross Clifton. He's not a man to be trifled with. I'd hate to see you get in over your pretty red head."

Brigid sat up straight. "Sure, you don't seem to have much confidence in me, Larson. And here I've been bringing you cases for two years—cases your flatfoots haven't been able to crack."

"Cases that haven't been worth the police department's time, Miss. You going to sit there and bask in the glory of busting three ten-year-olds who were fencing stolen bubble gum?"

Brigid batted her eyes again. "A sticky case, that was. But look at it this way, Larson: by catching those mugs while they were young, we turned 'em away from a life of crime and set them on a godly path. There's three less hoodlums you and your boys have to worry about, sure." She slid off the desk and leaned in to Larson's face. "If you'll not help me, I'll go it alone. And when I do crack the case and find the necklace, the reward money'll go it alone as well. Right into me pocket!" She wheeled away and stalked out the door, Larson leaning over to watch her depart.

"Cut! All right! Very nice, very nice! An excellent beginning!" Peter beamed. Vera came back onto the set and catching my eye blew me a kiss. Peter and the camera operator conferred about the shot and, satisfied, begin to reposition the camera and lighting for close-ups.

"That was great!" I said, shaking Doyle's hand and giving Vera a quick hug. I was careful not to mess up her hair or makeup; I didn't want to be responsible for shutting down production for half a day. I turned back to Doyle. "So you go from police lieutenant to outlaw, huh?"

Doyle chuckled and held up the dog-eared copy of a script. "Yes, I've got six days here in the orbit of this lovely star before I have to report to Sam Levin and start working with horse asses."

"Sam's not so bad," Vera laughed.

"I wasn't talking about Sam!" Doyle chuckled.

I checked in with Beeker Douglas on the set of *Jungle Command* and met the Marine Corps colonel who was serving as the technical advisor. He was a powerfully built man named Cobham with a courteous but professional mien. He'd fought the

Japanese at Guadalcanal and, like me, Okinawa. Unlike me, his time on Okinawa had lasted from the initial landings all the way to the end of the fighting. I had no doubt he would help Beeker make the most realistic picture possible—which really wasn't saying much. The public would have run screaming from the theater if they'd been forced to watch a "realistic" war picture. There was no way to capture the heart-breaking sights, smells, sounds and pains of battle. Besides, a true-to-life war picture would have violated too many tenets of the production code, which set forth acceptable content for motion pictures released in the United States.

The code had been adopted by the motion picture industry in the 1930s as a self-governing agreement to forestall efforts by some self-appointed moral policemen in Congress and elsewhere to censor movies. The code, which had been approved by all the studios, set forth general rules on dealing with a variety of subjects, including crime, violence, sex and religion. For instance, Beeker's war picture, despite Colonel Cobham's input, couldn't include scenes of brutality or gruesomeness. And in Vera's picture, we had to be careful not to overemphasize her abundant sex appeal. Violating either of these rules, or dozens of others, would result in the rejection of our pictures by the codes office. At a minimum, that would mean reediting the film and in some cases would require reshooting whole scenes. Either eventuality could quickly turn a picture into a financial nightmare, a situation in which the studio never won.

Chapter 14

Compared to my garage apartment at the Smiths', my new house on Taft Avenue was a mansion. Compared to the Baum's Bel Air home it was more like a lean-to. Still, I was highly satisfied with my two-bedroom castle. While it was no closer to the studio, it was away from some of the traffic, since Taft Avenue was not only north of Hollywood Boulevard, but also north of Franklin. Plus, it offered more room and greater privacy when Vera spent the night.

The 1,500-square-foot house was situated on a quiet street of homes just at the foot of the hills. It was a rare find, for in addition to the two bedrooms, it boasted two full bathrooms. I felt fortunate to have acquired it for $9,900. Abe's banker, Mr. Harley, had personally assisted me in filling out the mortgage application.

"Guess who came to see me this afternoon?" I said to Vera as we snuggled together in the double bed of the master suite.

"Clark Gable."

"Close."

She propped up on one elbow, the sheet falling away from her shoulder, and looked me in the eyes. "Not Terry?"

"The very one and only."

"What did he want?"

I recounted Thorpe's visit. Gladys had buzzed me on the intercom and said, "You have a visitor, Mr. Russell." Despite entreaties to the contrary, she persisted in calling me "Mr. Russell."

"Does my visitor have a name?" I asked, trying to keep the sarcasm out of my voice.

"Terry Thorpe." That got my attention. Despite my personal animosity toward Thorpe for the way he'd treated Vera, he was still the studio's biggest star. He was also someone I had never met, except for that brief encounter in the commissary. I didn't think he even knew who I was; yet he was waiting in the reception area to see me.

"Be right out," I said into the intercom. I grabbed my coat off the back of my chair and slipped it on as I stepped into the corridor and out to the waiting area. "Mr. Thorpe," I smiled as my eyes landed on the tall, handsome man wearing western rig.

He flashed his famous smile and shook my hand, "Please, call me Terry. Everybody around here does."

"Well, come on back to the office where we can talk," I said, turning to lead the way.

We entered my office and I waved him toward one of the matching chairs in front of my desk. I took the other. "Don't let your spurs scratch up the legs," I said. Thorpe shot a startled look at the chair legs and then back up at me. "I'm just kidding. Don't worry about it."

"Oh, okay," he fidgeted in his chair. For a big-time movie star, he seemed a little shy. "I, uh, hope you don't mind me showing up like this, no appointment and all, Mr. Russell."

"Frank," I corrected him. "Everybody around here calls me Frank."

"Oh," he smiled without confidence, "sure. Frank. It's just that everybody around here says you're the surrogate now, you know." I didn't, but I didn't want to spoil whatever illusions he had about my omniscience and authority. "I talked to Nestor Dawes and he said I should come see you."

I slouched in my chair, mirroring the way Thorpe sat. He'd left his Stetson elsewhere, but other than that, he was the quintessential cowboy, from his silver-toed boots to his chaps to the kerchief knotted about his neck. If Vera were here, I thought, I bet she'd love to pull that knot a whole lot tighter. "Well," I said, spreading my hands and smiling, "and here you are. What can I help you with, Terry?"

"I know you're still sort of new around here," he hesitated. "Now I don't mean that in a critical way. It's just that you may not know that I'm the best box office draw the studio has." I thought he might be leading up to asking why he hadn't gotten a shot at *Midnight Shamus*. I thought wrong.

"Believe me, Terry, I am well aware of your box office appeal. That's why we want to make sure that we continue to find the right vehicles for you."

"Well, that's fine, just fine, Frank. You see that's what I wanted to talk to you about. I'm good at westerns. I know that and I'm not trying to upset the apple cart. But do you think, Frank, that maybe once in a while, maybe just every year or two, the studio could put me in a picture where I didn't have to ride a horse? You know, maybe wear a suit. Cooper and Wayne, why they're great in the westerns, but every now and then they get to branch out a little. I mean, it took me years to get rid of my sidekick, you know. And after what he did! Well, I'm getting off the subject," he offered an apologetic smile.

A little red flag went up when he talked about his sidekick; there was some undercurrent that I didn't understand. I thought about mentioning my relationship with Mickey Moreno but decided revealing that to Thorpe might not be my best course of action. I came back to Thorpe's request. "So you'd like to be cast in some non-western roles. That should be easy enough—on one condition."

Thorpe perked up. "Condition? What condition?"

"You can't slug any of your co-stars."

The big man shifted in his chair, an uncomfortable look crossed his face. "I'm not sure what you mean, Frank."

"Sure you are," I said, staring directly into his famous blue eyes. "You know exactly what I mean."

He looked down, the healthy tan of his face giving way to the flush of embarrassment. "Abe said it would stay between him and me. He chewed me out pretty hard over that. How did you find out?"

"I'm the guy who kept it out of the papers," I said, giving myself more credit than I deserved.

"Oh. I figured Goz had taken care of things. Listen, Frank, that's not the kind of man I want to be, a man who hits a woman. I'd just had one too many, I guess." He looked back up. "That'll never happen again. You have my word."

I sat for a long moment, still staring at him. Then I smiled. "That's good enough for me, Terry." I reached over to my desk and flipped open a folder that contained the master feature film production schedule for 1946. I made a show of quickly scanning a list I could have reproduced from memory. "We've got you slated for *Long Road Home* next, that's another western. But after that, we've got a couple of projects we could talk about. Nestor's going to be making a submarine picture this fall. We don't have a title for that one yet. And Chas Simpson, you ever work with him?" Thorpe shook his head. "No? Well, he's going to make one about wounded veterans returning from the war. We're calling that one *On the Mend.* Either of those sound like something you'd be interested in?"

Thorpe smiled and nodded. "You know, I was a little nervous about coming up here to see you, but I really didn't want to bother Abe. I know how busy he is." Oh? Like I'm just sitting up here twiddling my thumbs, I thought. "I can see why people are saying nice things about you. Do you mind if I look over those two scripts you mentioned?"

"Of course not," I smiled as I wondered who the people were and what nice things they were saying about me. "I'll have copies sent over to your dressing room." We stood up and shook hands. Thorpe thanked me again and then loped off down the hallway, spurs jingling, and back to work.

I pulled myself into a sitting position and looked deep into Vera's blue eyes. "What did he mean 'surrogate?'"

Vera leaned across me, her breasts brushing across my chest as she reached into the drawer of the bedside table. She pulled out a glass ash tray and then sat back up beside me. She sat the ash tray on her lap, pulled a cigarette from her pack of Kools on the bed beside her and lit it with a small gold lighter. "I've heard a couple of people refer to you as the 'surrogate son,'" she said exhaling blue smoke toward the ceiling. "I don't think they mean anything by it. Everybody thinks you're doing a good job. Especially me," she grinned.

"So people are calling me Abe's surrogate son? Wonder how he feels about that."

"I doubt anybody's saying that within Abe's earshot."

"I sure as hell hope not. What's the real story with his son? What happened to him?"

"I told you." Vera pulled her knees up and balanced the ash tray on top. "He was in a car wreck and it messed him all up. That's what I know."

"When did it happen?"

"Back before the war. I hadn't been in town that long."

"Damn. That must have been a nightmare for Abe and Ruth. I'd hate somebody to slip up and call me 'surrogate' in Abe's presence. That would have to be pretty painful."

"Don't worry," Vera replied, stubbing out her smoke. "That's not something Abe's likely to hear."

I could only hope not.

Pacific Pictures' sole release for the month of May was *Redheaded Shamus*. It was our most expensive film planned for the year and our first in Technicolor. Max and Peter had done a good job adhering to the shooting and post-production schedule and the film was timed for release the Thursday before Mother's Day at the Chinese Theater on Hollywood Boulevard.

Goz had gone all out in preparing for the premiere. He and I had arrived hours before the start of the event to review a hundred details and make sure everything was in order for the arrival of the official party. A thousand VIP invitations had been mailed and the waiting line for the remainder of the available seats stretched all the way down to Las Palmas Avenue. Giant spotlights swept the night sky as limousine after limousine pulled up to the entrance plaza of the theater. To the right of the plaza was a wooden camera platform draped with bunting atop which George Burke was directing a trio of newsreel cameramen. Down on the red carpet leading into the auditorium, Hedda Hopper and Louella Parsons, wisely kept as far apart from each other as possible, interviewed the arriving royalty of Hollywood. The Baums arrived in their chauffeured limousine along with the Hoopers and the Shaws. Donovan Keegan escorted Vera while Janet Cantrell adorned Doyle's arm. Flash bulbs popped like Fourth of July fireworks as dozens of photographers angled for the best shot, the one that would perfectly capture the glamour and gaiety of the evening. Terry Thorpe, Tom Evers, Beverly Skardon, and every other Pacific Pictures star, bright and dim, was in attendance, along with screenwriter Hopkins Morton and all of the studio's other producers. Every time a familiar face would alight from one of the automobiles, the crowd, held back by glimmering brass stanchions supporting red velvet ropes, would applaud and cheer. The actors and actresses, especially those whose names were listed below the title, would shake hands, sign autographs and mingle with their fans and well-wishers.

The cast of *Redheaded Shamus* had no such opportunity. After obligatory interviews with the press, for which Goz had prepared them with key points, the stars all outfitted in glamorous evening attire, were whisked inside. As he'd done at the private showing of *Downtown Division*, Abe stood before the packed house to welcome the audience. He was outfitted in a tailored, double-breasted black tuxedo, a fresh white carnation on his lapel. The bright white beam of a spotlight pinned him to the stage like a butterfly to a display case.

"Thank you, friends, for coming out for this wonderful show tonight," Abe began. He was confident, smiling, clearly in control. "Before we run the picture, let me quickly introduce the creative team that made this outstanding motion picture possible." To enthusiastic applause, Abe called upon each member of the cast to stand while he briefly complimented each performance. He also introduced director Shaw, producer Hooper and writer Morton.

"I know you folks didn't come out tonight to hear a long-winded speech from me," he said, smiling, and drawing an appreciative laugh from the audience, "so let's get on with the show!" The spotlight winked out. The curtain parted and the first public showing of *Redheaded Shamus* began.

I stood with Goz and Max at the very back of the auditorium, underneath the balcony. I savored every laugh from the audience, every gasp of suspense, every delighted exclamation. When the screen finally went black after one hour and fifty-six minutes, the theater erupted with an ovation the likes of which I had never encountered inside a movie house. I reached over and shook Max's hand. Goz slapped me on the back.

"Nice work!" he shouted to be heard above the crowd.

In four weeks, the box office results for *Redheaded Shamus* surpassed all of Pacific's previously released pictures for the year. The film had earned good critical reviews too. Doyle's performance had been excellently received, but the superlative accolades had been reserved for Vera. She was riding a new wave of popularity and both she and the studio were eager to capitalize on it.

Vera had showered me with affection of a most intimate nature following the release and success of *Shamus*. Now, midway through June, she was itching to identify her next role. Abe was interested too.

"What's that old saying, my boy? 'Strike while the iron is hot!'" Abe pointed his finger at me from across his desk. "Miss Vance is a hot property. We need to take advantage of her good reviews and her box office success. What projects are available to showcase her talents?"

"We've got a few to choose from Abe, but candidly, nothing as strong as *Shamus*. We've got *Slap-Happy Sailors*, the musical that JJ is working on, but the female part is minor. Beefing it up would require us to seriously rework a script that is built around a bunch of musical numbers. Plus, I don't know if Vera can sing. Chas has got *On the Mend*. That's about a wounded veteran coming home and trying to fit back into his hometown. It's a good story, but the emphasis is on the soldier, not his girl. She'd be good in it, don't get me wrong, it's just that she wouldn't be the picture's focus."

"What else?" Abe asked, clearly not satisfied with the options I'd presented so far. Of course that had been the way I'd planned it. Offer two mediocre ideas and then come in with a concept he couldn't turn down.

"Well, we've got a romance on the schedule that Max is set to produce. It's called *A Lovely Evening* and it's sort of a Pygmalion-type story. Society guy meets a working-class girl in a diner and things develop from there." That's when I turned on the inspiration. "But, listen to this!" I slapped the top of Abe's desk and stood up, looking out the window toward the dressing rooms. "Suppose we do the same thing with *Evening* that we did with *Shamus*?" I looked back at Abe to gauge his reaction. He hadn't put all the pieces together yet.

"What' d'ya mean, 'the same thing?'" he grunted.

"You know, we switch the roles! Make Vera a society dame. She gets caught out in the rain, dashes into a diner to keep dry, meets a handsome guy trying to work his way through night school or something and *Bam*! They click! She takes him under her wing, polishes him up and helps him climb the corporate ladder."

"Did you just now come up with that?" he eyed me suspiciously.

"Just now," I fibbed, quite pleased with myself.

Abe began to laugh and leaned back in his chair. He wagged his finger at me again. "I'm going to have to keep my eye on you!" He liked my idea and that made me happy.

Vera was even happier. She threw herself into my arms and there was nothing I could do but catch her—and hold on. We'd been sitting on the sofa in her living room, looking out her back windows at the lights of Los Angeles sparkling in the darkness. She'd brought up the subject of her next role, something that had been on her mind a lot lately. She too was eager to capitalize on her box office success.

"As a matter of fact," I began with a knowing look, "I had a meeting with Abe on the subject this morning."

"And?" she said, tensing, leaning away from me and searching my face for clues.

"He wants us to be very careful not to overexpose you." I continued to stare out the window, biting my tongue to keep a straight face. "He says young actresses, if they aren't managed properly, can wear out their welcome with the public. Look at Anna Sten for example."

"Who?"

"See? So Abe thinks you lay low for a couple of months. Go out to dinner once a week with a handsome young studio executive, have your picture taken, get in the columns— " Vera jumped me and pushed me over, pinning my shoulders to the cushions of the sofa, her knee in a very uncomfortable position.

"Listen, buster," she commanded through gritted teeth, "you need to use your influence with Abe to get me another starring role in another good picture and you need to do so in one quick hurry! You savvy?"

I grabbed her by the shoulders and bear-hugged her so she couldn't get away and couldn't damage me. She was squirming, but I held her as tight as a straitjacket and then whispered in her ear, "*A Lovely Evening,* in Technicolor no less. With you in the Professor Higgins role."

She stopped wiggling and turned her head to look at me. Her face was so close I thought I might fall right into her eyes. When she finally smiled, I actually felt a warm glow. But then that may have been because she replaced her knee with her hand.

Chapter 15

Even I was surprised at how well things had been going. When I'd first proposed that we produce fifteen films in 1946, I figured we'd be lucky to complete twelve. But as the calendar flipped its page from June to July, we were only one film behind our projected pace. One of the key actors in *Streets of San Antonio* had fallen ill causing a two-week delay in shooting. Despite that blemish, we were within a month of equaling the studio's total output for all of last year.

Redheaded Shamus was on pace to become the studio's all-time box office champion while *Streets of San Antonio* and *Downtown Division* were also performing well. *Jungle Command*, the "realistic" war picture, was the only film not meeting financial expectations. That was likely due more to the public's fatigue with anything to do with the war than to the quality of the picture. Overall, Abe was pleased. So was Mr. Harley at the bank.

Vera had become such a hot property that other studios were calling to gauge her availability. Abe was generally reluctant to loan out Pacific's biggest stars. But, in Vera's case, we were still a couple of months from beginning production on *A Lovely Evening*, a couple of months during which

Pacific would have to keep paying her salary even though she was idle. So, when RKO proposed that Vera co-star with Maureen O'Hara in a drama about a family of Irish immigrants adapting to life in 1880s Boston, Abe gave it careful consideration.

"She'd be below the title," he explained one July afternoon in his office. "It's a good part, but small, so she wouldn't carry the weight of the picture if it doesn't perform. She still gets good exposure, though, so the public won't forget about her between our pictures." I nodded. I was a little reluctant to let go of Vera, but this was in everybody's best interests, Pacific's, RKO's, and Vera's. Everybody's except mine. A nagging insecurity tugged at my brain. Did I really want her working for another studio, a studio where I would have no influence or authority to make sure things went her way?

As if reading my mind, Abe fixed me with a direct stare and asked, "You know how to avoid this in the future, don't you?" I must have given a dumb look, because he didn't wait on me to answer. "Line up projects for her one-after-another. She's emerging as our top star. Every man in America wants to hold her hand. Line up three or four pictures for her for next year and we won't have to let RKO benefit from her box office appeal."

"Yes sir," I mumbled in agreement.

Abe had already spoken to Vera by the time we met for dinner at Perino's. She was excited by the prospect of working with O'Hara and the rest of the cast. Her blue eyes danced as she talked about the confidence Abe had expressed in her and how eager he was for her to do a good job at RKO and then return to film *A Lovely Evening*. The loan-out to another studio made her feel like a real movie star. I made a feeble attempt to reflect her excitement, but Vera could tell I wasn't as keen on the idea as she was.

"What's the matter?" she asked over her onion soup. "You don't seem happy."

I set my spoon down and stared at my bowl. "I don't want you going over there and falling in love with Cary Grant." I tried to make it sound like a joke, but it sounded more like self-pity.

"Ha! Cary Grant can't get me parts like you can. If that's all you have to worry about, cheer up! Life could always be worse."

Boston Irish was a moderate success at the box office for RKO. Vera and I continued to spend as much time together as I could manage even while she was filming for a rival studio. And I didn't lose her to Cary Grant.

Hopkins Morton had done another superb job on the screenplay for *A Lovely Evening*. He had made Vera's character, Dorothy Simon, into a confident, yet emotionally vulnerable career woman, the publisher of a toney women's magazine. We'd cast Tom Evers as the young waiter struggling to pay for night school. Vera and Tom worked well together—and I had no worries about losing her to her leading man. Arthur Porter had a well-earned reputation for working smoothly with actresses and had directed several of the studio's more successful romances over the years. Max Hooper had selected Arthur to direct the picture, which would be filmed in Technicolor.

Pacific generally avoided Technicolor. The process was both expensive and very technical, requiring special proprietary cameras that had to be rented from Technicolor, Inc. Unlike a conventional black and white movie, which was captured on a single negative, the Technicolor camera used three strips of film. Technicolor's patented system captured different colors on the three different negatives. In order to use the Technicolor process, the studio had to pay a color consultant from the company who would be on set daily and work with the film's director to achieve the desired results. The consultant advised the production team on everything from sets and costumes to lighting. In addition, unlike black and white film, Technicolor film could be developed only at the Technicolor Lab on Cahuenga Boulevard. Technicolor added a great deal to the cost of a picture, so we saved it for those projects we thought had the greatest box office potential. It seemed a perfect fit for *A Lovely Evening*, starring Vera Vance, which began filming on September 20th. We projected a five-week shooting schedule and planned to premiere the picture during the holiday season.

As Vera and the rest of the cast and crew commenced filming, I took Abe's advice to heart and began tinkering with the next year's production schedule to ensure that Vera would remain gainfully employed at Pacific Pictures. I already had some projects lined up for her. In the spring, we planned to release *Return of the Redhead* in which she would reprise her role as Brigid O'Dell. Marty French, another of the studio's able writers, was adapting *Flash of the Switchblade,* a recently published book about juvenile delinquents, into a vehicle for Vera as well. In *Night Over Africa*, we planned to re-team her with Donovan Keegan in a story about big game hunters in the 1920s using airplanes to track their prey.

For the current year, we'd had to schedule pictures on the fly, pushing them into preparation and production almost as fast as we obtained story rights. For 1947, I vowed we would stay ahead of the curve, so to speak. As September raced past, we had half the schedule for the next year fleshed out.

We were also caught up with our production plan for 1946. We had released eleven films so far, and *State House*, the picture about a political corruption scandal, was due to hit theaters by the end of the month. The start of *A Lovely Evening* had been delayed when we decided to flip the roles, but given Vera's box office success, that looked like a smart move. Of course, sometimes even smart moves can lead to trouble.

The strike by carpenters working in the movie industry, which I had encountered on my first visit to Pacific Pictures a year earlier, was still going on. At the heart of the strike was a dispute between which union, the International Alliance of Theatrical Stage Employees or the Conference of Studio Unions, would negotiate with the studios and therefore represent the workers. As things stood, most of the studios recognized the former and so the latter continued to picket. Warner Brothers had been hit hardest the previous year, but the other studios were often picketed as well. Pacific got off fairly easily because we weren't considered a major studio—yet.

The battle between the unions came to a head in late September when IATSE workers took over all the carpentry work at the major studios. The CSU members went on strike and picket lines went up at all the studios, even ours. Again, Pacific was spared the worst of the strikers simply because of our small size. The head of the CSU, a former painter named Sorrells, decided to put most of his workers on the gates at the big studios, MGM, Paramount, Warner Brothers, RKO and Universal. The problem was, Sorrells had only so many CSU members to work with. Maintaining pickets at all the gates of all the studios all the time was a tall order.

Whenever I could, which was most days, especially if Vera was going to be present, I'd sit in on the late afternoon screenings of the dailies from the previous day's filming. From where I sat, it looked like *A Lovely Evening* was going to be another smash at the box office. The on-screen chemistry between Vera and Tom was captivating, combining equal measures of drama and comedy. Max Hooper and Arthur Porter were, so far at least, only one day behind on their shooting schedule. We hoped to wrap up the filming by October 25th. Then, trouble arrived in the most colorful way.

"We're sidelined, just totally stuck!" Max Hooper was stalking back-and-forth in front of my desk while Arthur Porter sat patiently in one of the arm chairs. Realizing they couldn't shut down all the studios, the Conference of Studio Unions had taken its limited manpower and put it in the one place in Hollywood where it could damage all the studios at one time: the Technicolor Lab. Although Technicolor was staffed by members of the IATSE, the lab's workers had suddenly decided to honor the CSU picket line. "They've shut the place down. We've got two days' worth of film over there and it's just sitting in the cans. We can't get to it," he waved both his hands in the air, "and even if we could, we'd have no way to develop it. Now listen, Frank, I know I'm not always the fastest worker around here, but this is not my fault! You can't hold me responsible for things I don't control!"

"Relax. Of course if isn't your fault." I leaned over and flipped the intercom switch. "Betty, is Abe in his office?" Receiving an affirmative reply, I led the others down the corridor and knocked on Abe's door.

"Ah, come in, come in, my boy," he said, looking up with a smile from a script on his desk. "Have you read this *Switchblade* treatment? We may need to brighten it up." Then, seeing Max and Arthur behind me, Abe sat up a little straighter, his smile fading away. "You three look as if you're on the way to the guillotine!"

"Something like that," Max snorted. "They've shut down Technicolor!"

Abe didn't have to ask who "they" were and he didn't need us to explain the damage this would cause our business. "That bastard Sorrells!" he spat out the name of the CSU leader. He pressed his lips together and looked away from us, shaking his head. "That's what happens when you put a painter in charge. A Communist, at that." Abe switched his intercom on. "Betty, please place two calls for me. First, get me Herbert Kalmus at Technicolor; then Roy Brewer at IATSE." Abe looked up at us and directed, "Hold on a minute and let's see what we can find out." The phone on Abe's desk offered a muted ring and he snatched up the handset.

"Herbert? Abe Baum. I'm hearing some disturbing news. What's going on over there?" We could hear squeaking from the other end of the line, but couldn't make out any words. "Yes, I understand it's a union issue, but our contract is with Technicolor, not the union. We're deep into production on *A Lovely Evening*. We've completed about …" -- Abe looked over at me and I mouthed "sixty percent," while holding up six fingers -- "sixty percent of filming. We can't have that kind of investment sitting around in your lab."

"Well, no, I don't want to have to get the lawyers involved either, but if we do, Technicolor is going to pay for them." Abe paused, listening. "Well, how about you figure out what you're going to do to get our picture back in production. We can't proceed without our film and I don't have to tell you the liability Technicolor is incurring for every day we sit idle." He listened again. "Yes, well, I'll look forward to hearing back from you today." As soon as Abe set the handset back on the cradle, the phone rang again.

"Roy? What the hell is going on over at Technicolor?" Abe was intense, controlled, but obviously angry. "Oh, don't give me that! You just negotiated a raise two months ago!" Here was the difference between Abe Baum and every other soul that passed through the gates of Pacific Pictures: he could get the industry's key players on the phone at his whim. "Don't tell me your boys are getting in bed with that Communist bastard." The sound leaking from the earpiece this time was higher in pitch and volume, the speaker on the other end clearly on the defensive. "You negotiated the contract, Roy, you live with it!" Abe frowned as he listened. "Your men walked off the job when they have a valid contract. That's bad faith, Roy. You know it, I know it, the newspapers will know it and the courts will rule on it."

I glanced at the others, but they were completely engrossed in the one side of the conversation we could hear. "No good, Roy, no good. We've got $10,000 sitting over there right now. This is nothing but a union issue and your union represents the lab workers. You deal with Sorrells or President Truman or the Pope for all I care, but you get your men back to work." Abe sighed. "I know, I know you are. I am very upset, as you can tell. Yes, I would appreciate that. Make sure they know it's you and they will put the call through at any time. I look forward to it."

Abe hung up the phone. "Brewer says his IATSE technicians walked out of Technicolor in support of the CSU pickets. These guys are like lemmings headed for a steep cliff. He says he's working to get the lab back open. Quite frankly, he didn't sound too optimistic. What are our options?"

"We don't have any," Hooper snapped, reverting to his familiar refrain, "we're dead!"

"We could switch to black and white," I offered.

Abe waved the idea away like an annoying insect. "Too late for that if we're sixty percent complete. We'd lose a fortune."

"We could keep shooting," I offered. "I know that's a risk when you can't see dailies, but at least that way we wouldn't have to shut down for however long this strike lasts."

Arthur spoke up for the first time and addressed his reply to me. "I don't like that option. It takes much longer and costs a lot more to fix mistakes if we have to reconstruct sets after the fact." He then looked at Abe. "It's your call, Abe. It's a money call. If that's what you want, we'll do it, but it's risky."

Abe leaned back in his chair. What ten minutes ago had been a routine afternoon had turned into a disaster. "Film what you had planned for today. Reconvene here at six o'clock." Ironically, six was the hour during which the dailies were usually viewed. "Let's see if our friends at Technicolor or the union come through with a reasonable plan."

They didn't.

"Don't be discouraged," I told Vera as we walked on the beach at Malibu, carrying a wicker picnic basket between us. "It'll get worked out."

We'd taken a pleasant drive out to the beach along Alternate Route 101. Vera was wearing sunglasses, white linen shorts and a red and white checked shirt knotted above her waist. A blue, flower-patterned silk scarf covered her honey-blonde hair. It was a warm Sunday and with no immediate prospects of returning to the set, I'd invited her to the beach for the afternoon. "Look," she complained, "my career as an actress won't last forever. There's a clock ticking somewhere. I've got to make my mark while I'm still young, before I start to lose my looks. How many old actresses do you see getting parts these days? How long is this thing going to last? A week? A month? Longer?"

"I don't know, but worrying about it will make you age faster."

Vera stopped and turned toward me, a look of panic on her pretty face. "Seriously?"

"No! I'm trying to loosen you up a little bit. Relax. Abe's working on it. He'll get it fixed. Just give him a little time."

We set the picnic basket on the sand and spread out a pale yellow blanket--actually the bedspread from the spare bedroom at my house. Vera kicked off her white sandals and stretched out, pulling the scarf from her head. She was stunning and I stared at her for a moment.

"What are you doing?" she asked, looking up and shading her eyes.

"I'm just checking to see if your looks are fading."

She stuck out her tongue. "Comedian," she smiled, patting the blanket. I dropped down next to her and opened the basket. I'd brought cold chicken salad, Saltine crackers, apples and beer. Vera had brought her Kools. She sat up and lit one. "Do you think we'll be able to get it to the theaters before Christmas? That would really help me."

"It depends on how long this strike locks things up."

"Damn it! How could we have been so stupid?"

"What?"

"To let the Communists run things!"

I laughed. "You're starting to sound like Abe. He said the CSU is being run by the Communists and that's why the industry is in this mess. Look at the bright side," I said without considering my words, "MGM's got five pictures tied up over at Technicolor; Paramount three. We've only got one.

"Yeah," Vera looked at me with a sneer, "but it happens to be *my* picture, buster! Look all you want for a 'bright side,' but get me back to work."

Getting Vera back to work was tougher than we thought. Even Joan Roswell, whom I never really considered an ally, weighed in on the side of the movie-going public. "It's a shame," she wrote in her daily column, "that a mere 500 workers are jeopardizing the livelihood of the 30,000 film industry workers in and around Hollywood, not to mention the weekly entertainment of millions of American movie lovers. It's time the unions cleaned their own houses and sorted out this mess which really has nothing to do with the wages and working conditions provided by the studios."

Brewer and the IATSE officials eventually succeeded in removing the strikers and replacing them with new workers, but the strike had done its damage by tying up twenty-one motion pictures for thirty days. Instead of releasing *A Lovely Evening* in time for the holiday movie season, the earliest it would be ready for release was early January, typically a rather slow time for theater patronage.

Ironically, Max Hooper had managed to go yet another year with only one finished film under his belt. While there had certainly been delays beyond Max's control—a pause to rewrite the *Evening* script and the Technicolor strike—I vowed to learn from the experience and to put Max into a position to fulfill his three-picture obligation in 1947.

Likewise, I was going to make sure Vera had an unbroken stream of projects ready to take advantage of her present appeal.

I'd been working with Mary Goldman, the studio's story editor, on our line-up of projects for 1947. We didn't really function on a calendar basis as we were constantly on the lookout for new story material. Even so, because of my financial agreement with Abe, I tended to think of our motion picture production as an annual project. So in December, while Max and Arthur were finishing post-production on *A Lovely Evening*, I scheduled an appointment with Abe to review 1946's body of work and preview 1947's.

We sat on the small, wine-colored leather sofa to the left of his desk. Lovely Betty brought in a silver tray with coffee and sat it on the low table in front of us. I handed Abe a sheet of paper listing the thirteen feature films Pacific Pictures had gotten into theaters during the year. "Max and Arthur are almost done with *A Lovely Evening*, but I don't think we should be in any hurry to distribute it," I said. "After the holidays is a slow time for the box office; I'd rather wait and release it in March, when somebody will actually be in the theaters to see it." Abe nodded, but didn't speak. "The rewrite on *Evening* and the Technicolor strike threw us behind, Abe. We'll only get thirteen features out this year." I started to hand out a second sheet but Abe held up his hand to interrupt me.

"What happened to *A Matter of Discretion*? I told you I wanted that produced."

"Yes sir. It was to be Hooper's next project after *Evening*. The strike fouled up our timing. I know *Discretion* is important to you, and I'm sorry. Maybe I should have reassigned it to another producer, but Hooper had committed to making three films this year and, well, I just didn't adjust my plan like I should have." Abe sat for a moment staring down at the piece of paper I'd given him. Then he looked up at me.

"Don't let Hooper land you in the doghouse. What are you going to do about it?"

I handed Abe the second sheet. "I've got it scheduled to begin production as soon as Hooper finishes up. We release it and *Evening* in March. That's a little aggressive, but I think it's a feasible target."

Abe scanned the page, which in addition to *Discretion* and *Evening*, listed all the other films planned for release in 1947. Four pictures were contemporary dramas, then there were two musicals, one romance, two historicals, two comedies, two westerns, two adventures, and two crime dramas. There were seventeen in all, including four pictures starring Vera Vance. I thought it was a good line-up that would appeal to many specific segments of the broader movie-going public.

"Most of these already have scripts in the works, though they aren't all in a final form yet," I said.

Abe rubbed his chin. "I want you to add one. A tribute to this great country of ours. I'm sick and tired of the hooligans and Communists trying to tear America down. I want a picture that will highlight our values, our great leaders of the past, our natural beauty—what makes us different from the Europeans or the Asians. This is still a country where a man can pull himself up by his bootstraps, where if you are willing to work hard you can make a good life for your family. I want Pacific Pictures to tell that story, Frank. Add that to your list. I want Pacific Pictures to produce a film that will send a message about how America is still a land of opportunity. Get me a treatment by, let's say, mid-January. Can do?"

"Yes sir." In truth, while I kind of liked the concept, I didn't see how we could make a feature film out of Abe's idea. I was of the school of thought that if you wanted to send a message, you should go to Western Union.

I bought two tickets at the Egyptian Theater box office on Hollywood Boulevard and we timed our entrance for right after the lights went down for the start of the cartoon. Vera and I slipped into a row near the back of the theater to enjoy *Duel in the Sun*. Produced by David Selznick, *Duel*, like *A Lovely Evening*, had been delayed by the Technicolor strike. In addition to battling the strike, Selznick had had to fight with the production code office to get his big budget picture to the screen. According to scuttlebutt around town, the picture had been heavily edited to get it past the censors.

"She auditioned for this part on her back," Vera smirked when Jennifer Jones appeared on the screen.

"Shhh!" I whispered. "Not everyone can excel on talent alone like you." Vera smiled.

After the show, we dropped in to the Tikki Bar at Don's Beachcomber Café a block east. "Here's what I wanted to show you," I said, pulling the new production plan from my inside coat pocket. "We'll have four Vera Vance pictures hit theaters this year." Vera snatched the paper from my hand, spread it out on the table and scrutinized it. I pointed to her pictures. "*A Lovely Evening* in March, *Return of the Redhead* in May, *Flash of the Switchblade* in August, and *Moon Mission* in December. You are going to be one very busy movie star, Miss Vance," I smiled.

"Has Abe approved this?"

"He has. Every quarter, American movie-goers will see a new Vera Vance film. And what variety!" I teased. "America's favorite girl-next-door will dazzle movie audiences with the range of her talents as she disappears into one demanding role after another, no two alike! Why, she'll probably set the single year record with five Oscar nominations for just four pictures!"

Vera was smiling now, taking a sip of her rum and Coke. "Do you really think I'm 'America's girl-next-door'?" she purred.

"You're not like any girl I ever lived next door to," I winked, leaning in close to her and savoring her presence.

"Well, well, Hollywood's most attractive power couple," Joan Roswell said, approaching our table as though she was leading a coronation procession. She was wearing a gray suit trimmed with white, a white fox fur, head and feet and all, draped over her shoulders. I wondered if she'd stalked and skinned it herself. She carried an ebony cigarette holder in her right hand as though it was her scepter. The smoke from her cigarette mingled with her signature scent of rose perfume and powder.

"Uh oh," I muttered under my breath. Then I smiled and stood. "Join us, Joan?" I pulled a chair over from a neighboring table.

"How sweet of you, dear!" she trilled, sliding in to the chair and smiling at Vera. "Where have you two been tonight?"

"We just saw *Duel in the Sun*," I explained.

"Jennifer Jones was terrific!" Vera enthused.

"Mmmm. She got that part from sleeping with Selznick, you know."

"Really?" I asked, trying to sound shocked. "How do you find out stuff like that, Joan?"

"Oh," she chirped, "people just like to tell me things, I guess. Especially when they feel like someone is hiding behind a false screen of respectability. The average Joe hates hypocrites, you know." She waved over a waiter and ordered a rum drink. She plucked a fresh Chesterfield from a gold case, fitted it to the holder and lit it with a matching lighter. "Secrets. Secrets fascinate us. And when we know one, we can't wait to share it. The darker it is, the more compelling it becomes. Who's sleeping with whose wife? There's a lot of that around Hollywood. Always has been." She flipped an ash. "Who's a pain in the ass to work with? Who drinks too much? You've had some experience with that I'm sure." She gave me her knowing look. "What boys like girls and which ones like boys? Who hates Jews?" She paused, took a pull on her smoke and exhaled toward the ceiling as the waiter set her drink in front of her. "What happened to David Baum?" She stared at me with her green cat's eyes.

I stared back. I didn't intend to be intimidated, especially not in front of Vera. "Why don't you ask Abe? He's bound to know."

"Abe Baum won't give me the time of day." She waved her cigarette holder dismissively. "Oh, he's cordial enough--when he has to be. Otherwise he won't even return my calls."

"How about Goz?" I suggested.

"I think this is the one Pacific Pictures secret that even Goz doesn't know. I've tried, believe me."

"Sorry, I can't help you," I said. "But it's like I told you before, Joan, I really have no idea. I wouldn't know David Baum if he walked through that doorway right now." I pointed toward the door from the bar. "Maybe there's not really a story there. Did you ever think of that?"

"Oh, there's a story there all right. There's a story and I'm the person to uncover it and to tell it. Patience and perseverance, Frank, those are the tricks of my trade. And discretion, of course. If anyone wanted to tell me something that he knew, he could be sure that it would remain between him and me."

"And your readers?" I smiled. I didn't want to make Joan mad. That was a risky business move. But I also wanted her to know that I understood why she wanted to know about David Baum. It wasn't idle curiosity. She wanted to make money off the story, boost her distribution, build her following.

"My readers would certainly get a juicy story, but they'd never know where it came from. That part of the mystery would never be revealed. Who was involved in that car wreck, Frank?"

"Well, I wouldn't know anything about that," I laughed, trying to reduce the tension that had been building. "I'm just a simple lad trying to make my way in the world."

Joan blew another cloud of smoke toward the ceiling and tittered.

Chapter 16

With some deft scheduling, we were at work on four separate pictures in February. I was pushing our producers to front-load our feature film efforts so that if another strike came along or some other disaster struck, we wouldn't be stuck without pictures to distribute. Abe made it a point to show up often on the set of *A Matter of Discretion*, something he did infrequently on other pictures, preferring instead to view the dailies from each film in a small projection room off of his suite.

"What do you think?" he asked me one afternoon as the operator flipped off the projector. We'd just reviewed the previous day's footage from the *Discretion* set.

I hesitated, searching for words that would accurately convey my opinion without sounding too negative. "You know, Abe, it's just not a subject that I warm up to."

"It's an important issue," Abe stressed, "an issue the movies can help shed light on."

"I get it," I replied, "but, well, when I go to the movies, I want to be entertained. I want action or adventure or romance. I want to go back in time or forward into the future. Social issues just aren't very appealing as entertainment." I hoped I hadn't offended him; I knew this was an important picture to him.

"You're too young," Abe waved his hand in dismissal. "Life hasn't knocked you around enough."

I thought about reminding Abe that during my three days on Okinawa I'd been knocked around enough for one lifetime, but fortunately my brain was more mature than Abe was giving me credit for. "Maybe so," I replied. "What did you think?"

"There's a temptation to go for schmaltz when you're dealing with an issue like retardation, but people need to see that the retarded or those with brain injuries are still real people with real feelings, aspirations, needs. I think the public will see this as an honest attempt to bring attention to an issue that too often gets hidden away in a dark corner. Shining light into that corner can only result in a positive response."

"Maybe so," I repeated. "So what do you think of the picture so far?"

"I think Janet is doing a fine job. Doyle too. This material requires more nuanced acting than we typically encounter. I think the whole Pacific Pictures family will embrace it." Maybe, I thought, but the ticket-buying public wasn't going to.

"Walk me back to my office," Abe directed as he stood. I followed him out of the projection room and down the corridor to his office. He walked around behind his desk, opened his top drawer and removed an envelope. "We made a deal, you and me, at the end of 1945. Remember?"

"How could I forget," I laughed. "You slashed my proposal in half."

"True," he smiled, extending the envelope toward me. "But you still made a pretty shrewd bargain. Of course, it was only shrewd because you changed the way we approach production—and because it generated results. Open it," he nodded toward the envelope. I stuck my finger up under the flap and tore it open. I looked at the check inside and swallowed hard. "The way I see it," Abe commented, smiling, "you forfeited $2,600 in annual salary for a performance bonus of $10,500. Next time I have to negotiate my contract with the board, I want you in my corner." Abe came from behind his desk, reached up and threw his arm around my shoulders. "I'm very proud of you, Frank. Our output was up more than fifty percent and profits were up more than $2 million. You've already got us on pace to improve again this year. Well done, my boy."

"Thanks, Abe," I said sincerely. "Thanks for giving me the opportunity."

"I'm a good judge of character," he smiled. "And now some more good news for Pacific Pictures in general and a certain lady friend of yours in particular. *Variety* is about to report that our Miss Vance ranks number twelve among top box office stars for last year, coming in just below Betty Grable and Roy Rogers. That's the highest finish ever for a Pacific star! I believe the projects you've scheduled for her for this year will put her squarely among the top ten." I smiled, fairly certain that Vera would credit me with making at least part of her success possible. "You two make quite the attractive couple." Abe beamed like a proud father.

Vera was on break from the set of *Return of the Redhead* and we were having lunch in the studio commissary. "How's the new guy?" I asked. Ordinarily, we wouldn't have entrusted our newest director with our biggest star, but Arthur Porter had come down with pneumonia and we'd had to substitute David Wistar as the director just a week before shooting started. Wistar had come over from Monogram Pictures where he'd directed several well-received features.

"He's worse than you are," Vera pouted.

"What'd you mean?"

"He's always putting his hands all over me. He pretends that he's 'directing,' but he's really just copping a quick feel. Well, not always quick."

I wiped my mouth with my napkin and laid it on the table, pushing my chair back. "I'll go speak to him right now." Vera reached out and grabbed my hand.

"Oh, I wish you wouldn't," she shook her head. "I can handle him. If you get involved, it'll just disrupt things on the set, maybe even slow us down."

Ever since I'd been named director of production, "slow" was a word and a condition we tried to avoid. "Okay," I said after a moment's hesitation, "but if you can't handle him, I guarantee you that I can."

"Don't worry, darling. He's just annoying, that's all. If it gets out of hand, I'll let Max deal with it."

"Fair enough," I said. Then I recalled why I'd invited her to lunch in the first place. "I had a meeting with Abe yesterday. Know what he told me?"

"That Betty Hutton can't sing?" she said, digging into her spaghetti.

"He said *Variety* is about to report the top box office stars for 1946 and you came in at number twelve!"

Vera squealed and clapped her hands, causing the other diners to stop and stare for a moment. As I laughed at her delight, I thought back to my first visit to this dining room and felt a sense of pride that I could now sit with the "talent."

Vera's smile was as wide as Kate Smith's hips as she reached across the table and laid her hand on top of mine. "This year's going to be even better," she gushed, "I can feel it! And next year …" she paused looking up toward heaven, "who knows!" Her gaze returned earthward and settle on me. "I'm going to the top, you know." Her smile cast a sun-like warmth over our table. "And I'm taking Pacific Pictures with me."

"It's no secret, sweetheart," I said, diving into her blue eyes, "that the studio has positioned you to be its top star. Through the strenuous efforts of one young executive in particular, you are being cast as the lead in the studio's most promising pictures."

"I know," she grinned. "And it's time for him to renegotiate my contract." This comment hit me like a dropped option, but before I could reply, Vera continued. "I'm still making $2,500 a week and you said the studio doubled its profits last year. I'm partly responsible for that, don't you think?" She smiled sweetly as she twirled a noodle around her fork.

I was flustered by the sudden and unanticipated twist in the conversation. "I haven't really been involved in negotiating contracts with talent," I replied, thinking as fast as I could. "Besides," I laughed, "given the special nature of my relationship with you, I'm probably the wrong guy to negotiate your contract."

"Maybe I'll go see Abe then."

"He might call you a Communist."

"Brother," Vera laughed, "this is pure capitalism! Supply and demand. The public creates the demand and I am the supply."

I knew better than to argue with the woman I loved, but I vowed to warn Abe as soon as possible.

After I walked Vera back to Soundstage 3, I strolled over to No. 1 to check in with Beeker Douglas. Beeker was producing *The Butler Did It*, a comedy set in the 1920s and starring Tom Evers as the title character. Tom's butler served a wacky, titled English family on its country estate.

The soundstage door was open, so I went in knowing that I wouldn't be interrupting filming. Once my eyes adjusted to the dark interior of the set, I realized that nothing much was going on. Only working lights were on and the few crew members I saw were sitting or standing around reading the newspaper or talking. Beeker was over in a corner on the telephone. He hung up as I approached.

"Things look kind of slow around here," I smiled.

Beeker frowned. "How'd you like your old job back?"

"Tom again?"

He nodded. "Tom again. Third time in a week. With him, one drink's too many and a hundred is not enough! He goes out in the evening, starts drinking, falls asleep, can't wake up, can't get to work. I've already revised the shooting schedule so we don't film any of his scenes until after lunch. I need some help with him, Frank, or we're going to be shooting for three months."

"I'll talk to him. I'll also make sure Goz stops sending him on publicity dates when he's scheduled to shoot the next day. You've sent somebody after him?"

"Yeah, Dewayne. He's not quite as skillful at handling Tom as you were. He tends to want to push Tom around. Tom doesn't like that."

"Make sure Dewayne remembers who the star is. And keep me informed, okay?" I shook hands with Beeker and headed over to Soundstage 5 to look in on Sam Levin who was filming interior scenes for *Dust Clouds in the Desert.* Sam, as usual, had Terry Thorpe and the rest of his crew on schedule, so I headed back to the main building.

"Gladys," I said entering the outer office, "please let Mr. Evers know I'd like to meet with him here first thing in the morning. And is Abe in?"

"Yes sir and yes sir," Gladys replied, scribbling a note on her steno pad. I headed down the hallway and stopped at Abe's open door. Lovely Betty was leaning over the corner of his desk.

"… and Mr. Schary's office called. You and Mrs. Baum are invited to a private screening on Sunday the 20th at the Scharys' residence."

"All right. This one is signed and ready to go," Abe said, handing Betty a letter to be mailed. "I've redrafted this one, a couple of little changes, if you don't mind retyping it. And please accept Mr. Schary's invitation." Betty checked her pad, took the letters and turned to leave.

"Hello, Frank," she smiled as she passed me.

"Well, a nice surprise!" Abe's face brightened as my presence registered. "Come in! Sit down." I plopped down in the leather chair in front of his desk. "Do you come bearing good news or bad?" he peered over the top of his reading glasses.

"Oh, I don't think it's bad," I replied, "but it clearly isn't good. I stopped by and talked with Beeker Douglas after lunch. He's having trouble with Tom Evers' drinking again. It was after lunch and Tom hadn't shown up yet. I've invited Tom to come talk to me first thing tomorrow."

"First thing?"

"Yeah. He'll either come, demonstrating that he is in fact able to make it to work on time, or he'll fail to show up, in which case we can refer to the clause in his contract that requires him to report to work as scheduled. Either way, I think we'll get Tom's attention." I paused for a moment, considering my divided loyalties. "Speaking of contracts, I had lunch with Vera today. I shared with her that she'd made the top dozen at the box office." At the mention of contracts, I had snared Abe's full attention. I caught his gaze and then glanced away. "She mentioned that she wanted me to renegotiate her contract."

Abe's face hardened. "And you said?"

"And I said that I didn't negotiate contracts with talent. Anyway, she may come to you about it. I didn't want you to be caught off guard."

Abe sat for a moment, an uncomfortable moment because his eyes never left mine. "Remember what I told you about actresses." It was a directive, not a question. "Most of them are focused on one thing: their careers. Success goes to their heads like heroin into the veins of an addict—and with similar results."

"What do you want me to do?" I asked, not sure if I was ready for his answer.

"Do? Nothing. Just watch out for yourself, my boy. Don't let her pin you in the middle. If she wants to talk contracts, my door is open to her."

My intercom buzzed. "Mr. Evers to see you," Gladys reported.

A quick look at the clock caused me to smile. It was precisely 9 a.m. "Fine. Send him in." I stood up and met Tom at the door. "Good morning, Tom," I smiled shaking his hand. "Have a seat."

"Good morning, Frank. It's nice to see you," Tom replied with a sheepish grin.

I sat back down behind my desk and tried to sound and look as authoritative as I could. "I paid a visit to Soundstage 1 yesterday Tom and – "

Tom interrupted me, "I'm sorry, Frank! I've had a rough spell of it here lately." He was looking down at his shoes.

I resumed. "Beeker tells me you've missed call three days in the past week. Tom, you know we're all counting on you. If you don't show up, the whole crew is idle. It's hard for Beeker to adjust on the fly like that and make the day productive."

"I'm sorry, Frank." He was still looking down.

"Tom, I know you want to do the right thing here. Tell me the problem and let's come up with a solution."

"Alcohol just knocks me out. I have a few drinks and I just get loopy and I fall asleep and can't wake up."

"Maybe you shouldn't drink," I offered.

Tom just smiled. "I don't think that's a realistic solution," he replied.

"Well, what is? Because, if you can't make it to work as scheduled, you're going to find yourself relegated to second-rate pictures at a third-rate studio."

Tom sat silently for at least a minute, a minute I refused to interrupt. He was the one causing the problem and he needed to be the one to propose a solution. He began haltingly, "Remember when you would come out to my house each morning?" I nodded, but didn't speak. "Well, when I knew that you were coming, that motivated me to get my lazy ass out of bed and be ready. Maybe something like that would work."

"I'm not available to come to your house every morning, Tom."

Tom laughed and I smiled, pleased that he'd taken my comment in the light-hearted manner in which it was intended. "No, not you," he gave me his "aw shucks" grin. "But not that Dewayne kid either. He's an asshole and he forgets who he's talking to."

"Okay," I nodded, "if I can get someone with a little more tact and diplomacy to come pick you up each morning, then you promise you'll be ready?"

"I do," Tom said with the assurance of a groom.

"I'll also ask Goz not to schedule you for any more evening publicity events for a while. Beginning tomorrow, somebody will be at your door every morning at seven-thirty. You be ready, Tom, understand?" I stood up.

"Sure, Frank. Thanks." We shook hands and Tom left.

I flipped the intercom. "Gladys, please get me Mr. Douglas on Soundstage 1." Beeker was desperate by this point to move his picture along and so was more than agreeable to replacing the disagreeable Dewayne. The new guy, whoever he was, would become Tom's de facto chauffeur for the balance of filming on *The Butler Did It*.

By the middle of April, Pacific Pictures had finished and released its first six feature films of the year, including *The Butler Did It*. *Dust Clouds in the Desert* was due for release at the end of the month, followed two weeks later by *Return of the Redhead*, Vera's *Redheaded Shamus* sequel. Goz had added an assistant to help with the increased publicity load of fifteen annual releases but was still having to work long hours to keep up. He was in the midst of planning the *Redhead* premiere when I dropped in to see him.

"Were you able to book the Chinese Theater?" I asked hopefully. The Chinese Theater was the most famous movie house in Hollywood, which made it the most famous in the world. It was the place the stars appeared to immortalize their hands, feet or whatever in concrete squares in the theater's large courtyard. It had also been the site of the first *Redhead* premiere the previous year.

"No," Goz replied with a frown. "It's booked for *Miracle on 34th Street.*"

"What's that about?"

"It's a Christmas picture, believe it or not. According to Larry, the booking agent at the theater, Zanuck thinks more people will see a Christmas movie in May when the weather is nicer." Darryl Zanuck was the head of 20th Century Fox.

"What other options have we got?"

"I've got a call into the Egyptian. That'd be the next best. Would you consider opening out of town?"

"Like where?"

"Well, the picture's set in Boston isn't it?"

"Yeah, but we didn't shoot a single scene there. Besides it would cost too much. Vera's got to start filming *Flash of the Switchblade* the following week. I don't want to tire her out going back and forth to the east. Let me know when you hear from the Egyptian, will ya?"

The next day was a Friday, notable because shooting had wrapped on *Return of the Redhead,* thus freeing up Vera Vance for her contract meeting with Abe Baum. My plan was to make myself scarce as I in no way wished to be caught in the crossfire between my two favorite people at Pacific Pictures.

I was in my office with the door closed, trying to read several treatments the story department had sent over. We were already working on next year's line-up. Plus, if any outstanding stories popped up, we could always reorganize our plan, bump one scheduled story to a later date and fit the new one in its place. In addition, I'd asked Hopkins Morton to draft an outline for Abe's tribute to America. I'd suggested the title *This Great Country*.

I was having a hard time concentrating. My mind kept wandering down the hall and trying to imagine what was going on between Abe, my patron, and Vera, my love.

The buzz of the intercom startled me. "Mr. Gosnell for you, Mr. Russell." Gladys was the only person on the lot who called Goz "Mr. Gosnell" and me "Mr. Russell." I picked up the handset.

"We got the Egyptian," Goz said and I could hear his smile over the phone line.

"That's great, Goz! Good work!"

"It's going to cost us, though. Assuming *Redhead* does well—and I've seen some of the dailies and it is going to do very well—they want Vera's next premiere also. I agreed but told them you and Abe would have to confirm."

"I agree. I'll talk to Abe as soon as he's free. I hate not to premiere at the Chinese, but if they're going to run a Christmas picture in May, maybe we shouldn't be going there anyway."

Goz laughed. "Let me know after you talk to Abe."

I was two-thirds of the way through Morton's outline when my intercom buzzed again.

"Yes?"

"Can you come over here?" Abe asked, his voice sounding deeper and more tired than normal.

I was standing in his office doorway within a minute. "How did it go?" I asked.

He looked down at his desk, frowning. His eyes were puffy, his nose red. "Not so well that I care to revisit it just now," he growled. "I feel wretched and I'm going home. Your lady friend wore me out." He wasn't smiling as he shrugged his suit coat on. "She's a tough negotiator."

"Well, she's powerful at the box office," I said, not wanting to take sides, but not wanting to say nothing either. "Did you come to terms?"

"We agreed only to continue talking," Abe said, as he moved past me and into the hallway. "I don't want to put you in the middle, so I'll say no more for now."

"Thanks, Abe," I said, and I meant it.

"Betty," Abe said as he reached the front desk, "would you please ask Charles to get the car and meet me out front. I'm done for the week. Also, please call RKO and regret the Scharys' invitation to the screening on Sunday. I'm going to spend the weekend in bed and hope for a miracle to arrive so I can be back here on Monday." Abe turned toward me and said, "Ride down with me, Frank."

We walked along the corridor to the elevator. Henry, the operator, was waiting with the door open and we both stepped in.

"Ground floor, Mr. Baum?"

"Yes, thank you, Henry." We rode down in silence and I wondered why Abe had asked me to come along. When we exited the building and walked to his waiting car, I found out. "I'm hearing some troubling rumors, Frank."

"What kind of rumors?"

"It seems some of the Republican pea heads in Congress believe they can run against Hollywood next fall. An informal subcommittee of the Un-American Activities Committee may be coming out here next month to investigate the Communist influence in the motion picture business."

"Does that worry you? I haven't noticed any Communists around here," I said trying to lighten his mood.

"Well, at worst it's a distraction. We have to play nice with these characters because, like it or not, they have political power and a bully pulpit. If they had half a brain between them, they'd investigate Sorrells and his CSU bunch which is taking orders straight from Moscow." We'd reached the car, which I figured was a good thing for Abe's blood pressure.

"I'm sure the politicians won't cause us any trouble," I said. "You just rest up and get to feeling better. Is there anything you want me to do for you?"

He placed his hand on my shoulder and offered a weak smile. "I can't think of anything right now. In fact, I can't think at all. If something comes up, I'll let you know." He turned to slide into the back seat.

I placed my hand on the door and leaned in. "Goz arranged with the Egyptian for the *Return of the Redhead* premiere. The Chinese was booked, a funny story I'll tell you when you're feeling better. The Egyptian asked for some concessions."

Abe waved his hand and shook his head. He was clearly fatigued and ready to go. "You go over it with Goz. I trust you to handle it."

"Hope you feel better," I said closing the car door.

Chapter 17

Vera was clearly feeling better for having spoken with Abe and gotten her desire for greater compensation off her chest and on to the table. By the time I reached her home high up in the hills, she was in a cheerful mood and cooking dinner.

"A beautiful movie star who can act and cook!" I said by way of greeting. She had a spoon in one hand and a bowl in the other, but turned her head for me to kiss her. Even with her hair pulled back and wearing an apron, I thought her the most beautiful woman I'd ever known. "What are you making?"

"Pancakes," she giggled. "Don't you like breakfast for supper?"

"I do, actually," I answered, taking a seat on a stool next to the counter where she worked. 'How'd it go with Abe today?"

"What did he say?"

"He said you were the brightest star in the Pacific galaxy and that he had decided to hand you the keys to the studio; that whatever you wanted was yours for the asking as long as you fulfill my every whim and continue to make me happy."

She smiled and shook her head while she mixed the pancake batter. "What did he really say?"

"That you were a tough negotiator. He wouldn't tell me anything else. You must have really worked him over, because he went home early."

"He wasn't feeling well when I got there," Vera said setting the bowl on the counter. She opened a cabinet and pulled out a frying pan. From the Kelvinator, she took some butter and a bottle of milk.

"Well, how did it go?"

"I told him I wanted a bump up to $5,000 a week plus 25 percent of each of my pictures."

I whistled. "Pretty aggressive don't you think?"

"You have to be aggressive to start with," she explained, "because they never give you what you ask for."

"Aren't you afraid Abe will just walk away from the table with a demand like that?"

"Before I answer," she said placing her hand under my chin and turning my face square with hers, "I have to know whose side you're on, Abe's or mine."

"Yours," I said, because I knew that was the correct answer under the circumstances even if it was not wholly accurate. "Yours because I want you to be happy at Pacific so you'll stay at Pacific because I work at Pacific. Make sense?" I smiled.

She smiled back, which I took as a good sign. "Abe's not going to walk away," she said, putting the pan on the stove and coating it with butter. "I'm the first star he's ever had reach the top fifteen in annual box office. I'm not up there with Bing Crosby yet, but this year, thanks to you, darling, I'm going to make four pictures. Four quality pictures. And that's going to get me a lot closer to the top of the money list. Abe needs me. You know how many top fifteen actresses there are? Six. And only four of them are ahead of me. Of those four, Margaret O'Brien is the only one younger than me and she's only on the list because two movies she made three years ago, *Jane Eyre* and *Meet Me in Saint Louis,* are still circulating. She won't be back on the list this year, you can bet your pancakes. The other three are all over thirty. And little ol' me? Only twenty-four. So, let me ask you," she continued, "how many studios are there in town?"

"Oh, I dunno, eight or ten."

"Eleven, not counting Disney," Vera corrected me. She ladled batter into the pan. "Get the syrup bottle out of the pantry, will you? Eleven studios who might be interested, just might be, in a young actress who's already cracked the money list and she's not even twenty-five yet." She picked up a spatula and began turning up the edges of the pancakes. "So, when you look at it that way, I think maybe Abe needs me worse than I need Abe. What do you think?"

"I think Abe's right." She looked up from the pan, a startled expression on her face. "I think you're a tough negotiator."

When Vera Vance first appeared on the screen during the premiere showing of *Return of the Redhead*, the audience burst into applause. Goz and I, outfitted in tuxedoes, were standing in the very back of the 1,700-seat auditorium looking more like ushers than studio executives. Vera had been escorted by co-star Doyle Burton, and with Goz's publicity plan in motion, there was really no place for the boyfriend. It was my lot at these premieres that instead of sitting with my girl, I got to assist Goz with whatever he needed and make sure that Abe and Ruth were comfortable. The long, narrow courtyard leading from Hollywood Boulevard to the theater had been lined with movie fans eager to catch a glimpse of the industry's fastest-rising star—and they weren't disappointed. On the arm of the distinguished Burton, Vera sparkled in a dazzling blue gown and her ermine stole. When she stopped to speak with Hedda Hopper, who was covering the opening night on live radio, Vera was charming and humble. She thanked the fans for their response to the first Brigid O'Dell picture and promised they'd like the new one.

The enthusiasm of the crowd never waned. Throughout the picture, the audience responded with laughs, gasps, sighs and finally applause as Brigid and Lieutenant Larson toasted the resolution of another sticky case. After the lights came up and the satisfied and happy audience filed out of the theater, the cast, director, producer and writer gathered at the foot of the Egyptian's stage to answer questions from the press and pose for pictures. The Baums escorted some of their invited guests to a private dinner at the Ambassador Hotel.

"Miss Vance!" the reporter from *Variety* barked, holding up his hand to be recognized, "will you be making more *Redhead* pictures?"

"I certainly hope so," she replied, smiling. "We had such a wonderful story by Hopkins over there and our whole crew worked so well together. We had marvelous fun. I'd love to work with that whole family again to bring our fans another great picture."

I slipped up behind Goz and whispered, "Did you write those lines?"

"Just like she said 'em," he muttered from the corner of his mouth.

Flash bulbs were popping as a trio of photographers jockeyed for the best shot. Hopkins Morton was asked if he was working on another episode of the Brigid O'Dell saga. He also gave the correct answer, though not nearly as convincingly as Vera. Still, I was glad to see Hopkins getting some public credit for the good work he'd done in crafting two successful feature films from one short story.

I was enjoying the spectacle, wondering which quote would make the morning papers, when Joan Roswell fired off a question, her eyes as sharp as a hungry tiger's moving in for the kill. "Miss Vance, we understand your contract with Pacific Pictures expires at the end of the year. Any truth to the rumor that you're considering offers from other studios?" The small knot of reporters, photographers and studio people surrounding Vera fell as silent as a Buster Keaton picture.

Goz started to move forward, but I put my hand on his elbow to hold him back. It would look a lot worse if he had to rescue his star from an out-of-order question. Fortunately, no rescue was needed. Vera lifted her chin, smiled and said, "Absolutely not! Pacific has been my professional home since I broke into this business. Abe Baum has been gracious to me throughout my career and I consider him a father figure. I'd hate to leave Pacific after all the studio has done for me, after all we've done for each other."

It was clear that Goz hadn't written that response, but I could guess who had.

I didn't bring the matter up when we finally got back to Vera's house about eleven o'clock. By the time she got out of her gown and makeup and brushed out her hair, she was nearly beat. I massaged her feet for a few minutes to help undo the trauma caused by her high heeled sandals. As I was doing so, I started to ask about the question she'd planted concerning offers from other studios, but when I looked up, she had fallen asleep.

Abe was in a foul mood the next morning. On his desk were copies of the *Times* and *Variety*. "I'm not sure which one of these rags contains the worst news," he frowned after I'd taken a seat in front of his desk. "Vance Denies Offers" read the caption above an excellent picture of Vera from the previous evening's premiere. The page one article carried Vera's denial pretty much as she said it, but the clear effect was to put Vera on the market and to invite rival bidders. "This is going to make hanging on to our Miss Vance a good deal more expensive," Abe declared. Clearly, this was an issue he hadn't planned on dealing with. "And then more good news," he said sarcastically, holding up the *Times,* which showed a picture of Representative Parnell Thomas boarding the Santa Fe Super Chief in Chicago. "Thomas and his group of stooges are due to arrive here today. Apparently, Mr. Thomas believes it will be easier to run for reelection against the Communists in the motion picture business than against the Democrats next fall. Here, read this," Abe said, handing me the paper.

"Mmmm. 'Mr. Thomas said, "I have been besieged by requests to investigate the influence Communists are exerting in the motion picture industry. This industry not only helps fashion public opinion here at home, it also reflects American values abroad. If the power brokers of the industry refuse to clean the Communists out of their positions of influence, then I promise to use the full authority of the United States Congress to do the job."' Wow," I said looking up at Abe's tired eyes. "He sounds pretty intense."

"Intensely stupid," Abe snapped. "If he wants to boot the Communists out of Hollywood, he ought to start with the labor unions!" The newspaper report went on to say that the lawmakers intended to hold private hearings the following week at the Biltmore Hotel in downtown Los Angeles. "Your friend Joan Roswell has jumped onto Thomas' bandwagon. See her column?"

"No," I replied, flipping over to the entertainment section. "Let's see. Here it is. 'This reporter commends Mr. Thomas and his colleagues for realizing the harm that Un-American influences can have on our nation, its citizens and movie-goers around the world. The motion picture industry holds the attention and fascination of the world.

Mr. Thomas, through his hearings, has a chance to ensure that the patriotism of the men and women in Hollywood is beyond reproach.' That's not too bad," I said looking up at Abe. "At least she didn't call us *all* Communists."

Abe grunted. "I'll bet she knows who they are. Can you imagine the little black book she must keep? I'll bet she'd make J. Edgar Hoover turn green with envy. Now, what about Miss Vance? What's her game?"

"Capitalism. She's got supply, you've got demand."

"She's got supply all right," Abe acknowledged with a shake of his head. He leaned back in his leather chair and pinched the bridge of his nose. "We've done everything for that girl. She was nothing but a pretty face when she first came here. Acting lessons, singing lessons, dancing lessons. She's got talent, but she's also benefitted from Pacific Pictures' rather generous investment in developing her skills. She'd do well to remember that."

"We didn't talk about any of the contract stuff last night," I said, avoiding the discussion we did have following Vera and Abe's initial meeting. "I'm sure she doesn't expect you to give her the keys to the studio. She probably just wants to feel some acknowledgement of her contributions to Pacific's financial success."

"We take all the risk and turn her into Hollywood's most popular young actress. You'd think that and a weekly salary more than most Americans make in a year would be sufficient to produce some loyalty. Ha! I can't decide which are more bothersome, politicians or actresses!"

I chuckled and that seemed to help break Abe's mood.

"I suppose Miss Vance will have some time to think while she's on location. When does she leave?"

"She and Tom Evers are leaving early Tuesday morning. I've assigned Vera 'Tom duty' while they're up in the Valley. She's tough enough yet gentle enough to handle him. He likes her, they've worked well together before. I think they'll be okay."

Abe nodded. "Good plan. So then I imagine you're free Tuesday evening?"

"Tuesday, Wednesday, Thursday … " I let me voice trail away. I was happy when Abe smiled.

"Good! Go to the movie with me Tuesday night. *The Farmer's Daughter* is playing at Pantages. That's the picture Dore Schary screened at his home last month. I felt too poorly to attend, but Ruth went and thoroughly enjoyed it. She said I should see it, that I might learn a thing or two about movie-making. Why don't you go with me?"

"I'd love to."

Vera and I spent most of Sunday afternoon together at my house. She needed a break from packing in preparation for three weeks on location up in the Valley. Producer Nestor Dawes had contracted with authorities of the City of Van Nuys to film street scenes in parts of their fair city. *Flash of the Switchblade* featured Vera as a psychologist specializing in juveniles and working with a dedicated police detective to address gang vandalism and general misbehavior. Tom would play the detective. *Switchblade* was a grittier role for Vera and the movie was straight drama, without the playful banter that had so appealed to viewers of the Brigid O'Dell films. The capable Peter Shaw was directing.

We spent part of the day running lines, with me reading all the male parts, including those of the juveniles. It was kind of fun. I'd make up different voices for the different characters to try and break Vera's concentration. Couldn't do it. She was far too much the professional. I grilled a couple of steaks for supper and baked two potatoes. I set up some candles on the kitchen table and opened a bottle of wine. It was a pleasant way to spend the evening and I was sorry when Vera decided to go home.

"I've got to recheck my packing. I want to make sure I've got everything I need," she said.

"But I'll see you tomorrow, right? Musso & Frank at seven for dinner." She reached up and kissed me on the cheek.

"Make sure you pack wisely," I teased, "because tomorrow night you really should stay with me. Going to a wild location like Van Nuys, you never know how long it will be until you see me again."

She laughed and blew me a kiss then disappeared out the front door.

Chapter 18

Monday was a typically hectic day at Pacific Pictures. I'd started early with a story conference on *Night Over Africa.* It was scheduled to begin filming in less than a month, but so far we still didn't have a decent screenplay. I couldn't recommend committing one of the studio's limited number of stars to such a mediocre script and none of our contract players would have the box office muscle to attract an audience. From there, a meeting with our story editor, just back from New York, and then a quick visit to our operating sound stages. Over on Soundstage 3, Sam Levin was working on the interior scenes for another western, *Fast Runs the Pale Horse*, and Arthur Porter was filming a detective picture over on Soundstage 5.

I had lunch with Abe in his dining room upstairs (chicken salad on lettuce) and then struggled to stay awake as I read through early treatments of half a dozen scripts. Some of the writing was pretty good. Some of it was pretty lousy. But I knew now that a lousy first draft wasn't necessarily fatal. If I saw something an audience could latch onto, I could always take it down to the writers' floor and hand it off to one of the more talented scribes Pacific kept on the payroll.

I glanced at the round face of the clock on the left corner of my desk. It was already after six and I was meeting Vera for cocktails at Musso & Frank on Hollywood Boulevard in less than an hour. That's when my intercom made that annoying, grating sound, like somebody feeding a cat into an oscillating fan.

"Mr. Russell?"

"Yes, Gladys," I answered with my finger on the switch.

"Mr. Baum left early to drive up to Van Nuys and tour the locations for the *Switchblade* project. He asked me to remind you about attending the movie tomorrow night."

"Got it! Thanks for the reminder." I reached to switch the intercom off, but Gladys wasn't finished.

"Also, a Mr. Mickey Moreno is here to see you. He doesn't have an appointment."

Mickey Moreno! I hadn't seen or heard from him since my final morning on Okinawa. It seemed a lifetime ago.

"Mr. Russell?" Gladys interrupted my reminiscence.

"Thanks, Gladys. Send Mr. Moreno in."

Mickey Moreno was as handsome as ever, his dark, wavy hair stylishly cut, his clear brown eyes dancing above a white smile. He wore a stylish brown suit over a white shirt with a blue striped tie. He was fifteen pounds heavier than when I'd seen him last, but everybody should gain at least fifteen pounds once they leave combat, and besides, he carried it well.

"Sergeant Moreno!" I said with a broad smile, greeting Mickey at the door to my office. "What an unexpected pleasure!"

"Frank!" he said grabbing my hand. Our hand shake got sandwiched between us as I gave Mickey a great bear hug. "How great to see you! And look at this office! Things have changed a bit since we last met, eh?"

"Sit down," I waved him into one of the chairs in front of my desk while I settled into the other. "Tell me what you've been doing. I've wondered about you and Lieutenant Brooks and Righetti and the others. How did you ever make it out of there?"

"With a little skill and a whole lot of luck," Mickey laughed. "Brooks got wounded the same day you did. He's back in the States now. He had some friends in Washington. I think he went back there. Righetti came through all right. He sent me a letter not too long after we got home. Said he'd seen our unit in a newsreel."

"I can explain that," I chuckled. "You remember that tall Aussie fellow, the newsreel cameraman?"

"Sure," the smile vanished from Mickey's face. "I remember how he ended, how you almost ended. You were crazy running out to help him like that."

"Yeah, I guess I was. I was out of it for about ten days. When I finally came to, I was in a nice clean, white hospital. I was there when we dropped the bomb and the Japs finally surrendered." Mickey nodded. "To make a long story short, on the boat home, I'm digging through my duffel bag looking for a clean pair of khakis and I find Cameron's ruck sack: camera, film, even that little Jap pistol he had. I figured you or whoever scraped me up had grabbed it and thrown it in with my gear by mistake."

"To tell you the truth," Mickey grimaced, "there wasn't much left of poor Cameron. Once we got you back under cover and in the care of the medics, we let loose with everything we had. We were shooting so fast we ruined one firing tube. Dog Company's attack petered out eventually, but two more companies passed through our guys and kept the pressure on the Japanese. We heard later that night that our guys had flanked that big-ass ridge and gotten in behind the Japs. It wasn't until the next day that we packed up your gear and shipped it back to division. I guess that's when you got Cameron's stuff."

"You know, Cameron's stuff is the reason I'm sitting here now." I told Mickey all about my first visit to Pacific Pictures and how I'd met George Burke in the newsreel department and how things had played out from there. "So that's why I'm here. What brings you back to Pacific Pictures, Mickey?" I asked after I'd thoroughly bored him with my story.

"I came to see you."

"Me?"

"Yeah. Heard you were over here and I'm trying to get back into the business. Thought maybe you'd be willing to help an old Army pal."

I clapped my hands. "You bet I would! Especially one who saved my life!" Vera's face suddenly flashed into my mind. "Oh gosh! What time is it?" I looked at my watch. It was five minutes until seven. I jumped up from the chair and snatched my jacket off the coat rack. "Come on! I'll buy you dinner," I said, grabbing him by the arm and pulling him up and out of the chair.

Musso & Frank was only a few blocks away, but by the time we got to my car and to the restaurant, we, or rather I, was fifteen minutes late.

"Good evening, Mr. Russell," Phillip the maître d' greeted me as we burst through the door. "Miss Vance is waiting in the bar."

"Thanks, Phillip. Listen, there's going to be three of us for dinner instead of two."

"I'll take care of it personally," Phillip smiled. He waved a waiter over, leaned in toward his ear and personally delegated the issue. He turned back to Mickey and me and said, "This way, please, gentlemen."

Vera had a cigarette in one hand and a drink with a little pink umbrella in it in the other. When she saw me approach, she set her drink down, gave me a one-armed hug and pecked me on the cheek.

"Hi!" I said, then remembering my manners, stepped back so I could introduce her to Mickey. "Vera Vance, meet my old Army pal Mickey Moreno." Vera started to flash her movie-star-meets-adoring-fan smile, but then her eyes widened in recognition. "Ah, I see you recognize the famous Mr. Moreno." Vera's expression dissolved into what I took for a more genuine smile.

She offered Mickey her hand and said, "Pleased to meet you, Mickey. You're not all scarred up like Frank, are you?" All three of us laughed and then Phillip showed up to escort us to our table.

Sometimes you go places to be seen. Sometimes you go places because you want a good meal and you want to be left alone. This occasion was one of the latter, so Phillip put us at a table in a back corner of the dining room where few patrons would pass by. I ordered shrimp cocktail for an appetizer. Vera ordered the lamb chops while Mickey and I opted for steaks. Mickey asked that the tomatoes be left off his salad.

"What brings you to Hollywood, Mickey?" Vera inquired.

"A couple of things. I'm ready to break back into pictures," he said with a confident smile. "I heard Frank was running things at Pacific Pictures so I thought I'd start with him."

"'Running things' is a little bit of an exaggeration," I said modestly.

"No it's not," Vera countered, exhaling smoke and keeping her eyes fixed on Mickey. "He's director of production. He *is* practically running things. What have you been doing since the war ended, Mickey?"

"I've been knocking around Mexico City. I'm something of a celebrity there, believe it or not. Apparently the Mexican audiences identified with Pepe Ramos in the old Kit Justice serials."

"I always thought you were the smarter of the two. But then I've worked with Terry Thorpe," Vera quipped. Mickey laughed.

"Excuse me for a moment. I need to wash up," I said, pushing my chair back. "This isn't like the last meal we shared together, is it Mickey? Sitting in the mud, blowing away the flies and eating out of a can."

Mickey laughed and nodded. "And the company is much more pleasant too."

I took care of my business and then weaved my way back through the dim dining room. I could see Vera and Mickey before they were aware of my return. Their heads were close together, serious expressions on their faces. For a moment, I wondered if I should be jealous.

"Hope you didn't miss me too much," I said to lighten the mood. Vera smiled, sitting back in her chair.

"I was just telling Mickey that we actually worked together once. I had just signed a six-month contract with Pacific and I was used as an extra in a lot of films. One of them was a Justice serial, but I can't remember which one."

"We were cranking them out every three weeks," Mickey added. "It was kind of hard to keep them all straight."

Our meals arrived. Phillip brought two bottles of wine, a white for Vera and a red for Mickey and me. He poured and after he stepped away, I proposed a toast. "To friends, colleagues and comrades. May our best days be ahead!"

"Here, here," Mickey replied lifting his glass. We all drank.

Vera reached over and placed her hand on mine. "How sweet." I felt pretty good sitting there between this beautiful woman I loved and this brave man who'd saved my life. Now that I'm wiser, I know that when things feel that good, you need to start looking over your shoulder.

The steaks were great and I enjoyed listening to Vera and Mickey swap Terry Thorpe stories. Poor Thorpe came across as a mostly likeable but insecure man with more ego than talent. Our waiter cleared away our dinner plates and we were considering dessert when I picked back up on our earlier conversation.

"Mickey, you said 'a couple of things' brought you back to town. Getting back into pictures is one, what's the other?"

Mickey sipped from his wine glass and glanced around at the nearby tables. An older couple sat two tables away from us, but other than them, we were pretty isolated. He brushed some bread crumbs off the white table cloth and onto the floor. "I'm looking to serve my country."

I chuckled. "You already did. You saved my life. War's over. I saved Pacific Pictures. What more could your country ask of you?" I meant it as a joke, but Mickey wasn't smiling.

"There's a new danger, Frank. As deadly as the Japanese, but more insidious." Mickey was serious and intense. "The Communists have infiltrated our business, Frank. They're sneaking propaganda into motion pictures. Movies are the most powerful medium of communication we've ever known. The Communists understand that and they're using Hollywood to undermine American values."

I searched Mickey's face for a twitch, a glimmer, anything that would help me determine if this was a hoax or if he believed what he was saying. I realized then how little I knew him. I'd spent less than three days in his presence, after all. I cleared my throat. "How do you know all this?" I asked.

"Simple. I used to be one."

"One what?"

"A Communist. When I first got into pictures in 1936, times were really tough. The Depression was so bad, all my family had to eat were tomatoes. The Communists were promising a better future, a utopia where everyone worked together to eliminate poverty and suffering. It sounded pretty good compared to the reality all around us. They provided me a place to fit in, a sense of community. And the contacts I made helped me get jobs. As long as I went along, they looked out for me." He shifted his gaze from me to Vera, who was holding her cigarette over a heavy glass ash tray. "Hitler starts menacing Europe and the Communists saw him for what he was. We protested against him, held rallies, raised money for refugees. Our movement was growing, we were flexing our muscle, united in battling a common enemy, the Fascists."

Mickey looked back at me. "Then, the strangest thing happened. Stalin and Hitler became allies. The party stopped criticizing Hitler and started protesting against the British who were standing up to Hitler. I got very confused, and when I started asking questions I was told to 'shut up' and do as I was told. All of a sudden, instead of feeling like a community where everyone had a voice, it began to feel a little like Hitler's Germany. I got the feeling that people were watching me, ready to rat me out if I crossed some line."

"What did you do?"

"I walked away. I joined the Army. And now I'm back and I have a story to tell."

"A story to tell?" I asked. "To whom?"

Mickey took another sip of wine and glanced around our darkened corner of the restaurant. "There's a Congressional committee in town. They're investigating Communists in Hollywood. I'm testifying on Wednesday. I'm going to tell them the real truth behind these guys. They pretend to be this great brotherhood of equality, but they're just like the Russians. Do what they say and everything's jake. Disagree with them and the hammer falls. That's what they want for America, a worker's paradise just like in Mother

Russia—where nobody has enough to eat and where nobody has the strength to speak out."

Mickey scared me. I knew Abe hated the Communists, but I had interpreted his loathing to be related more to economic self-interest than to politics. Mickey painted a picture of a dark, cynical conspiracy threatening to undermine American society by attacking the freedoms on which it was based. I was in no mood for dessert.

I settled the bill and we left the restaurant. We were standing out front waiting for the valet to bring our cars up when Vera asked, "Where are you staying?"

"The Alhambra Courts Motel. It's over on Formosa. It's not fancy, but it's clean."

"Well, good luck," Vera said, smiling and shaking hands, "with your testimony and your job hunt too. I'm sure Frank will do all he can to help you."

I got the number of the motel and promised I'd check in with Mickey in a day or two.

Vera was spending her last night in town with me. In the morning, she and Tom were leaving early to head up to Van Nuys for three long weeks of location shooting.

We parked both cars in the driveway alongside the house and went inside. I locked the door and turned off the porch light.

"Oh, Frank," she cooed, "kiss me as though it was for the last time."

"*Casablanca*, right?" I laughed and she giggled. But I kissed her anyway.

She took me by the hand and pulled me toward the bedroom. "This is our last chance for three weeks," she whispered. We helped each other out of our clothes and enjoyed spirited love-making. I remember seeing the orange glow of her cigarette in the darkness before I drifted into a restful slumber.

Chapter 19

Vera was up before six o'clock. I heard the shower running and I was tempted to get up and go scrub her back. Instead, I turned over and snuggled down in the warm covers. She didn't need my help. I supposed she had to fix her hair and makeup so she could drive north for an hour and then have her hair and makeup redone before reporting to the set. How someone as naturally beautiful as Vera could spend so much time worrying about how she looked was beyond my comprehension.

I heard the scraping noise as Vera opened the drawer in the bedside table, for the ash tray I guessed, then the scratch of a match as she lit a morning cigarette. I drifted in and out of sleep as she puttered around in the bedroom and bathroom.

At some point, Vera leaned over to whisper in my ear, her jasmine-scented perfume a pleasing sensation. "I better not hear about you catting around while I'm working my ass off in Van Nuys. Make sure you have an alibi, mister." I heard the front door open and close and then the sound of her car starting up in the drive. I rolled over and looked at the clock: seven-fifteen.

Goz was reading the morning paper in the outer office when I arrived on the third floor at eight-thirty. "Good morning, Goz," I greeted him.

He folded the paper, stuck it under his arm and stood, a grim set to his lips.

"See you for a minute, Frank?" he asked without a trace of the good humor I always associated with him.

"Sure," I hesitated, "come on." I headed down the hallway with Goz trailing behind. We entered my office and I removed my coat and hung it up. As I did, Goz closed the door. "What's up?" I asked. It was obvious that Goz wasn't here to hand out good news.

"I always check the gate house every morning," Goz began. "If anything unusual happened overnight, I need to know about it so I can deal with the press if they start asking questions." I nodded and he continued. "End of the day yesterday we had a guy named Mickey Moreno pay a visit. That name mean anything to you?"

"Of course it does. Mickey and I served together in the war, on Okinawa. I think I mentioned that to you when I first visited the lot. He saved my life." I peered at Goz to see if he remembered ever hearing any of this before. "Any of this ringing a bell with you, Goz?"

He rubbed the side of his face with his knuckles. "Maybe, maybe," he mumbled. He looked me in the eyes and waved the newspaper as if he was swatting a fly. "It doesn't matter. Do you know who Mickey is?"

"Goz," I said, sounding a little frustrated as I sat down behind my desk, "I just told you! What am I missing here?"

Goz shook his head and sat down across from me, tossing the newspaper on the corner of the desk. "What did he want?"

"He wants what any red-blooded American boy wants; he wants to get back into the movie business. He'd heard I was here now and thought maybe I could help him."

"Well, you can't!" Goz snapped. He leaned his head back, staring up at the ceiling for a moment before he started to speak again. "Right before the war," he began slowly, "Moreno was a key player in the Kit Justice serials, the sidekick. Good part. He played it well; got along with everybody on the lot. Always ready to work, always professional. So he's a friendly, popular guy, right? Abe likes him and he's one of the reasons the studio decides to expand the Justice storyline into feature films. Thorpe at this point is gaining popularity and we think it's a good move. Moreno's part of our calculation. Gives the stories broader appeal. Anyway, Abe's son David is hanging around the studio when he's not in school. Abe's happy about this because he figures David is picking up the movie business, you know, learning how things work. Abe's hoping that someday David will take over from him and Pacific will enjoy a second generation of Baum leadership. He was crazy about that boy, I guess like all fathers. Abe told me once that David had saved his and Ruth's marriage." He paused.

"Go on." This was more than I'd ever heard about David and I still felt that I didn't know anything. Joan Roswell's calculating green eyes popped into my mind.

Goz took a deep breath and continued. "So David starts hanging around Mickey. David's an only child; he looks up to Mickey like he's a big brother. Mickey was a pretty good guy, like I said, but no angel. We were filming the first full-length Kit Justice picture and after work one day, Mickey and David jump in Mickey's convertible and head off to the Strip. It was a Friday and we weren't scheduled to shoot the next day. I was working late, looking over some poster concepts when my white phone rings. It's a friendly cop I know who works along the Strip. He says that there's been an accident with injuries and that I need to get there as fast as I can. It seems our hero Mickey and his pal David had gotten too well lubricated. Mickey wrapped his convertible around a light pole. He gets thrown clear of the wreck, but David, David gets pinned between the car and the pole."

Goz stopped for a moment, the memory vivid and painful. He cleared his throat and resumed. "Mickey's got some scratches on his face, but he's in such a relaxed state that he's otherwise unhurt. David? Well, David's another story. By the time I get there, the cops aren't sure he's gonna live. Shit, by the time I get there, they're not even sure he's alive. I throw Mickey in the back of my car and tell him to lie down on the seat and stay there and not to look out the windows. The fire department and the ambulance come and they cut David out of the wreckage and lay him out on the stretcher," Goz choked up for a moment. "His head, Frank, it was mashed in on one side; purple and squashed. He looked like something out of a Lon Chaney movie. It was the worst thing I'd seen."

"But he lived, right?" I felt as though an electric current was being run through my body.

"Sort of. He's been in a private sanitarium above Malibu for the past six years. He doesn't speak, he doesn't walk. He just sits in his wheel chair and stares straight ahead. Traumatic brain injury. That's what the doctors called it. Abe brought in a specialist from the Mayo Clinic, but nobody could do anything. The damage was done and couldn't be undone. Abe and Ruth still go to Malibu to visit every Sunday."

I sat stunned for a moment, trying to comprehend the anguish Abe and Ruth Baum must have felt. And all because of my friend. "What happened to Moreno?" I asked, feeling guilty but not understanding why.

Goz lifted his head and sat back in the chair. "Scratches. Nothing more. I get there in time to keep him out of the press. I fixed it for Mickey. I couldn't fix it for Abe."

"What happened for Mickey here at the studio?"

"He finished the picture. Then he joined the Army. This was the summer of '41. Lots of guys were being drafted, even actors. Only a few of us knew why he turned so patriotic so quickly. It was the best thing for Abe. We couldn't have Mickey around Pacific. Plus, going into the service like that, he wouldn't be making pictures for another studio either."

"Good Lord, so that's the story Joan can't sniff out," I whispered. "Poor Abe. Poor kid."

"Frank, don't even think about sharing any of this with Joan. And don't think of helping that bastard. He's already ruined David's life and Abe's life. Pacific Pictures doesn't owe him anything. Neither do you."

I wasn't sure I agreed with Goz's last statement, but this clearly wasn't the time or place for a debate. "Goz," I said, meeting his resolute gaze, "thanks for telling me all this. I can tell it wasn't easy. And don't worry. I'll do the right thing."

“Right.” Goz stood up, his lips pressed together, sadness in his eyes. He nodded, then opened my office door and disappeared into the hallway.

I stood up and paced the length of my office a couple of times while I considered what I needed to do. I’d made a commitment to help Mickey, but I also had a commitment to Abe. I needed to take an honorable course of action with respect to both men. The only problem was that I wasn’t sure what that would be.

I picked up the newspaper Goz had left behind. The front page headline trumpeted that the House Committee on Un-American Activities had commenced its hearings the previous day. Apparently things hadn’t gone well for the visiting team. Their key witness had developed some memory problems and couldn’t tell a consistent story. The unreliable witness had torpedoed the committee’s plan for the day, so it had adjourned early. According to the article, the chairman, Mr. Thomas, along with his colleague, Mr. Roberts, had then driven down to the Mexican border to inspect the crossing point at Tijuana. Thomas had described the security measures there as “shoddy” and declared that it would be easy for a person to illegally enter the United States at that crossing. “This is a critical point,” he had elaborated, "because the Communists in Hollywood are being directly controlled by the Soviet Embassy in Mexico!" I wasn't too worried about the Communists in Hollywood. I had bigger problems to think about.

My normal routine helped take my mind off of the Mickey issue for a while. From a management perspective, I thought it was wiser for me to meet our producers where they worked rather than interrupt their efforts to have them report to me in the main building. I took my daily stroll to the soundstages again. Since *Switchblade* was filming on location, only two of them were in use. Soundstages offered no economic benefit when they sat empty and silent and I made a note to consider renting space to some of the independent producers when we weren't operating at full capacity.

I stopped by to check on post-production work on two pictures slated for release in June. *Dark Night Big City*, a gritty drama, and *Can't Carry a Tune*, a carefree musical, would pull in audiences from the opposite poles of the movie-going public. Hopkins Morton and I discussed Abe's tribute picture, *This Great Country*, over a quick lunch in the commissary. Hopkins had some good ideas that he'd outlined on a single piece of lined tablet paper. In his version, the film would be beautiful and inspirational. I made a couple of minor suggestions and suggested he make a formal presentation to Abe and me after the next weekly producers' meeting. I was thinking this project might be a good fit for George Burke's newsreel division. I wondered what George and his team might be capable of, if given a decent budget. I also thought the prestige of producing a feature length film would appeal to George.

I was back in my office trying without success to concentrate on some new script treatments Mary, our story editor, had sent over. There was one about a heroic dog that would appeal to children. With the success Disney was having, I thought we should be on the lookout for more family-oriented projects. Another idea was an adaptation of a popular Broadway play that had just closed after a two-year run. I figured anything that was good enough for two years on Broadway ought to be good for two hours at the movies.

My intercom buzzed. "Mr. Russell," Gladys reported, "Mr. Dawes on the line for you."

"Hello, Nestor," I said, picking up the phone.

"Good afternoon, Frank," replied the producer of *Flash of the Switchblade*. "I wanted to let you know that our cast and crew are all present and accounted for here in Van Nuys."

"Great!"

"We're doing some equipment checks this afternoon and then a meeting with everyone at five. After that, I'm turning them all loose to get a good night's rest. We start up in the morning with crew call at seven and cast at eight-thirty."

I asked Nestor if there was anything he needed, but as I would expect from an old pro like him, he had everything well in hand. After I hung up the phone, I decided that I had procrastinated as long as I could. It was time for me to go see Abe.

"Got a minute?" I asked leaning around the frame of Abe's office door. Abe looked up, removed his glasses and smiled.

"Of course, of course, come in. What ideas for improved profitability have you got for me today?"

"We're on schedule through June," I answered. "Hopefully those financial statements," I pointed at the documents Abe had been reading, "are reflecting the benefits of our production strategy."

"As the youngsters would say, 'and how!'" Abe chuckled. "I'm planning to go visit with Harley at the bank next week. Our first half results make this an advantageous time to acquire additional funding."

"Abe, did you know that one of our soundstages is dark right now? We've got *Switchblade* filming up in Van Nuys."

"Yes, I drove up there yesterday and had Nestor Dawes show me around the location," Abe reminded me.

"Right. Well, I was thinking that we could block time on our soundstages and then when we're not going to be using them, we could rent the space to some of the independents. I'd have to check on the going rate, but I'm sure we could be competitive. We don't have the overhead that MGM and Paramount and RKO have."

"I like that idea. But we don't rent to Goldwyn. That man is so contrary his dog doesn't even like him." Abe laughed and I joined in.

Now, I thought to myself. I stood up and closed Abe's office door. A puzzled look covered his face and his brown eyes followed me as I came back to his desk and sat in one of the armchairs facing it. "I need to tell you a story," I began. Abe nodded his head at me and leaned back in his chair, giving me permission to proceed. I told Abe about arriving on Okinawa and being sent forward to the 77th Division, about meeting Lieutenant Brooks and Sergeant Moreno. If he remembered me ever telling him about my brief time on the front lines with Mickey, he didn't reveal it. He did seem to remember hearing about Oliver Cameron before. I reminded him of why I'd come to Pacific Pictures in the first place and of the kind greeting he'd extended. I skimmed over the work we'd done together the last twenty months and arrived as quickly as I could at the previous evening.

"About six o'clock last night, I was finishing up in my office. I was meeting Vera for dinner at seven and you'd gone up to Van Nuys. Gladys buzzed me and said that Mickey Moreno was here." Abe shifted in his chair, but held my eyes. "We had a nice visit and I invited him to have dinner with us. He accepted. He told me that he wanted to get back into pictures and asked if I would help him." I paused for I knew my next statement would at best make Abe uncomfortable. "I told him I would."

"This morning, Goz was waiting for me when I got here. He took me into my office and closed the door, much as I've done here. He told me, with a great deal of personal sadness, what happened to your son, David." Abe drew in a deep breath. "I didn't know any of this until Goz told me this morning, Abe. First of all, I want you to know that I am very sorry about what happened to your son. Secondly, I want you to understand that this changes the way I view Mickey Moreno. I would never think about offering him any work here in light of what I now know."

Abe nodded and continued to stare at me for a moment. Finally, he cleared his throat, and with a raspy, low voice, spoke. "Worst few days of my life." He had tears in his eyes now. "I saw my son on that hospital bed and instinctively knew that his life was ruined. The doctors, the specialists, they merely confirmed it." He looked out the window at the sunny afternoon. "One minute. One second. One stupid mistake and my son pays with his future." Abe paused and brushed away a tear. "Ruth and I still go to see him every Sunday. Did you know that? Every week, we're greeted by the same vacant stare." He turned back to face me. "Oh, we've come to accept it on some level, I guess, that things will never return to normal. David's not really there at all, I think. And yet he lives." He stopped for a moment and stared blindly at the papers on his desk. "What are you going to do for Moreno? You made a commitment to him, Frank. I will think no less of you for helping him."

"I don't know," I said softly. "I just needed you to hear this from me."

"Thank you, my boy."

"There's something else you should know." Abe raised his eyebrows, an invitation for me to continue. "Moreno said he was in town to testify in front of that Congressional committee. He told us he'd once been a Communist, back before the war."

Abe looked back out the window again, as though he could reverse the sun and turn back time. "I should have killed that bastard," he said.

I wondered if he still might.

I left Abe alone and went back to my office. It had been a difficult conversation, more so for Abe than for me. The mistakes I had made had been innocent. For Abe, the mistakes others had made had been tragic. I did the best I could to focus on my work, but without much success. My mind kept wandering back down the hall to check on my mentor and friend. About 5:30, I got up and went back to Abe's office. He was staring out the window, his feet propped on an open desk drawer.

I rapped my knuckles on the door. "Say, Abe, we're still on for the movie tonight, right?"

He looked confused for a moment, then smiled weakly and said, "Right. *The Farmer's Daughter*. I don't want to attract any attention, so why don't you plan to drive? Let's leave in an hour. There's a taco stand on the way and I'll treat."

"Sounds good! See you in an hour." He was still aching, he always would; but he seemed to be putting Mickey Moreno behind him. Again.

The taco stand was over on El Centro Avenue, not "on the way" at all. But the tacos were good and helped Abe shove his heartache back into a distant corner of his mind. We arrived at the Pantages Theater a little before the scheduled seven-thirty show time. Abe and I stood off to the side of the lobby and watched the patrons. I was curious as to who composed a typical audience. As this picture featured a strong female protagonist, I expected there to be more women in the audience. Certainly women were well-represented, but there were plenty of men as well—probably because gorgeous Loretta Young played the female lead.

The lights in the lobby dimmed and we headed into the theater, taking seats about two-thirds of the way back. The cartoon started promptly at seven-thirty.

"Ever think about adding animation?" I whispered as Mickey Mouse appeared on the screen.

"No. Very expensive. Besides, how could you compete with Disney? It's cheaper to do what RKO's doing here: just buy cartoons from the best."

The newsreel was next, describing a plan put forth by Secretary of State George Marshall for massive amounts of aid to starving Europe. A fairly unfunny comedy short feature followed and then RKO's radio tower logo appeared as an introduction to *The Farmer's Daughter*. Abe chuckled a few times, but I was still fighting the battle of Mickey Moreno. About halfway through the picture, I gave up. Something would come to me, I reasoned. Somehow it would work itself out.

Abe had dismissed his chauffeur, Charles, for the night, so when the picture ended about ten o'clock, we got back in my car and headed to Bel Air.

"A pleasant evening," Abe said. "I can see why Ruth enjoyed the show. Do you know why audiences like political comedies?"

"Why?"

"Because politics is by nature part farce. Listen to any candidate's stump speech and you'll hear five percent truth, seventy-five percent hyperbole and twenty percent outright lies. People aren't stupid. They feel stories like this which make the politicians look foolish are just and proper. I'm inclined to agree with them. Of course these charlatans out here now pretending to 'investigate' Hollywood don't need our help to look foolish, do they?" he chuckled.

"No sir," I agreed.

I drove west along Santa Monica Boulevard and then, in Beverly Hills, turned right onto Wilshire. Abe tapped me on the arm.

"See that corner," he pointed to our left. "We owned that, Morty Aaronson and me." There was a Thrifty Drugs store there, its blue and white sign bright against the darkness.

"I'll bet you collect a nice rent from a tenant like that."

"Ha! 'Owned,' as in past tense. We had a deal, Morty and me, that either one of us could buy and sell assets. I expected we'd talk it over first, but that didn't happen on this deal. Morty had got himself into some money trouble and so he sold that lot right out from under me. I nearly choked him!"

"When did he pass away?" Nobody had ever mentioned Aaronson to me except for George Burke during that first morning tour he'd given me.

"Long time ago now," Abe mumbled, staring out into the darkness as we began to climb the ridge that would lead us up to his mansion. After that, he fell silent.

I dropped Abe off at the massive wooden doors of his castle-like estate just after ten-thirty.

"I enjoyed that, Frank," he said, one hand on the top of the car, the other holding open the door. "We'll have to plan another outing soon."

"I look forward to it. Good night, Abe."

It was after eleven by the time I parked the Ford in my driveway. It had been a long, sometimes difficult day, but it had ended well.

Chapter 20

In keeping with my habit of going to where the action was taking place, I left early Wednesday morning to drive up to Van Nuys to see how things were going on the *Switchblade* set. The sun was just peeking over the mountains as I started the trip north on Route 99. I passed through the mountains and turned west at Burbank with Lockheed Airport on my right. My time working there on the P-38 assembly line seemed an eon ago. I pulled into a diner at Universal City and paid forty cents for a plate of bacon, eggs, potatoes and toast and a cup of coffee.

It was kind of fun to be out of Hollywood, to sit and eat a casual breakfast in a place where no one knew me. I watched the other patrons come and go for about twenty minutes, silently making up little stories about each one. There was an older man, he must have been in his forties, dressed in dungarees and an oil-stained work jacket who took a seat in a booth a couple of tables away. With him were three neatly-dressed little girls who ranged in age from about five to twelve. They chattered happily while they waited on their food. The man, I guess he was their dad, didn't say a lot, but he smiled often. Another customer dropped a catsup bottle on the tile floor. The resulting mess would have fit perfectly in *Jungle Command.*

I finished my breakfast, jumped back in the Ford and finally pulled into Van Nuys about nine o'clock. According to what Nestor had told me the day before, everyone—including Tom Evers—should already be on the set. I parked my car outside the barricades that had been set up to control spectators and curious passersby. A Van Nuys policeman was controlling access to the shoot. I introduced myself and told him I was with the studio and he passed me right on through. I guess he hadn't had many visitors yet.

It was quickly apparent where the filming was taking place. All you had to do was follow the cables. Light cables, sound cables, power cables all entwined and snaking hither and yon. I saw Nestor talking to the head grip. Peter Shaw was standing off to the side nursing a mug of coffee and talking with Tom Evers. I took that as a good sign.

Peter waved when he saw me, causing Tom to turn around. When he recognized me, Tom's eyes registered panic. He walked straight to me and grabbed me by the elbow, pulling me behind an equipment truck. "Nothing happened," he was shaking his head, "nothing! I swear!"

"What are you talking about?" I was totally bewildered.

"We went out and had a few drinks, that's all. You know me, Frank. You know I'm not that kind of guy. Really," he pleaded, "you know."

"Slow down, Tom," I said. "I'm about two reels behind you. Who, what, when? Give me some basics."

Tom took a deep breath and squeezed his eyes shut for a second. "We had a crew meeting with Nestor yesterday afternoon, you know, just to kind of get everybody oriented, rooms assigned, call times, that kind of stuff. Once it was over Vera and I went out driving around. We stopped and had a couple of drinks."

"How many?"

"Three or four. And then we left and drove around some more."

"Well, Tom, how many places did you have three or four drinks?"

"Only two," he paused. "Maybe three."

"Okay, so then what?"

"Well, this is where it gets a little sensitive."

"I'm a sensitive guy, Tom, you can trust me."

"Well, like I said, Frank, nothing happened. Nothing." He put his hands on my shoulders and stared into my eyes. I could clearly see the effects of the previous evening on Tom's eyes. "This morning," he paused again, "this morning I woke up in Vera's room. But I was on the floor, Frank. On. The. Floor."

"Okay, Tom," I nodded. If Vera Vance was going to cheat on me, it wasn't going to be with

Tom Evers. He wasn't that kind of guy. Literally. "Come on," I said, this time taking him by his elbow. "Let's get back to work. We can sort all this out later."

"Thanks, Frank. I knew you'd believe me."

"Of course I do." I slapped him lightly on the back. We stepped over some more cables and around the truck. Peter was still drinking his coffee, but was now conferring with Nestor.

"Good morning, gents," I called.

I shook hands with them and they gave me a rundown on preparations for the opening day of shooting. They were just a few minutes from filming the first scene and were waiting on the grips and gaffers to finish setting up for the shot. This first shot would take place in the parking lot of a high school, where Tom's character, the police detective, would have a heart-to-heart talk with one of the delinquents played by Wyatt Todd, one of the studio's young contract players.

Peter and Nestor went to inspect the set-up while I enjoyed the warm rays of the morning sun. "Hey, good looking," Vera's voice came from behind me.

"Hey yourself!" I replied smiling at the sight of her. "You look particularly beautiful this morning." I leaned over to kiss her and she turned her face to offer her cheek.

"The effects of an hour in the makeup chair," she laughed. "Don't mess it up."

"What in the world happened with Tom last night? When he saw me I thought he was going to pee in his pants."

Vera threw back her head and laughed. "Tom and I went out for drinks last night. He got wasted and fell asleep. So I brought him back to the motel. Have you seen the motel our studio booked us into for three weeks?"

"No."

"Luxury it ain't."

"Well, this is Van Nuys," I answered. "I doubt there were a lot of options."

"Sure," she said, clearly of the opinion that at least one better option was available. "Anyway, my room is on the ground floor, Tom's on the floor above. I wasn't willing to carry him up the stairs so I dragged him into my room, dropped him on the floor and covered him with the bedspread and stuffed a pillow under his head." She laughed again. "You should have seen that poor boy's face when I woke him up this morning! Pure panic. I'll bet he hasn't woken up that fast since Prohibition ended. And you know what?"

"What?"

"He was on the set on time. I bet he doesn't miss a day." We both laughed. Then Vera's face grew serious and she put her hand on my arm.

"Hey, I'm really sorry about your friend. What a shock!"

For the second time since I'd arrived I was dumbfounded. It seemed the stars of this picture both knew things that I didn't.

"My friend?"

"Yeah, Mickey." Vera searched my face for comprehension. "Jesus," she muttered. "You don't know, do you?" She hooked her arm inside my elbow and led me over to a canvas chair that had her name stenciled on the back. A copy of the *Times* was on the seat. She picked it up, unfolded it and held it up for me to see. Below the fold was a picture of Mickey Moreno and the headline "HUAC WITNESS FOUND DEAD AT HOLLYWOOD MOTEL."

As I stood there in the warm sunshine, my peripheral vision began to narrow from both sides like the curtains of a movie theater closing after the end credits. I felt light-headed and I dropped into Vera's chair.

"Connie," I heard Vera call out, "bring us a glass of water over here, would you, honey?"

A glass appeared directly in front of me. It was the only thing I could see. The sensation was eerily similar to what I experienced on Okinawa when Oliver Cameron had simply disappeared. I sipped some water and closed my eyes. When I reopened them, Nestor, Peter, Tom and Vera were fanned out in front of me, concern reflecting on their faces.

"Are you okay, darling?" Vera was asking. "You want us to call a doctor?"

"Mmmm." I shook my head. "No. I'll be all right. I just need to sit for a minute." I tried to smile. "Sorry to scare everybody. I'll be okay." This brought relieved smiles. I felt the warmth of the sun again. My vision expanded back to normal, the theater curtains slowly opening once more.

"I'm sorry I shocked you," Vera apologized, once the others had wandered away to give us some privacy. "I figured you'd heard."

I shook my head again and took another sip of water. "I left early. I didn't see any papers and I didn't listen to the radio. It was a pretty morning, so I just enjoyed the drive."

I must have dropped the newspaper, so I leaned over carefully to pick it up. I looked at the now lifeless eyes of Mickey Moreno, his smile staring at me from page one. Vera's hand was on my shoulder. I scanned the story. Mickey's body had been found in a parking lot next to his hotel. The police said he'd been shot at close range by an unidentified assailant. The police were looking for witnesses and anyone who had seen or heard anything was asked to phone the detectives at the Hollywood Division.

"You never know, do you?" I looked up at Vera. "One day he shows up, the next day he's dead. It makes me sick to think of all he survived in the war and then he gets shot by some punk on the street."

"I'm sorry, Frank," she repeated.

The filming of the first scene lasted until about two o'clock, after which Peter declared a lunch break. A catering truck had been brought on-site to minimize the amount of time lost for meals. Vera, Tom and I grabbed sandwiches and Cokes. I could tell Tom craved something stronger, but once he got on set, his discipline improved.

After lunch, I kissed Vera goodbye and shook Tom's hand. I thought a lot about Mickey on the drive back to the studio. I wondered if his murder was the work of some random street junkie or if … or if. I refused to take that thought any farther.

I got back to the studio a little after four and headed upstairs. When I pushed through the office doors, Lovely Betty caught my eye and with a barely perceptible nod indicated two gentlemen in nondescript suits. They were seated in the waiting area, one reading a newspaper, the other a recent edition of *Photoplay*.

"Mr. Russell," Betty said, smiling, "Detectives Driscoll and McKale are here to see you." Unlike Gladys, Betty never called me "Mr. Russell." The two detectives looked up at the mention of my name. I introduced myself to them and they showed me their credentials. I invited them back to my office.

I motioned for them to sit down and asked if they'd like anything to drink. Predictably, they declined. "What can I help you with?" I asked, sitting down in my desk chair. McKale, the older of the two, took the lead.

"We understand Mickey Moreno came to see you on Monday."

"I figured that was it. Yes, he did." I'd seen enough cop movies to know that I shouldn't volunteer too much until I could determine what direction our conversation would be taking.

"Why?"

"Mickey and I were in the Army together. Okinawa. He saved my life there and he came here to see if I could help him get back into the motion picture business."

"Did he tell you he was going to testify in front of the Congressional committee?" McKale continued the questioning. Driscoll was busy taking notes.

"He did. He said he wanted to expose the Communists in Hollywood."

"Did he mention any names?" McKale and Driscoll both watched me.

"No and, candidly, I didn't ask him to. A man's politics are his own business." I must have sounded a little defensive.

McKale glanced at his partner and then back to me. "Just so we're all clear here, Mr. Russell, this isn't about politics. We don't give a rat's ass about who you voted for or what party you think ought to run America. We're interested in finding a killer."

"I understand, detective. Mickey didn't give me any names. If he had, I would share them with you. He was a friend of mine, in my mind, a war hero."

"Did he say where he'd been working, what he'd been doing?"

"Only that he'd been in Mexico. He said they treated him like a celebrity south of the border." I realized how very little I actually knew about Mickey and how little I'd be able to help the police.

"Did he use those words: south of the border?"

"No, I don't think so. Those are my words. He just said they treated him like a celebrity in Mexico."

"Please tell us where you were last night, Mr. Russell."

"Well, I worked here until about six. Then Abe Baum and I went and bought some tacos and went to a movie. After the show was over, I drove him home and then I went home."

"What time was the movie?"

"It started at seven-thirty. It let out about ten. Abe lives up the mountain in Bel Air. I guess it took us about thirty minutes to get there and then another thirty for me to get back to my place. I live on Taft, just north of here."

"So you would have gotten home about eleven?"

"Right. Maybe a little after."

"And from about ten-thirty to eleven-ish, you would have been in the car alone?"

His question made me a little nervous. "Yes, that's right. What time was Mickey killed?" I asked figuring his answer might give me a clue to whether I was a suspect.

"Sometime around ten."

"How precise is that?" I asked.

"You'll have to ask the coroner, Mr. Russell. Do you have any witnesses that can corroborate your alibi?"

"Abe Baum," I said, figuring they would recognize the name. The detectives traded quick glances telling me my hunch was correct. "Like I said, we were together from six o'clock until ten-thirty."

"You wouldn't have a ticket stub from the theater would you?"

"Well, I might, but it would be in the trash can at home. Or still in my pants pocket."

"Mr. Russell, do you know anyone who had a grudge against Mickey Moreno, anyone who might like to see him dead?"

"No," I lied.

McKale looked at his partner, who shook his head. "Thank you for your time, Mr. Russell. Condolences for your friend."

"Sorry I wasn't more helpful," I said. I opened my desk drawer and pulled out one of my business cards. "Here's my office number," I said, and then flipping it over, I jotted my home number on the back. "If there's anything I can do, please call me, day or night." I handed the card to McKale who handed it to Driscoll who stuck it inside his little notebook. "Do you mind if I ask a question?"

"You can ask."

"Was Mickey robbed? Was it some junkie looking for quick cash so he could get high again?"

"We don't think so. He still had cash on him, about forty dollars. Powder burns on his clothes. Small caliber bullet. Like I said, we think it happened about ten o'clock, but we don't have any witnesses so far. It's not the best part of town for finding people anxious to cooperate with the police."

"Well, again, if there's anything I can do to assist your investigation, please call me."

The two detectives stood and thanked me, then they left. Once I was sure they would have cleared the front reception area, I buzzed Betty.

"Yes, Frank?"

"Has Abe been here today?"

"Yes. He only left a few minutes before you arrived. He had a haircut scheduled."

"Did those policemen ask to speak to him?"

"Nope, only with you."

I'd been in my office only a few minutes the next morning when I heard a knock on my door. Abe stuck his head in and asked, "May I come in?"

"Sure," I said, coming around from behind my desk and sitting across from him in the facing chair.

"I'm sorry your friend was killed, Frank," he said without making eye contact. "You know how I felt about him and what he'd done, but I know he was important to you."

"He is, indirectly at least, the reason I'm here," I replied.

"I admit there's some closure in this for us," Abe resumed, "though it will never be complete, of course. Anyway, I just wanted you to know that I feel for you."

I nodded. "Thanks. That means a lot. It was a rough night last night." We sat silently for a minute and then I asked, "Abe, have the police talked to you?"

He shook his head. "Why should they?"

"To get you to confirm my alibi."

His posture stiffened. "Your alibi?" he asked, concerned.

"Yes. Two detectives were here yesterday when I got back from Van Nuys. They knew Mickey had been to see me. They asked where I'd been the night he was killed. I told them we'd been to a show. They starting asking for times and stuff like that. I think they were deciding whether I was a suspect. Anyway, you're my alibi."

"Then you have nothing to worry about, my boy. You were with me. I'm sure that the two of us were seen at the theater and, all modesty aside, I was probably recognized. No, if they come sniffing around again, send them to me. I will disabuse them of any notion that you could have been involved."

I was still at my desk, staring vacantly into space two hours later when my phone rang. Gladys was gone for the day, so I picked up on the second ring.

"Frank, darling!" It was Joan Roswell. "I just heard the most curious bit of information."

"What's that?" I asked, keeping my voice as flat as I could.

"Well, I heard that Mickey Moreno paid a call on you the night before he was killed. What's the story?"

"The story? The story is that Mickey Moreno was, for two whole days, my platoon sergeant on Okinawa. He probably saved my life when I was wounded. He came to see me on Tuesday and asked for my help in getting back into the picture business. Then he got killed. That's the story, Joan."

"Why do you think he was killed?"

"Ask the police. Look, Joan," I said with a little more anger than was prudent, "Mickey was my friend. He's dead and I'm sad about it. I don't know who killed him or why. If I did, I would have told the police."

"Have you talked to the police?"

"I have. I am confident they will quickly solve the case and bring the murderer to justice."

"Can I quote you on that darling?"

"Hell, yes!" I snapped, slamming the receiver down on the cradle. Sometimes I'm right, but this wasn't one of those times.

Joan Roswell's column in Friday morning's paper felt like someone scraping a raw wound with 40-grit sandpaper: "Police have already questioned Pacific Pictures executive Frank Russell in the mysterious shooting death of former film star

Mickey Moreno. This reporter has learned that Russell, who served in the same platoon as Moreno during the war, is a suspect in the L.A.P.D.'s murder investigation."

Just like that, the readers of the *Times*, the vast majority of whom had never heard of Frank Russell, now considered me to be a likely murderer. I was sipping a cup of coffee in the kitchen, staring at Joan's pretty, smiling face above her harsh, accusatory words and trying to decide what kind of bouquet I could send her that would make her break out in hives, when I heard a knock on the front door.

"Mr. Russell," Detective McKale nodded in greeting when I opened the door. Behind him stood his partner Driscoll and a couple of uniformed officers. A squad cruiser and an unmarked car stood at the curb.

"Detective," I replied, confusion at his presence joining the lingering anger over Joan's column.

He held up a buff-colored piece of paper. "This is a warrant to search these premises in connection with our investigation of the Moreno murder. While we're having a look around, we'd like you to ride downtown with us and answer some more questions."

"Am I under arrest?"

"No sir. We just want to look around, that's all. It's better that you aren't here to get in the way."

"Do I need to call a lawyer?"

"Not if you haven't done anything." McKale nodded to Detective Driscoll and the uniformed officers, who pushed past me and into my home. McKale looked me squarely in the eyes, well aware that he was in complete control of the situation. "Just come on downtown with us, Mr. Russell, and we can keep this nice and easy and out of the papers."

I tapped the newspaper lightly against his chest. "Too late for that," I said. "Let me get my wallet and my coat."

McKale's questions weren't the reason he wanted me to ride to headquarters. The questions he asked me were pretty repetitive of the ones he'd already covered Wednesday afternoon at my office. What was different, what they couldn't do at my office, or at my house for that matter, was a paraffin test.

McKale escorted me to the police lab in the basement of their headquarters building. It was several interconnected rooms with concrete floors broken here and there by drains. The walls were covered floor to ceiling with white, shiny tiles. Various pieces of equipment, including calipers and microscopes, covered the neat work counters. The whole place had a dank, chemical smell and I wondered what mysteries it had helped solve—and if the death of Mickey Moreno would be added to the list. McKale led me over to a white metal table upon which sat a hotplate and a simmering pot of something and introduced me to one of the lab's technicians, a Mr. Boykin. He had all the style and personality of a laboratory test tube.

"Sit here," Boykin directed, pointing to a metal chair next to the table, "and put your hands flat on those two pads there." Two small rectangles of light pasteboard sat on the table top. I did as I was told and Boykin stirred the small pot from which steam was rising. "When a gun is fired, small particles are expelled from the back of the weapon and from the muzzle. You were in the service, weren't you, Mr. Russell?"

"The Army, yes," I replied.

"Well, then you understand," Boykin resumed in his flat monotone. "This will feel hot to you," he said, continuing to stir the pot, "but it won't burn your hands. You're right-handed or left-handed?"

"Right."

Boykin drizzled some hot wax across my right hand, causing me to flinch. "Keep still," he directed. McKale stood silently behind me, just out of sight. "We're going to make wax casts of your hands and then treat the casts with a chemical that reacts with the residue left behind when a weapon is fired. Blue specks on the casts indicate the presence of potassium nitrite and potassium nitrate which would be indicators that you've fired a gun."

"Well, I haven't," I replied grumpily. "I haven't fired a weapon since I got out of the Army." The truth was that even during my short time in combat, I hadn't fired my weapon. "Besides, I've washed my hands a half dozen times since the night Mickey was killed."

Boykin laughed, "Oh, that doesn't matter. The wax opens up your pores and lifts out particles. We'll find them."

"If they're there," I frowned.

"If they're there," Boykin repeated.

It took Boykin about twenty minutes to finish the casts and for them to cool enough for me to remove my hands. "That's it, Mr. Russell," he said, carrying the cooling casts to a work counter.

"That's it? What about the results?"

"Detective McKale will show you out." I glanced quickly at McKale, who nodded toward the lab door. Reluctantly, I pushed through the doors and up the stairs.

"How long until you get the results?"

"We'll be in touch," McKale answered.

I was annoyed, angry really, by the time I finally made it to the office at about eleven o'clock. I nodded to Lovely Betty and Gladys and headed straight towards Abe's office. I didn't like being treated like a criminal. I didn't like having my name linked with murder in the newspaper. I didn't like it that my friend was dead.

"Got a second?" I asked, sticking my head into his door.

"What's wrong?" Abe asked, reading my face immediately.

I shared my morning's experiences, including the details right down to the heat of the wax. Abe listened attentively and nodded. Talking about it helped a little—but only a little. At the conclusion of my story, Abe leaned back and folded his hands together. "Let me see what I can find out. I've got a few connections with the city."

Chapter 21

I slept late on Saturday morning. When I got up, I scraped the leftover food from the skillet and fried a couple of eggs, brewed some coffee and sat down to read the newspaper. Congressman Thomas was calling for a "full-dress public hearing" on Communism in the motion picture industry. He called the Communists insidious, just like Mickey had, and said that Hollywood ought to "clean its own house." I'd had enough talk about Communists and so quickly flipped to page two. I'd worked my way through the sports section, checking the baseball standings to find Detroit a game and a half ahead of the Red Sox in the American League. Over in the National League, the Cubs and the Boston Braves were tied for the lead twenty-four games into the season.

Without thinking, I kept turning the pages, munching on my toast. When I hit the obituary page, my eyes were immediately drawn to a picture of Mickey. I realized that it was the same picture of my friend that had appeared on page one in Wednesday's edition, only in a smaller version. The underlying article announced that funeral services would be the following day at Hollywood Memorial Cemetery. There was no further information concerning the police investigation into Mickey's death.

Sunday morning dawned cool with high clouds, but by the time I pulled into the cemetery just off of Santa Monica Boulevard, the sun had broken through. I got out of my car and checked with the cemetery usher, who directed me to a plot on the west side of the forty-acre sanctuary. I got back in the car and drove slowly, passing hundreds of monuments, gravestones and sarcophagi until I came upon a small knot of people, all dressed in black, clustered around a flag-draped coffin suspended above an open grave.

I got out, closing the door quietly, and buttoned my suit coat. I stopped a few yards from the back of the group. I could still hear the priest while being respectful of the mourners' privacy. The sun was warm, pleasant, a cheery counter to the sadness of the occasion. Slowly, I scanned the mourners. I nodded when I made eye contact with Detective McKale. No one else from Pacific Pictures had come.

Abe checked on me Monday morning, which I appreciated. We had lunch together in the private dining room and talked about our business. Neither of us brought up Mickey Moreno. Abe had a 2 p.m. appointment with Mr. Harley at the bank. He planned to share our results through the month of April and preview our coming attractions.

"The best way to please a banker," Abe tutored me at lunch, "is to always exceed his expectations. As this is rarely possible for a variety of reasons, you should never pass up the opportunity to report excellent results. In person," he added.

With Abe heading to the bank, I decided to head back to Van Nuys. *Switchblade* was our biggest budget picture presently in production. Making sure things were running smoothly and that Nestor had the resources he needed seemed like a prudent way for me to spend my time. I also needed to see Vera. I needed to hold her, to touch her, to talk to her.

I reached the set about two-thirty. Traffic on the drive up had been heavier this time because it was so much later in the day. I'd gotten stuck a couple of times behind produce trucks, so the trip had taken longer than I planned. Still, there was plenty of daylight left by the time I reached the shooting location, and Nestor and Peter had the set humming.

I spoke briefly with both of them, soliciting their thoughts on how things were progressing. Nestor said everything was on schedule, that the city officials had bent over backwards to make sure our company had everything it needed. Peter was pleased with the spirit of cooperation of the cast and crew. "Sometimes," he said, smoking a cigarette and using his hand to shield his eyes from the sun, "the crew can get a little testy when they're with each other all day and into the night. Instead of going home after a day on the set, they go to the hotel and they're right next door to the people they've been working with all week. This crew's been really delightful to work with. No drama," he laughed, "except what will appear on screen!"

Having done my professional duty, I sought out Vera. She was sitting under a large beach umbrella covered with yellow polka-dots while one of the makeup experts gave her a touch up. "Hey, good lookin'," she purred when she saw me. "Thanks, Connie," she said to the makeup lady who took that as a clue to leave us alone. I kissed Vera carefully on her offered cheek, then pulled another chair over and sat beside her. "How're you doing, lover?" she asked.

"So-so. I just needed to see you. I miss you, you know."

"I miss you too, darling, but things are going swell here and we'll be back home for good in another week." She glanced around to ensure no one could hear her and then leaned in and whispered in my ear, "You could stay the night. I've got a double bed in my room. And I'm not planning to let Tom stay with me." She sat back and flashed a wicked smile.

"How is good old Tom?"

"Petrified of me and you!" Vera laughed. "I asked him if he wanted to go get a drink Saturday and he turned as white as Caspar the Friendly Ghost. He's still not sure you believe nothing happened, but he is sure that I am not to be trusted."

We sat under the gaudy umbrella for half an hour, just talking and joking. She was as beautiful as ever, vivacious, irreverent, funny, fun. She was the tonic my scarred soul needed. By the time Peter called her for her next shot, I felt normal again.

"Listen, Frank," she said taking my hands in hers, "we finish up this location stuff next Wednesday. Now about next Wednesday night, I want to go to bed really early, you understand?" The wicked smile again.

"Got it," I winked. "In fact, I got that so loud and clear that I'm going to haul my ass back to work and clean off my desk so that when you do get back there is nothing to get in between me and a certain heavenly body." I kissed her on the lips and she rolled her eyes.

"Now I got to do makeup again!" But she was smiling.

True to my word, I put in a lot of hours at the studio over the next eight days. With Vera out of town, there was no temptation to scoot out early for an evening on the town. Besides *Switchblade*, Pacific had two other pictures in production and two ready for June releases. One of the projects in the works was *This Great Country*, Abe's tribute to America. Hopkins Morton had drafted a script and he read through it for me after lunch that Friday.

"We start off with an aerial shot of the California coast and dissolve to a similar shot of the Grand Canyon," Hopkins explained. "'America the Beautiful' is playing underneath as we get a feel for the sweeping grandeur of the country." I'm not kidding; he said "sweeping grandeur." Only a writer would talk like that.

"Wait a minute," I interrupted. "So we're hearing 'spacious skies' and 'amber waves of grain' and you're showing us the rocky coastline and the Grand Canyon? Isn't that a little incongruous?" I really said "incongruous."

Hopkins appeared confused. "Well, you see, it's really the same idea, you know, sweeping grandeur, majestic landscapes…"

"Okay, go ahead and we can come back to that." Hopkins forged ahead, relieved.

"The great plains, maybe we can move that up to match the music." He looked up for affirmation so I nodded.

"Good idea."

"The mighty Mississippi. The Chicago skyline with that big lake in the background."

"That big lake?"

"Yeah, yeah, you know they have one of the Big Lakes up there." He was rolling now, so I let him continue. "Over the heartland, Independence Hall in Philadelphia, the Liberty Bell, up to New York and the Statute of Liberty, then that church in Boston. Finally, to Washington: the Capitol, Lincoln Memorial, Jefferson Memorial, the White House."

"Think about leaving the White House out. That automatically alienates half our audience," I suggested. Hopkins made a note on his page.

"Then we dissolve to the Declaration of Independence and the Constitution and we hear a voice-over reading key phrases. I'm thinking maybe we get Doyle Burton to narrate."

"Good choice," I agreed.

Despite a few minor flaws, Hopkins' script was pretty good. I offered a few suggestions to make it better and asked him to have another draft ready to review with me on Tuesday. Once we had a good working copy, we'd take it to Abe for his okay. It was his idea, after all.

Chapter 22

I spent the weekend cleaning house. My house. I was a fairly typical bachelor. Cooking and cleaning were not my strongest suit. I hauled the rugs out back and beat them like the Saint Louis Browns. I dusted, swept, washed and polished.

The kitchen had gotten a little bit nasty. I threw away all the green things in the refrigerator since none of them were vegetables. I soaked the dried up food off the dirty plates I'd stacked up over the previous ten days and then scrubbed them until they shone like Ingrid Bergman's smile. I wiped down counters and erased the evidence of old spills. I even washed the kitchen trash can.

I changed the sheets on the bed and cleaned the bathroom fixtures. I mopped the floors. I was going to wax, but decided that mopping would be sufficient. Vera had never shown any inclination to inspect the floors, after all.

I tidied up in the bedroom, making sure all my clean clothes were put away in the chest of drawers or hung up in the closet. It made for a full weekend, but by Sunday, the house looked good enough to pass a GI inspection. My last task was to wash the ash tray and put it back in the drawer of the bedside table.

I didn't see what wasn't there.

Abe had been pleased with the latest draft of the script for *This Great Country*, which of course was a big relief to both Hopkins and me. Abe had suggested we incorporate images representing America's military might and scenes depicting our economic power, like an assembly line running at full capacity. He also wanted to add a montage of images from some of the American military cemeteries in Europe and the Pacific, scenes that he said would show how America had sacrificed to rescue the rest of the world from tyranny and despotism. I thought his ideas added favorably to the draft Hopkins had presented. Abe asked us to show him a final draft when he returned from New York in two weeks. I also suggested that George Burke helm the project. Abe liked the idea.

After Hopkins was dismissed, Abe turned to me. "I had a chance to speak with Chief Horral yesterday. I asked him about your involvement in the Moreno matter. He promised to check on it and call me back, which he did just before lunch. He said that the police found nothing unusual at your house and that your paraffin test was negative." He smiled.

"That's great," I said with obvious relief. "Now I can focus on work without this nagging doubt in the back of my mind. Plus, Vera's due back this evening."

"Big plans?" he asked with raised eyebrows.

"Quiet evening," I smiled.

I left Abe's office and walked down to my own. I pulled the phone book out of my desk drawer and dialed Crossie's Flowers, a florist over on Gower. "Can you send a bouquet of poison ivy?" I asked.

I hadn't had any luck finding the right arrangement to send to Joan Roswell, but I did greet Vera with a dozen beautiful red roses when she arrived at my place at 7 o'clock. We enjoyed a light supper and then retired early to enjoy each other.

Nestor had given the cast Thursday off to help them recover from their time up in Van Nuys, so I had arranged to take a half day off and sleep in. About eight o'clock, I awoke to the sound of the drawer opening, the scratch of a match and then the aroma of Vera's cigarette. I rolled over and squinted as Vera exhaled a cloud of blue smoke.

"How do you do that?" I croaked.

"Do what?" she said, turning her head to look at me. She was wearing an old t-shirt and nothing else. Even with wild hair and a face creased by sleep, she looked stunning.

"Smoke a cigarette before you even get out of bed."

She grinned from around the butt of the cigarette. "It gets my blood pumping." She exhaled again and set the cigarette on the lip of the ash tray and then rolled over and squeezed me. "Just like you did last night!" She kissed me, long and wet and smoky.

It was a good thing I didn't have to be at the office any time soon!

I'd planned to take Vera back to the beach on Saturday, but she begged off. She had fallen behind on some personal business while on location, she said, and needed the weekend to help catch up. Plus, I'd brought her the script for her next role and she wanted to begin studying it and learning her character.

It would be Vera's last picture of the year, a science-fiction drama called *Moon Mission*. She'd play the only female member of a four-person crew traveling to the moon. Pacific hadn't done much in the realm of science fiction, but interest in the genre had exploded after the war. The rapid advances in scientific knowledge and technology brought about by the requirements of the military had whetted the public's appetite for more stories about science and exploration. I thought *Moon Mission* would be a good foray into science fiction and a strong final release. We'd assigned it a budget of nearly $900,000, small by MGM standards, but big for Pacific, and it would feature our top stars: Keegan, Burton, Evers, Thorpe and, of course, Vance.

So, instead of a pleasant day at the beach, I decided to continue with my new-found fetish for cleaning. I discovered two things. The first was that cleaning after a few days of getting things dirty is a whole lot easier than cleaning after a few months of getting things dirty. There were fewer dirty things and these fewer things were easier to clean. Take the ash tray, for instance. I had soaked and scrubbed it to remove months of accumulated ashes from Vera's cigarettes. When she'd returned, the ash tray had looked like I'd just bought it off the shelf at Thrifty Drugs. After only a couple of days of use, it was easy to return it to pristine condition. All I had to do was run some warm water over it and, presto, it was like new again.

When I went to put the ash tray back in the drawer, I discovered the second thing. I had dried the ash tray off and had pulled out the drawer of the bedside table. I set it in the drawer and it bumped up against the Nambu pistol. I pushed the pistol aside. I was about to close the drawer, but something wasn't right, so I looked a little more closely. I didn't see the pistol's magazine. I picked the gun up to see if the magazine was behind it, deeper in the drawer. I realized immediately that the reason I hadn't seen the clip was that it was inside the pistol. For safety's sake, I kept the magazine with the pistol, but never *in* the pistol.

I released the magazine from the Nambu and then cleared the chamber, ejecting an unfired bullet onto the bed. I picked it up and set it on top of the table. Odd, I thought. I lifted the gun and sniffed the barrel. It smelled faintly of smoke. Okay, it had been a long time since I'd paid much attention to the pistol and truthfully I wasn't sure how it should have smelled. I sat on the edge of the bed, and tried to remember when I'd last seen the pistol. Instead, I remembered when I hadn't.

I set the pistol on the bedspread beside me and stared at the magazine in my hands. I turned it over a couple of times trying to decide if I really wanted to do this. It was silent in the bedroom, in the house. I'm not sure how long I sat there staring at that damn thing, but at some point my thumb eased up and began pushing the bullets out of the clip: one, two, three. Empty. I placed them next to their mate on the table. Four bullets.

That's when I knew.

My face flushed and a clammy sweat popped out on my forehead. Bile rose in my throat and I stumbled to the bathroom just in time to vomit into the toilet. I retched twice and sat back, my vision blurry from tears, my throat burning. I spit into that nasty toilet as though doing so could clear my mind of the dark thoughts that had taken up residence there.

What the hell did I do now?

Chapter 23

For the next couple of days, I was like one of those zombies in the horror pictures, just sleepwalking through life without any awareness. Abe had taken Ruth to New York to see some Broadway shows and meet with the big publishers about upcoming books for which film rights were still available. That made it easier for me to sequester myself in my office. With the door closed and instructions to Gladys that I didn't want to be disturbed, I spent the first part of the week in a trance. I still made daily visits to the soundstage where *Fast Runs the Pale Horse* was about to finish shooting and I still chaired the weekly production meeting, but I could not concentrate for more than twenty seconds on anything.

Finally, after days of bewilderment, I worked up the nerve to call Vera. Without any shooting scheduled, she'd been spending most of her time at home.

"Hi," I said, trying my best to sound chipper when Vera answered the phone.

"Hi yourself," I could hear a smile in her voice. "I thought maybe you'd retired or got tired of me or something."

"No. No, it's not that." I was doing a lousy job of sounding chipper. "I, uh, we need to talk, Vera." Chipper had left the office by now.

Vera hesitated. "Okay," she said slowly, "I guess we do. How about I meet you at your place about seven?" I wasn't in the mood for sex, but I wasn't in the mood to argue either. I wasn't in the mood for anything.

"Sure," I said. "See you at seven."

I was watching out the front window when Vera pulled up to the curb in front of my house about seven-fifteen. As always concerned about her appearance, Vera adjusted the rear view mirror and applied fresh lipstick. I'd paced a rut in the floor over the last forty-five minutes, my hands cold and clammy, my mouth dry. I wasn't sure what I was going to say to her. And then she was knocking on the door.

"Hi, come in," I said, feeling as though I might throw up again at any point. Vera pecked me on the cheek and I asked, "Been getting a lot of work done?"

"You'd be surprised how far behind you can get when you're out of town for three weeks," she said lightly, but she was watching me with intense eyes.

"'Surprised' doesn't begin to cover it," I replied.

"You're really acting strange," she said, cocking her head to the side. "Are you all right?"

"No, I'm not," I said with all the strength I could muster, which wasn't much. We stood staring at each other. Vera broke eye contact. She opened her purse and I noticed her hands were trembling. She pulled out her pack of Kools, stuck one in her mouth and lit it.

"I guess you'd like an explanation," she said, still not looking at me.

"You're damn right."

Then, as though she'd walked onto a soundstage and assumed a role, she exhaled and seemed to relax. She looked me in the eyes. "I started working on it two months ago. We finalized it over the weekend. That's why I couldn't be with you. I'm sorry."

From lost and bewildered, I had advanced to hopeless and confused. "Wait, what are you talking about?"

Now Vera looked exasperated, like a shoplifter caught red-handed. "Okay, I'll just come out with it. I signed with MGM on Sunday night, effective January 1. Mayer offered me $7,500 a week, Frank, plus five percent. MGM, Frank. The greatest studio in the history of the movies. Abe couldn't match this offer even if he was of a mind to. Which he is not."

I stood there baffled. I must have looked like a half-wit. Vera looked down at her shoes, then with her head still tilted looked back up at me. "I hope you won't hate me for this. You've been great to me. I never could have done this if you hadn't found these great roles for me." I stood motionless, silent. "I should have told you. I'm sorry, Frank." Maybe she was.

"Vera," I said, my voice catching. She looked at me, her eyes beginning to mist. "I know, Vera."

"Of course you know," she coughed up a humorless laugh. "I just told you. MGM is the only studio that can afford me. Louis Mayer understands the value of talent."

"I'm not talking about Louis Mayer, dammit!" I snapped, raising my voice. "I'm talking about Mickey Moreno."

It was growing dark in the house by now, but I'd be damned if I was going to turn on any lights.

"Mickey Moreno?"

"Yes, Vera. Mickey Moreno. I know you killed him, or had him killed, I just don't know why."

She took a long drag on her cigarette. Then, coldly, calmly she began to talk. "The little bastard recognized me, Frank."

"Of course he recognized you!" I was almost shouting now. "You're one of the top movie stars in America!"

"I don't mean from my pictures. From the meetings, Frank, the meetings." She blew smoke and glanced around for an ash tray. "You had to bring him to dinner, didn't you? You couldn't have just said, 'Come back tomorrow, Mickey, and I'll see what I can do.'"

"He saved my life for Chrissakes!"

"Well, you ruined his!" she snapped. "I came here when I was seventeen years old, determined to make it in Hollywood. I worked, I studied, I cajoled, I humbled myself. I did everything I had to in order to get a studio contract. Everything. One of those 'everythings' was to go to meetings with a bunch of people who said they could help me get some work, get on a movie lot, appear as an extra. This little group met every other week or so and sure enough, they opened some doors for me. I got a job as an extra over at Monogram. A few weeks later I picked up another job at Republic, then United Artists. And I kept going to the meetings. They were political meetings, Frank. Get the picture?"

I was beginning to catch on. I nodded slowly.

"Your pal Mickey was there sometimes. I didn't know him except to say 'hello,' but then he started having some real success. Everybody liked him. Even after he got on in that serial he kept coming to meetings." Vera took another drag, her tone became angrier. "He recognized me from the meetings, Frank. Don't you see? He was going to that hearing and he was going to give that committee the names of Communists in the picture business. I wasn't going to let him ruin what I've worked for so hard and so long. I wasn't going to let him give them Vera Vance." She was breathing heavily now.

"How'd you do it?"

"I borrowed your little pistol. And I borrowed my co-star. The one who passes out after a few drinks. He's my alibi, Tom is. He thinks we went out for drinks and then spent the whole night together. The truth is, I poured a few drinks down his throat and then I'm just waiting for sundown. Mickey had told us where he was staying. That's a crummy part of town. The cops probably think he was robbed or something."

"No, they don't. Not robbed, anyway."

"It doesn't matter." She had calmed down. "I'm sorry about your friend and I'm sorry about you. But nobody was going to stop me, not now, not just when I'd reached the top."

"The police will."

"I've got an alibi. Besides you can't turn me in, you're an accessory."

"How do you figure? I didn't know about this until a few minutes ago."

"Really? You seem to have figured it out several days ago, yet you've done nothing about it. That's curious, don't you think? I'm sure the police would think so. They'd also be curious that the murder weapon belongs to you."

"I had no motive to kill Mickey."

"No? How about this: he was threatening to expose the woman you love, the one you've been sleeping with. Not enough? Let's add a financial angle: he was threatening to expose the woman who's been pulling your gravy train, who helped you earn a ten thousand-dollar bonus."

"Ten thousand five hundred," I corrected without thinking.

"Ten thousand five hundred. All the better. Still not enough? Moreno was going to ruin the second half of Pacific Pictures' year. He was going to rat out the only Pacific star to ever crack the top-fifteen box office list. You were going to lose the star power that helped increase studio profits two million dollars in one year. Motive? You've got plenty, buster." She wheeled about and stalked into the kitchen. I heard water running in the sink as she washed her cigarette down the drain. I stood rooted to the spot like a fifty-year-old oak.

It was the calm Vera who returned. I was looking down at my feet, a lump in my throat. "Look at me," she said, gently placing her hand under my chin and tipping my face up. "I've got an alibi. You've got an alibi. Mickey's dead. Nothing's going to change that no matter what you do or what unbelievable stories you spin for the police. Sometimes life is hard, Frank" she paused, "but it could always be worse." She continued to stare at me for a moment, her eyes cold and hard. Then she kissed me lightly on the lips and walked out of the house.

I greeted Abe with false good cheer on the Monday morning he returned and asked him how his trip back east had been. "Productive, productive," he smiled. "I've got some ideas to discuss with you later."

"Good. Betty put me on your schedule for this afternoon at three o'clock. I've got a couple of things to discuss with you as well." It was a long morning. I was nervous about facing Abe, telling him what I knew. It was going to sting. Half of me wanted the day to drag on forever so I wouldn't have to meet with him; half of me wanted three o'clock to arrive immediately so I could get this over with.

When it was finally time, I straightened up my notes and walked down the hallway to Abe's door. I knocked.

"Come in, my boy, come in!" he was smiling broadly, clearly happy to be back in his element, back behind his desk running the company that he'd built, that he'd put his energy and soul into—and that had stolen his most precious treasure.

I smiled weakly as he waved me into a chair. I presented the latest draft—I hoped the final draft—for *This Great Country.* We'd added a segment on American power, beginning with scenes from several manufacturers' assembly lines. We'd also included some shots of the atomic mushroom cloud. Our focus here, of course, was not to frighten people, but to emphasize the lengths to which Americans would go to protect our values and way of life. The closing scene was a slow tracking shot between the endless rows of white crosses and Stars of David that defined Arlington National Cemetery. I'd opted for scenes from Arlington because it told the same story at half the cost of similar scenes shot in one of the European cemeteries. The narrator here talked about American resolve, generosity and sacrifice.

"Very good. Yes, very good," he said glancing up from the script. "Much improved. I wonder," he paused, "if we should include anything about this European recovery plan that Secretary Marshall has put forth?"

"Well, it would certainly underscore the generosity angle," I said, "but I'm not sure how you do that without making the film seem dated right away. And what if Congress doesn't go for it? I think we create a timing problem by including it.

We sort of have to wait to see how things turn out and that delays our release. I recommend we go with this script as is. The themes represented are timeless ones."

Abe thought for a moment and then nodded. "You're right. We have to pick a moment in time and make a decision to move forward. This is the moment." He held the script up and nodded his head. "Let's go with it like it is. Who gets it?"

"I was thinking George Burke. It's right up his alley. Or, I can give it to Hooper. This one plus one more would give him four films for the year. He sort of owes us after last year." Abe and I both chuckled.

"Give it to George," Abe decided. "What else have you got for me?"

My stomach was spinning round and round like one of those little wheels hamsters run on. I felt that unpleasant icy sweat on my forehead as I stood up and slowly walked over to Abe's office door. He watched, an expression of concern replacing the smile on his face.

"I learned some unpleasant news while you were away," I began, looking down at the top of Abe's desk. "I had begun to suspect something and so I confronted Vera." Abe sat back, his eyebrows arched, his fingertips together. It was clear I had his full attention.

"Go on," he said.

"To make a painful story short, she's signed with MGM. Mayer offered her $7,500 a week and five percent on her pictures."

Abe whistled, impressed. "She drove a good bargain," he said grudgingly. "We could never have approached those kinds of figures."

"She knew that," I said. "I think she's sorry to be leaving, honestly. She knows how good you've been to her Abe."

"And how good you've been to her," he said quietly, looking out his window. "She's finished her work on *Switchblade*, correct?"

"Yes sir. We've got her cast as the female lead in *Moon Mission,* which is scheduled to begin filming in August. Abe, I think we should let her go, release her from her contract. If she doesn't want to be here, then why force her?"

Abe looked at me for a full minute before he replied. "That's your heart talking, Frank. Think with your head. Vera Vance is the most successful box office star we've ever had. This is a business and we make business decisions. I know her jumping ship like this is particularly painful for you, but keep in mind that her decision was based on business factors as well. As disappointed as you are—and I am too, by the way—we don't need to let our emotions rule us. We honor our contract with Miss Vance. Can you accept that?"

"Yes sir." To Abe's immense credit, he never said "I told you so." And I never mentioned Mickey Moreno.

Flash of the Switchblade, when it was released in August, was Vera Vance's third successful opening of the year. She was well ahead of her 1946 pace and had a shot at cracking the top five on the box office list for the year.

Abe brought Goz into the picture a week after *Switchblade* opened. "Her last Pacific Pictures film will be *Moon Mission,* now in production. It will be in theaters for the holidays. I'd like you to draft a press release thanking Miss Vance for the wonderful job she's done these past six years here and wishing her every success in the future. Quote me as complimenting Louis and MGM on adding such a bright star to their galaxy of talent, or something like that."

Goz made notes and nodded. "We'll stay on the high road, Abe."

The day after filming finished for *Moon Mission*, Abe invited several of us to lunch in his private dining room as a farewell send off for Vera. It was an awkward affair for all, me in particular. In addition to severing our professional relationship, she had destroyed our personal one as well. She was moving on up the ladder of stardom and success. The rest of us were falling a few rungs. Abe made some kind remarks, too kind I thought, and presented Vera with a framed montage of still photos from her most memorable roles. Most of them, ironically, had occurred since I took over production.

As the luncheon broke up, Jimmy, one of the photographers on Goz's staff, came in to shoot some group photos. Vera, the center of attention in every photo, looked every inch the glamorous movie star, smiling, beautiful, in control. She gave me a quick hug and peck on the cheek, then she was gone. I wandered back to my office, closed the door and lost myself in the dark recesses of my troubled mind.

Epilogue

The Hollywood film colony really wasn't that big and over the next few years, I would see Vera occasionally at industry events. She was always cordial. She always greeted me by name and insisted on introducing me to her escort, whether it was Gene Kelly, Van Johnson or MGM's newest male star. When we would part, she'd smile at me, give me a quick hug and kiss me on the cheek, as if to renew the lease on the secret we shared.

She was nominated for a best supporting actress Oscar in 1949, but lost out to Mercedes McCambridge in *All the King's Men.* That was the zenith of her stardom. The fading looks she had foreseen on that long-ago Sunday on the beach began to catch up with her. By the time Eisenhower took office, MGM had cancelled her contract. I lost track of Vera after that. Joan Roswell reported that she'd gone off to Europe and married a prince, but that he'd turned out to be broke.

Oh well, life could always be worse.

Author's Note

Hollywood in the 1930s and 1940s was arguably the center of American, some would say world, culture. The films turned out by the major studios played to more than 80 million domestic movie-goers each week—every other American went to the movies! When they did, they got to see more than just a "picture." The feature films were preceded by cartoons, short features and newsreels, giving millions of Americans their only look at the newsmakers of the day. The studio system was at the peak of its power and influence, drawing not only the attraction of millions, but envy as well.

The creativity, colorful characters and shenanigans of the film community of the era make for a great setting within which to tell a story! Here were America's royalty, actors, studio chiefs, directors and writers pulling in salaries that even seventy years later would allow for comfortable living—while many in the country were struggling under the effects of the Great Depression. It remains an intriguing period in the history of a place and an industry which continues to fascinate.

Thanks as always to those who took the time to read the early drafts of THE MOVIE STAR AND ME and to offer criticisms. Joe, Don and Chuck always provide thoughtful suggestions which improve the finished product. Special thanks to Ina and Harry for reading and commenting, reading and commenting and then reading again and commenting. Your recommendations greatly strengthened the story.

Thanks also to Kathryn Smith who edited the manuscript, applying not only her keen eye for style and substance, but offering historical insights as well. Natalie Obando and her Do Good PR team crafted an effective introductory campaign for this book. Special thanks for the good effort and sound advice!

In this digital age, many readers choose their next book based on the reviews others have posted. I'd appreciate you sharing your opinion—even if it's not filled with superlatives!—to help others decide if THE MOVIE STAR AND ME is a good fit with their preferences.

Yvonne, my wife, has been supportive of my writing habit since my first efforts eight years ago. Since I've been able to write full-time, her encouragement has never flagged. Likewise, our daughters, to whom this book is dedicated, tolerate my writing with their delightful mix of good humor, sarcasm and hugs. I'm a lucky fellow.

Kelly Durham
Clemson, South Carolina
June 2016

About the Author

Kelly Durham lives in Clemson, SC with his wife Yvonne. They are the parents of Mary Kate, Addison and Callie and also provide for their dog, George Marshall. A graduate of Clemson University, Kelly served four years in the US Army with assignments in Arizona and Germany before returning to Clemson and entering private business. Kelly is the also the author of THE WAR WIDOW, BERLIN CALLING, WADE'S WAR and THE RELUCTANT COPILOT. Visit his website, www.kellydurham.com, or contact him at kelly@kellydurham.com.

Frank Russell's adventures at Pacific Pictures continue with Book 2 in the series:

Temporary Alliance

Here's a sneak peek!

Prologue

Hollywood
June 28, 1950

"There's no water in the Pacific Ocean!" Max Hooper snapped over the telephone. Max was the producer of Pacific Pictures' biggest-ever motion picture, a naval war epic set in the Pacific Ocean around the Philippines.

"What's wrong?" As the chief of production for the studio, my job was providing Max with the support his project needed—including making sure there was water in the giant outdoor pool we'd constructed as a setting for many of his motion picture's scenes. Those scenes included this morning's scheduled filming of the model ships that would be standing in for the Imperial Japanese Navy in one of the big battle sequences.

"There's some foul-up with the supply valve or something," Max complained. "Harry's working on it, but right now we're just getting a trickle of water into the pool." Max paused, then asked, "By the way, how are you? I heard what happened last night."

"I'm fine." I wondered how the story of my encounter the previous evening had been embellished by the time it got to Max. “Where are you now?”

“I ducked into Soundstage 5 to use the phone. I’m going back over to the pool.”

“I’ll meet you there.”

Chapter 1

Hollywood, California
April 1950

"Epic, Joan," Larry Gosnell, said as he explained Pacific Pictures' new exterior seascape set to syndicated columnist Joan Roswell. I was tagging along to make sure Joan felt she was being treated with the respect due someone with her following. Every day except Monday, Joan's column was read in more than four hundred newspapers from coast to coast. Those of us in the motion picture business, and particularly here at Pacific Pictures, which was not her favorite studio, were cautious around Joan; her opinion could promote or destroy a motion picture—or even a studio.

I first met Joan Roswell on my initial visit to the studio back in October 1945. I was a twenty-six-year-old Army lieutenant just back from the war and I was returning some film that had found its way into my possession. The film had been shot by a Pacific Pictures newsreel cameraman who had been killed in action on Okinawa. I had been severely wounded by the same explosion. I never determined exactly how the film canisters ended up in my gear, but my decision to return the film to the studio's newsreel division changed my life. George Burke, who ran the studio's newsreel efforts, and Larry Gosnell, who was presently conducting Joan's tour, had taken me to lunch in the commissary. Joan had breezed in as though leading a coronation procession and had, without an invitation, joined us.

She hadn't changed much since that first meeting. Oh, sure, she was nearly five years older, but she was still a handsome woman with arresting, sly green eyes and expertly-coiffed blond hair. Not that she was my type. In fact, my last serious relationship had ended poorly. I'd fallen hard and fast for an actress, one on the Pacific Pictures payroll. I was sure it was true love, but after the fact I came to realize that she had ripped out my heart and stomped flat for her own personal ambitions. Even if I had been ready to jump back into romance, it wouldn't have been with Joan, no matter how attractive she appeared.

Sure, Joan's smile was pretty: white, straight teeth contrasted against full red lips. She had an appealing figure for a woman in her mid-forties and I never saw her when she wasn't impeccably dressed in a conservative suit, always with stylishly-matched shoes and purse. She favored furs draped across her shoulders and always carried an ebony cigarette holder which she often used to accentuate her conversations. She was quick, smart, and somehow invited confidences. I always found her to be warm, engaging, and wholly insincere.

"Oh my, Goz," Joan gasped, staring up at the thirty-five-foot tall framework being assembled. "What's all this?" Larry Gosnell launched into a technical explanation that I could only partially follow. As the chief of publicity for Pacific Pictures, Goz was a jack-of-all-trades and master of quite a few. He was a big fellow, hale and hearty, with a personality that instantly made others feel at ease. He had to be able to tell the full Pacific story, from the size of leading man Terry Thorpe's cowboy boots to the latest box office results for any of the eighteen pictures we'd produced the previous year to the number of Academy Award nominations the studio had received over its thirty-plus year history. He also, as he was doing today, had to be able to explain to esteemed members of the press and other VIPs how Pacific was utilizing the latest technology in order to produce motion pictures that would appeal to an ever more demanding movie-going public.

"This, Joan, and the area you see before you," he said, gesturing with a sweep of his arm toward a vacant parking lot just in front of us, "is in the process of becoming Pacific Pictures' exciting new exterior seascape set! With this set, we'll be able to produce high quality effects simulating ocean and other water settings without the expense--and hazards, I might add--of location filming. The structure there," Goz pointed toward the back of the lot where workers were framing a wall, "will support a giant panarama which will allow us to overlay realistic backgrounds to match our foreground action. And over there," Goz pointed to our left front, "we'll construct a 500,000-gallon water tank to supply our set. Those men over there," Goz pointed to a group of four workmen, one of whom was standing in a large, muddy knee-deep hole, "are installing the sophisticated drains, pumps and other plumbing apparatus that will allow us to control all that water."

"But, Goz, dear, all I see in the foreground is a parking lot. One with several potholes, by the way," Joan said, pointing with her cigarette holder.

"Sure, that's all you see now," Goz grinned. "But this whole parking lot will soon be resurfaced and a four-foot-high concrete wall constructed on all sides. Then we flood it with the water from the tank and it can become the Panama Canal or the Indian Ocean or the Mediterranean Sea merely with the change of the background. Pretty fantastic, don't you think?"

Joan took a pull on her cigarette and looked at me with her curious cat's eyes. "Why go to all this expense? What movie magic are you cooking up, Frank Russell?" Her question was accompanied by a sly smile.

Joan and I had gotten along pretty well since I'd first arrived at the studio. She'd been a skeptic when, although I had no movie-making experience, studio founder Abe Baum had put me in charge of feature film production. But when we increased our motion picture output by sixty percent in the first year, she had grudgingly conceded that maybe I had a little more on the ball than she'd realized. Except for one brief instance when her column had described me as a suspect in a murder investigation, we'd enjoyed a cordial, though wary relationship.

"It's like Goz said, Joan," I replied, shielding my eyes from the warm morning sunshine. "We're planning something epic. We need this seascape for that project."

She smiled her I-know-you're-holding-back-on-me smile, which I'd seen on more than one occasion. "Now, Frank, darling, this is Joan you're talking too. Surely you can share more than that with me."

I glanced theatrically at Goz, who just as theatrically shrugged his shoulders. So far, our little act was playing out as we had planned it. "Well, Joan," I said, lowering my voice and taking a step closer to her, "we've got a big picture in the works." I was close enough now that I could smell her orange and jasmine perfume. "In fact, it will be the most ambitious, most expensive project Pacific Pictures has ever tackled." I looked into her green eyes, enjoying both their beauty and the anticipation I could feel building.

"Tell me more, darling," she cooed.

"Well, I'd like to, Joan," I said looking away, "but we're not really ready to release details just yet. We're still in the early stages of the project. Still working on the script, casting, planning and all the technical stuff that will go into an epic film like this." I felt the hook had been set, but now I wanted to play with the fish a little.

"It's not the Red Sea, is it? You're not going to remake *The Ten Commandments,* are you? You know Cecil's been talking about that for years! He'd die if you stole that out from under him!"

I shook my head. "Of course not. Nobody could out-do Cecil B. DeMille."

"Oh, silly me!" Joan tittered. "Abe Baum would never spend the money to make an epic like that. You know," she threaded her arm through mine as we circumnavigated the parking lot, "if DeMille had made his picture at Pacific, it would have been *The Five Commandments*!"

I laughed just to be polite. I glanced at Goz and saw him roll his eyes. "No, it's not a Biblical epic, but it will be grand in scale." I stopped walking and took Joan's gloved hand in mine. "Listen, Joan, you've always been kind to Pacific Pictures." This was a lie. She knew it. I knew it. She knew I knew it. But sometimes that's how we play the game in Hollywood. We were about to risk more money on one picture than we'd normally spend on five. To help ensure a big return at the box office, we needed all the early buzz we could get and we'd need to keep that hum growing all the way to our release date, which was still several months away. "Can we go off the record for a minute, Joan?" I asked.

"Oh, dear! Why do you always want to tell me things you know I can't use?"

"Just for a minute, Joan. Then we'll go back on the record again. Okay?"

"All right, Frank." She smiled sweetly. "But only because it's you, whom I admire so much."

I thought I might vomit, but I smiled and thanked her. "Joan, with the cooperation of the United States Navy and the Department of Defense, Pacific Pictures is going to produce a film about the greatest naval battle of all time. The battle of Leyte Gulf finished off the Japanese Navy. It was the biggest sea battle in history and secured the landing beaches in the Philippines. Capturing the Philippines made Japan's defeat inevitable. This parking lot is going to be transformed into the

Pacific Ocean, Leyte Gulf, and the San Bernardino Strait. Right here, we're going to recreate the battle that secured American mastery of the Pacific and led to the end of the war." I paused, excited that the proverbial cat was now out of the bag, and waited for Joan's reaction.

"And when will this epic be released to theaters?" she inquired with a slight turn of her lovely head.

"Just in time for the holidays."

"Death, destruction, tragedy and triumph!" Joan cocked her head at me and smiled again. "What a perfect picture for Christmas!"

"How did it go with Joan Roswell?" Abe Baum asked that afternoon over lunch in his executive dining room on the third floor of the studio's headquarters building. Abe and I tried to see each other for a few minutes daily and for lunch at least once a week. At fifty-seven, Abe was still going strong. He ate sensibly, walked two miles every day before coming to work, didn't smoke and drank only socially. At five feet six, he was four inches shorter than me, but he made up for his stature with a forceful, energetic personality. And he looked every inch the head of a successful movie studio. He wore expensive, tailored suits, custom-made shoes and kept his gray hair cut close to his tanned scalp. His intense brown eyes drilled into me, waiting for my reply while I finished chewing a piece of baked chicken.

"It went pretty well, I think," I said, wiping my mouth on the fancy linen napkin. Abe's dining room was well-appointed with fine china, crystal, silverware and linens, all trimmed in gold and adorned with the studio's *PP* monogram. "Of course, we won't know for sure until we read what she says in her columns."

"I'm still nervous about this, Frank. So is the board," Abe said. "They're watching this thing very closely. We've never spent three million dollars on a picture before. Why, back when we started Pacific, we didn't spend a million dollars for the whole year!"

"Yeah, Abe, but in 1919 there wasn't much competition and the audience wasn't very demanding. Neither were the critics."

"Ha! The good old days! There weren't any critics! No Joan Roswell, either! I don't trust her. And I don't like her, either."

"Who does? But we've got a lot riding on this picture and we're going to have to play it smart. Goz has crafted a very creative publicity plan. It's got lots of parts, from star profiles to biographies of the true-life heroes of the story to 'making-of' features. It's really going to help build excitement for the picture. And, like it or not, Joan Roswell is a key part of that plan. I've also been over all the numbers with Erskine," I said, referring to the studio's finance director, Erskine Pierce. "He says the budget is realistic."

"Well, it better work!" Abe said between bites, "or we'll be sunk. Pardon the pun."

Abe had good reason not to like Joan Roswell. For years, he felt she'd been less than objective in her coverage of the studio he'd built. Her veiled animosity was based on a story she knew was there but had never been able to fully uncover.

In 1941, Abe's son David had been a passenger in a car driven by Mickey Moreno, an actor under contract to Pacific Pictures. Mickey, with whom I would briefly serve during the war, had been drinking, as had the teenage David. When Mickey rammed his convertible into a light pole, he was thrown clear. David was less fortunate. He was trapped between the car and the pole and suffered traumatic injuries to his head. Ever since, David had been confined to a wheelchair in a Malibu sanitarium. He couldn't walk or talk, feed or bathe himself. Nonetheless, Abe and his wife, Ruth, spent every Sunday visiting with their son.

Joan Roswell knew something had happened to David. She even knew he'd been in a car crash. But that, as far as I could tell, was all she'd been able to find out. Initially, Goz had buried the story to avoid bad publicity for the studio—and additional anguish for Abe and Ruth. But over the years I felt it had become a battle of wits to keep Joan from learning what had happened. It was as though keeping the secret and denying the story to Joan Roswell had become its own objective.

Even though construction of our seascape set was not yet completed, we had already been working on our war picture for several months by the time we gave Joan her peek. I had fought in the Pacific during the war, specifically on Okinawa, where I'd lasted less than three days before getting myself blown up. I'd come to in an Army hospital far from the fighting. In addition to a broken leg, I had suffered a ruptured spleen and a concussion. The spleen I didn't miss, but the leg still bothered me occasionally, especially in wet weather. Fortunately, we didn't have much of that in Southern California. I was proud to have served and felt that most of the guys who'd survived, come home, and picked back up with their lives felt the same way.

In 1946, the first year I'd been in charge of feature film production at Pacific, war pictures hadn't done so well. That year, we'd released *Jungle Command*, which followed Marine commandos in their fight against the Japanese on a fictional Pacific island. I thought it was a pretty swell picture, but it didn't perform very well at the ticket window. Sam Goldwyn's *The Best Years of Our Lives* had led at the box office that year, pulling in more than eleven million dollars and winning the best picture Oscar as well, but it really wasn't about the war itself. It was about the challenges three veterans faced in adjusting back to civilian life. In fact, over the next two years, no war film had cracked the top ten box office list.

That started changing in 1949. That year, *Battleground, The Sands of Iwo Jima,* and *Twelve O'Clock High* were among the top grossing pictures. And that got me thinking: maybe the guys like me who'd gone and done their duty, come home, started careers and families, maybe they were finally ready to look back on their time in the service. The Army, Marines and Army Air Force had been favorably represented by those three films. Maybe the time was right for Pacific Pictures to tell the Navy's story. Sure, the Navy guys got better chow and got to sleep in warm, dry bunks every night, but they'd served, too.

I had done my homework and decided to share my idea with a skeptical Abe Baum during our regular weekly meeting in his office a couple of weeks before Christmas. I normally had multiple reports with me for these meetings: production budgets, shooting schedules, story leads and the other information we needed to keep our feature film efforts moving ahead. On this occasion, I had one additional item stashed among my papers.

"People are tired of the war," Abe protested after I gave voice to my idea. He glared at me over the tops of his half-moon reading glasses. "Remember *Jungle Command*? Didn't make a dime."

"You're right, Abe," I countered, "people were tired of the war. But now they're starting to look back on it and say, 'Hey I was part of something pretty amazing—and I served with some swell guys.' I think a lot of these men are starting to look back with a little nostalgia. I mean, what if these really were the best years of their lives? Don't you think they're going to want to revisit that? Take their wives to the theater and say, 'Look, honey, this is what I did during the war.'"

Abe was sitting in his wine-colored leather chair behind his neat desk. I was always impressed with the way he kept his significant work load so well-organized. He pressed the fingertips of both hands together and leaned back. "War pictures don't make money."

"They haven't up until this year. But there are three war pictures in theaters right now and, according to *Variety,* all three are pulling in big audiences."

Abe chewed on his lip and stared at me for a couple of moments. "Let's say you're right, that there's some nostalgia for the war. What would our story be?" That's when I knew I had him, when he called it "our" story.

"The largest naval battle in history. The battle that sounded the death knell for the Japanese fleet and ensured the success of the Philippines invasion. The Battle of Leyte Gulf!"

"And you think we can make a coherent story out of this battle?"

"Yes!" I dropped a buff-colored folder on his desk.

"Oh," Abe said, nodding his head in comprehension, "so you've already been spending the studio's money on this even before you come to me?"

"This is just a story outline, Abe, but it's got everything we want in a movie: excitement, action, heroism, sacrifice—"

"How about romance?"

"Romance? No, it's a war movie. It's fact-based. There's no romance."

"Find a way to put some romance in it and bring me a draft." That was Abe's way of moving on to round two.

Made in the USA
Monee, IL
23 May 2021

69306624R00233